Lady Elinor's WICKED ADVENTURES

LILLIAN MAREK

sourcebooks
casablanca

Published by Sourcebooks Casablanca, an imprint of Sourcebooks,
Inc.
P.O. Box 4410, Naperville, Illinois 60567-4410
(630) 961-3900
Fax: (630) 961-2168
www.sourcebooks.com

Printed and bound in Canada.
WC 10 9 8 7 6 5 4 3 2 1

To my brother Joe, who was always brilliant, always encouraging, and who always laughed at my jokes.

One

London, 1852

CHEERFUL FRIVOLITY REIGNED IN THE BALLROOM OF Huntingdon House. The dancers swirled to the strains of a waltz, jewels glittering and silks and satins shimmering under the brilliant light of the new gas chandeliers. Even the chaperones were smiling to each other and swaying unconsciously to the music.

Harcourt de Vaux, Viscount Tunbury, an angry scowl setting him apart from the rest of the company, pushed his way to the side of his old schoolfellow. Grabbing him by the arm, Tunbury spoke in a furious undertone. "Pip, your sister is dancing with Carruthers."

Pip, more formally known as Philip Tremaine, Viscount Rycote, turned and blinked. "Hullo, Harry. I didn't know you were here. I thought this sort of thing was too tame for you these days."

"Forget about me. It's Norrie. She's dancing with that bounder Carruthers."

They both looked at the dance floor where Lady Elinor Tremaine, the picture of innocence, was smiling up at her partner, whose lean face and dark eyes spoke of danger. He was smiling as well, looking down at her with almost wolfish hunger.

"What of it?" asked Pip.

"He's a bloody fortune hunter and a cad to boot. How could you introduce him to your sister?"

Pip frowned slightly. "He introduced himself, actually. Said he was a friend of yours."

Harry spoke through clenched teeth. "You idiot. That should have been enough to disqualify him. Where are your parents?"

"Dancing, I suppose."

Harry caught a glimpse of the Marquess and Marchioness of Penworth on the far side of the room, dancing gracefully and oblivious to everyone else. Turning back to find Carruthers and Lady Elinor again, he muttered an oath. "He's heading for the terrace." When Pip looked blank, Harry shook his head and charged across the dance floor.

❧

Mr. Carruthers had timed it quite neatly, she thought. As the music ended and he twirled her into the final spin, they came to a halt just before the terrace doors. These were standing open, letting in the scent of roses on the breeze of the soft June evening.

"It is rather warm in here, Lady Elinor, is it not?" he said. "Would you care for a turn on the terrace?"

Before she could answer, a strong hand clasped her arm just above the elbow. "Lady Elinor, your mother wants you." When she turned to object to this high-handed treatment, she found herself staring up at the all-too-familiar scowl of Lord Tunbury. "Harry…" she started to protest.

"If Lady Elinor wishes to return to her parents, I will be delighted to escort her." Carruthers spoke frostily.

"Lady Penworth requested that I find her daughter." Harry's even icier tone indicated that there was nothing more to be said on the subject.

Lady Elinor looked back and forth between them and wanted to laugh. Carruthers was tall, dark, and handsome, or at least decorative, with a pretty bow-shaped mouth. Harry, equally tall, had broad shoulders and a powerful build. His square face was pleasant rather than handsome, his middling brown hair tended to flop over his middling brown eyes, and his wide mouth was more often than not stretched into a broad smile. Not just now, of course.

One would say the two men were not much alike, but at the moment they wore identical scowls. They did not actually bare their teeth and growl, but they were not far off. She could not manage to feel guilty about enjoying the sight. It was too delightful.

Carruthers stopped glaring at Harry long enough to look at her. He may have stopped scowling, but he was not smiling. He was stiff with anger. "Lady Elinor?" He offered his arm.

Harry's grip on her arm tightened and he pulled her back a step. His grip was growing painful, and she would have protested, but she feared it might create a scene not of her own designing, so she smiled. "Thank you, Mr. Carruthers, but if my mother sent Lord Tunbury, perhaps I should accept his escort."

Carruthers bowed stiffly and sent one more glare at

the intruder before he departed. That left her free to turn furiously on Harry. "There is no way on earth my mother sent you to fetch me. What do you think you are doing?"

He caught her hand, trapped it on his arm, and began marching her away from the terrace. "I cannot imagine what possessed your parents to give you permission to dance with a loose fish like Carruthers."

"They didn't, of course. He at least had enough sense to wait until they had left me with Pip." Harry was dragging her along too quickly, and she was going to land on the floor in a minute. "You might slow down a bit," she complained.

"You little idiot!" He turned and glared at her but did ease his pace. "He was about to take you out on the terrace."

"Well, of course!" She gave an exasperated humph.

"What do you mean, 'Of course'?" By now they had reached the end of the ballroom, and he pulled her into the hall and swung her around to the side so he could glare with some privacy.

She shook out her skirt and checked to make sure the pink silk rosettes pinning up the tulle overskirt had not been damaged while Harry was dragging her about. She was very fond of those rosettes. "I mean, of course he was going to take me out on the terrace. That's what he does. He takes a girl out on the terrace, leads her into one of the secluded parts, and kisses her. Marianne and Dora say he kisses very nicely, and I wanted to see if they were right."

Harry made a strangled sound. "Marianne and Dora? Miss Simmons and Miss Cooper...?"

"Among others." Lady Elinor waved a hand airily. "He's kissed so many of this year's debutantes that I was beginning to feel slighted, but I think perhaps he is working according to some sort of pattern. Do you know what it might be?"

He was looking at her with something approaching horror, rather the way her brother looked at her much of the time. "You and your friends discuss… What in God's name are young ladies thinking about these days?"

She shrugged. "Young men, of course. What did you suppose? That we discuss embroidery patterns? Don't you and your friends talk about women?"

He closed his eyes and muttered a prayer for patience. Then he began speaking with exaggerated formality. "Lady Elinor, under no circumstances are you to even dance with a rake like Carruthers, much less go into the garden with him. You have no idea what he would do."

"Fiddlesticks! I know precisely what he was going to do. He apparently has only two speeches that he uses to persuade a girl to let him kiss her, and I want to know which one he is going to use on me. Then I'll know if I am generally considered saucy or sweet."

"Norrie, no one who is at all acquainted with you would ever consider you sweet."

"Well, I should hope not. You know me better than that. But I want to know how I am viewed by the people who don't know me."

He grabbed her by the shoulders and turned her to face him. "Norrie, I want you to listen to me. A bounder like Carruthers will try to do far more than simply steal a kiss."

"I know that. You needn't treat me as if I am simpleminded. But I am hardly going to allow anything more."

"It is not a question of what you will allow. Just precisely how do you think you could stop him from taking advantage of you?"

She gave him a considering look and decided to answer honestly. "Well, there is the sharply raised knee to the groin or the forehead smashed against the nose, but the simplest, I have always found, is the hatpin."

"Hatpin?" Harry looked rather as if he were choking as he seized on the most innocuous part of her statement.

"Yes. It really doesn't matter where you stab. Gentlemen are always so startled that they jump back." She offered him a kindly smile. Sometimes he sounded just like her brother.

He went back to glaring at her. "Norrie, Lady Elinor, I want your word that there will be no strolls in the garden with disreputable rogues."

"Like you?" she interrupted.

"Yes, if you like, like me! Forget about rogues. You may not always recognize one. Just make it all men. You are not to leave the ballroom with any man at any time."

"The way we just left it?"

"Stop that, Norrie. I am serious."

He did indeed look serious. Quite fierce, in fact. So she subsided and resigned herself to listening.

"I want your promise," he said. "If you will not give it, I will have to warn your brother, and you know Pip. He might feel obliged to challenge anyone who tries to lead you into dark corners, and you know he is a hopeless shot. You don't want to get him killed, do you?"

He had calmed down enough to start smiling at her now, one of those patronizing, big-brother, I-know-better-than-you smiles. It was quite maddening, so she put on her shyly innocent look and smiled back. "Oh, Harry, you know I would never do anything that would cause real trouble."

"That's my girl." He took her arm to lead her back to the ballroom. "Hatpins indeed. Just don't let your mother find out you've heard about things like that."

She smiled. He really was quite sweet. And foolish. He had not even noticed that she gave him no promise. And then imagine warning her not to let her mother find out. Who did he suppose had taught her those tricks?

༄

Tunbury hovered at the edge of the ballroom and watched Norrie hungrily. He had not seen her in more than a year, and then two months ago, there she had been. It was her first season, and somehow the tomboy who had been his and Pip's companion in all their games and pranks had turned into a beauty. Her dark hair now hung in shiny ringlets, framing the perfect oval of her face. Her eyes—they had always been that sort of greenish blue, shining with excitement more often than not, but when had they started to tilt at the edge that way? And when had her lashes grown so long and thick? Worst of all, when had she gone and grown a bosom?

But she was such an innocent.

She thought herself so worldly, so knowing, when in fact she knew nothing of the ugliness lurking beneath the surface, even in the ballrooms of the aristocracy. That ugliness should never be allowed to touch her. Her parents would protect her and find her a husband worthy of her, a good, decent man who came from a good, decent family.

Not someone like him. Not someone who came from a family as rotten as his. The Tremaines thought they knew about his parents, the Earl and Countess of Doncaster, but they knew only the common gossip. They did not know what Doncaster had told him, and he hoped they never would.

Yes, Norrie would find a husband worthy of her, but he couldn't stay here and watch. That would be too painful. He had to leave. He would leave in the morning and disappear from her life.

Two

London, four years later

WHAT FIRST CAUGHT HER EYE WAS THE WAY HE WAS striding along Oxford Street, so unlike the languid stroll of most gentlemen, even in the chill of late January. He was turned away, of course, and it was already starting to get dark, so she couldn't be sure. After all, for years now her eye had been caught by glimpses of men who might be him. It had surprised her, the number of tall, broad-shouldered, brown-haired men in the world.

At the corner he stopped and looked to the side, and Lady Elinor caught sight of the high cheekbone, the angle of the jaw. She grasped her mother's arm. "Mama, isn't that…" She couldn't finish.

Lady Penworth looked at the young man her daughter was staring at. "Good heavens, it is!" She stepped forward and called out, "Lord Tunbury!"

He had to stop and turn, of course. Even if he hadn't wanted to, her mother's call—her shout, to be blunt—had drawn attention to him. At first he just stared at them, almost as if he were afraid. As if Harry had ever been afraid of anything. Harry, who had always been the first to race down a cliff or dive into the water or send his horse flying over the hedge. Didn't he recognize them? But he had to know that he couldn't just stand there staring. He finally did move toward them, even if not quite as quickly as she and her mother were moving to him.

He looked the same. Well, no, he didn't. He had the same square, solid face, so familiar, so…reliable, that was it. But different, somehow. The set of his wide mouth was firmer, harder, and there were slight creases at the corners of his eyes, as if he had been squinting a lot. His shoulders seemed broader—was that possible? And he looked older.

He was older, of course. After all, it had been almost four years. Still, he seemed to have matured more than Pip had in the same time. But after that first moment of surprise when he just looked blank, he smiled, and she had to smile back. That was Harry, who had been her friend since childhood. She would know that smile anywhere. How she had missed it.

Beaming joyfully, Lady Penworth put out her hands to greet him and he took them in his.

"Lady Penworth, Lady Elinor, what a wonderful surprise."

His voice was deep, deeper than she remembered. A rich, man's voice. Elinor could almost feel it vibrate in her but couldn't manage to say anything herself. She just stood there, feeling foolishly glad that she was wearing her new blue velvet capelet with the fur lining and the matching bonnet.

Her mother, of course, had no trouble finding her tongue. "Harry, look at you, so brown and handsome! You look like sunshine in this gray London drizzle. When did you get back?"

"Just yesterday, as a matter of fact. I'm putting up at Mivart's Hotel."

Lady Penworth frowned slightly. "At a hotel? You are not staying with your family?"

Harry seemed to freeze up at that, and his smile vanished. What was the matter? And he spoke almost roughly. "No, no, I am not."

"Well, in that case, you must come stay with us," Mama said firmly, ignoring his tone. "No, I insist. We can't have you staying in a hotel. You can come with us now, and we can send someone to collect your things from Mivart's."

Elinor couldn't hold back any longer. She flung herself at him to give him a hug. "Oh, Harry, I am so very glad to see you."

Her mother uttered an indulgent "tsk," but after a moment of hesitation, when Elinor feared he was going to push her away, Harry's arms wrapped around her and he hugged her back. "I missed you too." His voice seemed a trifle thick, and he held her longer than she had expected.

Lady Penworth took charge, of course. She sent Harry to fetch a hackney, explaining that it would have been ridiculous to bring their own carriage into this traffic, settled them into the cab when it arrived, and had them on their way in no time. Harry seemed to have been struck silent by all of this, and Elinor was struck silent by the amazement of having her friend

Harry not just back in England after all his adventures but right here in the carriage, only inches away, so Lady Penworth chattered away, filling Harry in on four years' worth of family doings.

❧

It was all so familiar. His feet fit automatically into the worn grooves on the steps of Penworth House, and the door swung open before them.

"Lord Tunbury!" Jacobs, who had been the butler here for God only knew how long, beamed at him. "Welcome back."

"Good to see you again." Tunbury couldn't help smiling back. Jacobs held himself as straight as ever, though most of his hair seemed to have disappeared. Had that been recent, or was he remembering Jacobs as he had first seen him?

There was no time to ask, or even to wonder. No sooner had his overcoat, gloves, and hat vanished than he was ushered into the sitting room and plied with tea while Lord Penworth and Pip were sent for. Rycote, not Pip. He should remember to call him Rycote now. After all, they were no longer children. The warmth of the fire was nothing compared to the warmth of the welcome. Not a word of reproach about his four-year absence.

Over dinner, the questions about his travels were curious and interested, not reproachful. And all different. Lord Penworth asked about political conditions. Lady Penworth asked about social conditions. Rycote asked about farming conditions.

And Norrie asked about his adventures. She wanted

to know about everything. What did places look like? How did people talk? What did they wear or eat? What did they do? What was it like in Brazil?

He laughed at that one. "It was hot. Horribly hot."

She laughed right back. "Oh, how could it possibly be horrible to be hot. London has been miserably cold and wet for months."

"Hot and steamy is far worse. You have no escape. The air is so thick and heavy all the time that the moment you move, the sweat pours down until you feel as if you're drowning. All the planters and their families, all the wealthy families in the cities, insist on dressing as if they were in Europe—tight collars and frock coats for the gentlemen, huge skirts for the ladies. Naturally, they can't do anything except sit around and fan themselves while they complain about the heat and order the slaves about. Slaves do everything."

Pip frowned. "I thought they finally abolished the slave trade."

That prompted a sour laugh from Harry. "That's no help for the poor devils who are already there." He caught the look of concern that shadowed Norrie's face. "But the jungles are incredible. Plants, creatures, birds, even butterflies in fantastic colors, the likes of which you've never seen. And the river—it's like nothing in Europe. Sometimes it's hemmed in by jungle, sometimes it spreads out into swamps so broad you don't know where it ends."

Norrie was looking at him skeptically, as if she knew he had changed the subject deliberately. She might not want to be protected from ugliness, but that wouldn't stop him from trying. There were horrors she should never have to face, not if he could help it. So he grinned at her. "And the most enormous snakes, snakes that could swallow you whole."

She gasped for a second, then grinned back. "Beast! I don't believe it."

"I swear. I saw one swallow a pig that was a good deal fatter than you." He put a hand over his heart, but she just shook her head at him.

When Lady Penworth rose to leave the gentlemen to their port and cigars, he thought Norrie would object. However, one look from her mother was enough to settle the matter. Everyone obeyed Lady Penworth. That was another thing that hadn't changed.

He couldn't restrain a grin as he watched Norrie leave the room. Without doing anything that could earn her a parental reprimand, she managed to display resentment in every line of her body. And while he regretted her departure, there was something he wanted to know, a question he could hardly ask while she was in the room.

There was a companionable silence while they slid the port along and got their cigars drawing properly. Tunbury leaned back, hoping no tension showed in his posture, and asked, "How is it that Norrie is still unwed? Or is there something in the offing?"

Rycote snorted, but Lord Penworth smiled gently and said, "She's very young yet, barely twenty-one. I'm grateful she hasn't wanted to rush into an engagement but is taking her time to look about her."

Tunbury felt able to breathe again.

"Taking her time is one way to put it," Rycote

said. "They come swarming around her, but as soon as one of them starts to show serious intentions, she sends him off. This one's too boring, that one is a fool, another one is only interested in her fortune. And they keep pestering me, asking how to win her favor. As if I would know."

"Is she wrong in her judgments?" asked Tunbury.

Rycote gave an irritated sigh. "No, to be fair she's been perfectly right. Hamilton is boring, and Wandsworth is rather a fool. As for Carruthers, probably the less said, the better."

"Carruthers?" Tunbury sat up in alarm. "But I warned you about him before I left."

"Yes, well, I don't know exactly what happened, but a week or two after that, he fell into a fishpond in the Coopers' garden. Norrie said he slipped."

The three gentlemen looked at each other and laughed.

❧

Later that evening Tunbury sat by the fire in his room, his slippered feet stretched out to the warmth of the blaze. A wood fire, not coal, because Lady Penworth preferred the smell of wood in the bedrooms. The room was as familiar as the smell, the room he always had when he stayed with the Tremaines in London. It had the same big carved mahogany bed with the posts he used to measure himself against. He remembered how proud he had been the year he grew so much that he had topped two whole knobs. There was the same mahogany wardrobe, the same marble-topped dressing table with the brown and white pitcher and basin. It was as if everything had just been waiting for him to return.

There were even some of his old books still on the shelves by the window—*The Three Musketeers, Waverly, The Deerslayer*. That last was the one that had made him determined to go to America on his travels, but he hadn't found any Indians in the woods of New England. On the western plains, but that wasn't quite the same. Well, that war had been a long time ago. He didn't suppose there were many Jacobites lurking in the Scottish heather anymore, either.

His clothes had been unpacked and put away, his shaving gear was set out, and the bed was turned down. It was as if he had never been away.

He was back with the Tremaines, in the one place where he had determined never to intrude again. Apparently, he was the only one who realized it was an intrusion, that he did not belong here.

They had all—Lord and Lady Penworth, Pip, and Norrie—welcomed him as if he had just been away at school for a term. The younger children actually were away at school.

It was not that the Tremaines had failed to notice his absence. They were all eager to hear about his travels. But there was no coolness, no resentment at his abrupt departure with no real explanation, no complaints about his failure to write. They had expected him to return, and they were glad he had.

Now he was trying to make sense of the day, trying to make sense of himself. This was precisely why he had fled England four years ago. He hadn't wanted to bring the ugliness of the sordid de Vaux mélange into this house, into this family. He had run away. Cowardly, perhaps, but he never wanted them to know his family secrets. What was common knowledge was bad enough.

He had tried to convince himself that he wanted to be forgotten. He had behaved in ways that were probably best forgotten. But the moment he heard Lady Penworth's familiar voice call his name, the years fell away, and he felt like a schoolboy again, reveling in the warmth of her welcome. When he walked into the drawing room of Penworth House, he felt as if he had come home. How could he cut himself off from all that had been best in his life?

And then there was Norrie.

She had hugged him right there on the street, and this evening she had teased him just the way she teased Pip. She twitted Pip for his new moustache and she twitted him for being still clean-shaven when even her father had grown a small beard. In short, she treated him like a brother.

He had thought that was what he wanted. He had told himself he would be able to think of her as a sister.

He had been a fool.

She was so damn beautiful, even more so than when he left. She had been a lovely girl then. Now she was a beautiful woman. Not one of those simpering little dolls that seemed to be the fashion. She had a luscious mouth that begged to be kissed, and a bosom that promised paradise. And then there were those aquamarine eyes. He could never decide if they actually did tilt up at the edge or if it was just the way her brows slanted. A man could spend hours just staring at her eyes.

She may not have been married, but it was still true that she treated him like a brother, just as she always had. Why wouldn't she? For all those years he had been turning up for school vacations along with Pip, and the three of them had played together, gone fishing together, gone riding together. He and Pip had even taught her to play Rugby football, and she had mastered the tackle very well. He could remember her delight the time—she couldn't have been more than nine—when she knocked him sprawling in the mud. Why wouldn't she think of him as a brother?

All right. He could manage that. One thing he had learned in his travels was a bit of self-discipline. It would not be easy to treat her like a sister, to have her treat him like a brother, but if that was all he could have, so be it. At least he would be able to see her and be part of her family. He would be able to protect her.

It would not be easy, but it was better than nothing.

❧

Lady Elinor allowed Martha, her nursery maid turned lady's maid, to remove her clothing, hand her the soap and towel to wash, brush and braid her hair, tuck it into a nightcap, and put her into a warm flannel nightgown. But instead of snuggling under the covers as she usually did, once the maid was gone, Elinor wrapped herself in a woolen shawl and curled up on the window seat to look out on the darkness.

She smiled when she saw that a few stars were actually visible in the London sky. What with the rain and the fog, that didn't happen very often. Perhaps it was a good sign.

She could hardly believe that Harry was back. She

hadn't realized how much she'd missed him. It was
as if she saw him on the street and thought, "Oh yes,
that's what I've been missing."

She didn't know why—it couldn't be anything
romantic, after all—but he just seemed so much more
real, so much more alive than any of the other young
men she knew. Maybe it was just that he had gone
off and had adventures, wandered around the world
and seen all kinds of different people, done all sorts
of things. Everyone else she knew had just done all
the expected things, turned up at dinners and dances,
said all the things they were supposed to say, done the
things they were supposed to do.

Just as she had.

Was she bored? She considered that possibility. No,
that wasn't it precisely.

She was envious—that's what it was.

Harry had gone to exciting places and met exciting
people while she had stayed home and done nothing,
nothing more exciting than flirting and dancing. It had
been fun, and she had enjoyed it, but it didn't seem to
be enough. She wanted more.

Did she seem terribly dull to him? He had probably
met sophisticated and glamorous women—and maybe
done more than just meet them. After all, he had
been gone for four whole years. It would be foolish
to assume he had led a monkish existence. Even Pip,
stuffy though he might sometimes be, had affairs that
she and Mama pretended not to know about.

But that didn't matter now. Harry had come back.
He even seemed glad to be back.

She was so glad to have him back.

Three

RYCOTE WAS A MEMBER OF WHITE'S. OF COURSE. Tunbury could not keep from grinning. Lord Penworth was a prominent reformer, an outspoken opponent of the Crimean War, a critic of the country's India policy, a proponent of universal education, et cetera, et cetera, et cetera. Naturally his son was a member of the stuffiest, most conservative club around.

Well, perhaps not completely stuffy. Tunbury caught sight of the famous betting book. This was, after all, the club where Alvanley had once bet £3,000 on the speed of a raindrop. Tunbury left Rycote to order a bottle of wine and strolled over to see what was occupying the minds of the aristocracy these days. One glance was all it took to turn him to stone.

"What's caught your eye?" Rycote looked over his shoulder. "Oh."

Of course. The thing might as well have been written in scarlet letters ten feet high. "Lord M wagers Lord B that Lady D will change lovers at least twice before Easter."

He felt his friend's hand on his shoulder. He didn't need the comfort. Not really. But he felt it.

"These fellows don't know what they're talking about most of the time. And there are half a dozen Lady D's."

Tunbury turned to face his friend. "But we both know they mean my mother, Lady Doncaster." His mouth twisted. He was trying for a smile but it probably came out a grimace. No matter. "Don't worry. I stopped fighting over remarks about her honor—her lack of honor—years ago."

Yes, he'd stopped fighting during his second year at Rugby. He'd gone home to Bradenham Abbey before going to Penworth Castle for Christmas. His sisters were babies then—Julia just three and Olivia still an infant—and he'd wanted to see them. But he'd made the mistake of opening the door to his mother's sitting room without knocking and found her copulating with one of the footmen.

He couldn't remember ever loving his mother. She had never been enough a part of his life to prompt any feeling one way or the other. But after that he had been unable to think of her with anything but disgust. Was his father's drinking a response to her behavior? If so, it was a cowardly, contemptible response.

He'd never told anyone about that scene, not even Pip, but thereafter he'd greeted comments on his mother's activities with an indifferent shrug, the same way he treated remarks about his father's drunkenness. As for the whispers about the bad blood of the de Vaux family, he pretended he didn't hear them. What he couldn't do was ignore the fear that those whispers might be true, that he had inherited that bad blood.

Rycote led him to a pair of leather chairs in a corner, leaving the fireplace seats to the elderly members, and began talking about the new orchards he was planting at the estate his father had turned over to him on his twenty-first birthday. He was discussing apple varieties—Foxwhelp, Tremlett's Bitter, Knobbed Russet, Winesap from America, and Muscadet de Dieppe from Normandy.

Tunbury let the names wash over him. It sounded so sane, so clean, rather like the entire Tremaine family. Rycote was doing this deliberately, he knew, trying to distract him. As if he could ever forget what his parents were like. "The Degraded de Vaux" one schoolboy wit had called them, and the fellow's friends had laughed. Harry had to fight that time, and Rycote had joined him. When it was over, he'd thanked Rycote but told him that he shouldn't have bothered. What they said about his parents was perfectly true. All the more reason they shouldn't say it, Rycote had replied.

How could he have survived without Rycote's steady friendship and loyalty?

What would have become of him without the Tremaines?

A wave of guilt washed over him. For all those years when he was growing up, he had the Tremaines. He could forget that he was the son of the Earl and Countess of Doncaster because he almost never saw them. After a while, it had become possible for him to go for months, even years, without thinking about his family.

To his shame, that meant he had ignored his sisters as well as his parents.

Did his sisters have anyone to help them? They certainly didn't have their brother. He had left them behind when he ran off four years ago, never giving them a thought in his eagerness to escape. Not that he had given them many thoughts before that. If anything, he had simply assumed that they were safe enough in the care of nurses and governesses. As a boy, he had been powerless to do anything for them, so it was easier to not think about them.

Had they been safe? They had no way to get in touch with him. Had they needed him? That was a joke. Why would it even occur to them that he might help them? He never had before. What had he given them? An occasional visit of a few days when he could be sure his parents weren't in residence at the Abbey?

But he was no longer a boy, and his sisters weren't babies anymore. Julia must be…seventeen. Was she making her come-out this year? Good God. The poor girl, to be introduced to society by the most notorious whore in it. There must be something he could do about that. He had no idea what, but there must be something.

He would have to go see them.

"What do you think?"

Tunbury blinked. What did he think about his sisters? But Rycote couldn't know he was thinking about them. "I'm sorry. I was woolgathering."

"Obviously. I was saying that my father is suddenly looking old. Is he ill, do you think? Or just tired?"

It immediately struck Harry that Rycote was right. The marquess couldn't be more than fifty-five or so by Tunbury's reckoning, but he had looked drawn and haggard. Harry had noticed it when Penworth came in the evening before, but the impression had faded in the pleasure of their talk.

"I don't know," he said slowly. "Are you worried?"

Rycote shrugged. "Yes, a bit. He spends too much time in the Lords, fighting too many losing battles. I think Mama is worried too."

Rycote was not one to parade his feelings. That he had even mentioned this meant that he was very worried indeed.

&

The next day a footman brought Harry an invitation to join Lady Penworth in her sitting room. A bit surprised, even unnerved, by the formality, Tunbury promptly presented himself at the door of the chamber overlooking the garden. It had not changed much since he first saw it as a boy, and it had been old-fashioned even then. Pale curtains were pulled back to allow as much light as possible to enter through the tall windows. The marquetry table had been there as long as he could remember, always with a vase of flowers on it. Hothouse flowers at this time of year, but still scenting the air.

The upholstery and draperies must have been replaced from time to time, but always in the pale colors of the past, not the deep hues currently in style. Lady Penworth was not one to let the coal dust of London defeat her. Light colors, painted wood, and walls covered with watercolor sketches of her children made the marchioness's room seem full of sunshine even in late January.

Lady Penworth's smile was full of sunshine as well

when she looked up to greet him. He could not resist smiling in return. She looked so much like Norrie, though he supposed he ought to say that Norrie looked like her mother. The same dark hair, the same lovely oval face, the same slightly tilted blue eyes. Well, Norrie's eyes had a bit more green than Lady Penworth's did. All in all, it was one more piece of good fortune for the man who married Norrie—his wife would be beautiful all her life.

"Harry, thank you for coming. I need your advice." She gestured to the chair facing her beside the fire. "I am worried about Penworth."

Harry halted for a second as he was sitting down, then settled himself carefully and took a long look at Lady Penworth before speaking. She might have been taken for a bonbon, covered as she was in frills and ribbons, but she did actually look worried, and he had a sudden, sinking feeling. "Is Lord Penworth ill?" he asked cautiously.

"No, that is not the problem. At least, it is not the problem yet."

Harry did not feel comforted. He had started to worry himself, especially after talking to Rycote. If his friend was worried enough to mention it, and if Lady Penworth was worried, something was definitely wrong, and that distressed Harry more than he could say. There was no man he admired—no, loved—more than Lord Penworth.

"He is tired. Far too tired." Lady Penworth frowned.

"He does seem tired, a bit depressed," he agreed carefully. It would have been overly blunt to say that Penworth looked terrible, but tired was a good deal better than truly ill. Could weariness be all there was to the problem?

"Depressed," she said slowly. "Yes, I suppose that is a good description. He has always been conscientious to a fault, but this recent war with Russia has worn on him. He was unable to prevent it; he was unable to convince anyone of the dangers of giving command to fools like Cardigan. And now he is worried that the army is going to create another disaster in India."

Harry acknowledged that with a grimace. "I spent some time in India. I wish I could say that his fears are groundless."

"What are your plans for the next few months, Harry?"

The abrupt change of subject startled him. "Well, I can't say that I have any specific plans. After talking to Lord Penworth these past few days, I have begun to think I might try for a seat in Parliament."

"That would make Penworth very happy."

Her approving smile made Harry flush. "It was just a thought," he mumbled.

"Is there anything urgent about it? I don't think any elections are coming up at the moment."

"No, not at all. Just a thought."

"Then perhaps you would be able to help me."

"Anything, my lady."

She smiled at him again. "Well, Penworth needs a distraction, something that will absorb him enough to take his mind off the iniquities of the British Army. He needs something he can sink his mental teeth into, something that he can enjoy with no feelings of guilt. Something scholarly. I think I know what will do it. You were in Italy for a while, were you not?"

"For more than a year."

"Then you speak Italian?"

"Yes, somewhat." He was confused. Could she want him to teach Lord Penworth Italian? His own knowledge of the language was thoroughly vernacular, not intended for reading Dante or Petrarch, or even for diplomatic correspondence. More for dealing with officials and getting in and out of gambling casinos with his skin intact.

"Wonderful." Lady Penworth beamed at him. "Now, I don't know if you have read Mr. Dennis's book on Etruscan antiquities."

He shook his head. "The Etruscans? Are they the ones with all the tombs, and the statues with the funny little smiles?"

"Yes, that's them. They seem to have been such a cheerful people. But you haven't read Dennis?"

He shook his head again.

"No matter," she continued. "I have and so has Penworth. We both found it fascinating and talked about someday going to Italy to see the ruins for ourselves. Now would be the perfect time."

By now Harry had a sinking feeling. If Lady Penworth was being this indirect, he suspected it was because she thought he would not want to do whatever she was proposing. And since he owed her and her entire family far too much to be able to refuse anything she asked, he was growing increasingly nervous.

"Do you wish me to help you plan a trip?" he asked hopefully.

"Nothing so simple, I'm afraid." She gave him a rueful smile. "What I really want is for you to accompany us."

"You and Lord Penworth?"

"And Rycote and Elinor. I thought to leave soon, while the younger ones are still in school."

The sinking feeling was replaced by panic. No. He could not possibly do this. "A family voyage? But surely you will not need me when you have Rycote and Lord Penworth."

"Oh, but I do! Lord Penworth knows almost no Italian, and I really do not want to burden him with the cares of dealing with officialdom. You know that Rycote is truly hopeless with languages, and his way of dealing with officials whose rules make no sense to him is to lose his temper and shout."

Harry bit back a smile at the memory of Pip at school battling what he saw as an usher's abuse of authority. Pip could never tolerate bullies.

"Elinor speaks French and Italian, of course," Lady Penworth continued blithely, "but it would be difficult if not impossible to get officials to take her seriously. The French and Italians seem unable to treat women as anything other than decorative ninnies. They are quite as bad as Englishmen, possibly worse. No, Harry, Penworth needs to relax. That will only happen if you are there to take care of things. He trusts you."

She looked at him seriously. "I know this is a great deal to ask, months of your life when you may have all sorts of things planned"—she smiled impishly—"things you might not want to tell me about, and you need not. You must just say so if I am asking too much."

Too much? Of course it was too much. How could he possibly set off on a trip where he would be with Norrie for months? There must be some reason why he had to stay in England. There must be responsibilities involving his father's—the Earl of Doncaster's—estates. He was the heir, after all, and it was unlikely that either the earl or the countess had been attending to things. They never had before.

He opened his mouth to say "No, I couldn't possibly," but what came out was "I would be honored."

Four

A WEEK LATER, HE WAS NOT SURE HOW IT HAD ALL come about, but somehow Lord Penworth was under the impression that he was indulging his wife by agreeing to this trip. Pip was under the impression that he was going along to protect his mother and sister. Norrie did not seem to care how or why the trip had been proposed. She was completely unable to behave with ladylike restraint and had all she could do to keep from jumping up and down with glee.

Lady Penworth was summoned to visit the queen.

"I don't entirely understand it," she told Elinor on her return. "Her Majesty seems to approve of me. Do you suppose it's because I have six children?"

"Don't be silly, Mama," Elinor said with a grin. "It's because you clearly adore Papa, just as she adores Prince Albert. You are a Good Example and show that she isn't foolish."

"She is, of course. If she weren't a queen, no one would take her for anything but a ninny." Lady Penworth settled herself comfortably and took a sip of tea. "But I am grateful that she approves of our trip. It does make things easier."

Things did not go entirely smoothly, of course.

Tunbury was relieved to be the one taking care of the minor problems, like arranging letters of credit, working out an itinerary to get them to Rome with the least discomfort, and getting passports and visas— France, Austria, and the Papal States were all involved, and some signatures could not be obtained until a week or two before arrival.

They would spend a week or so in Paris, and a hotel was needed there. Then Penworth said no— the ambassador was an old friend, so they would be staying at the embassy. So the ambassador had to be warned. Hotels would be needed in Chalons, Lyon, Aix, Avignon, and Marseilles. Then the British consul in Rome was requested to arrange for a private carriage to meet the party at Civita Vecchia, along with a *lascia-passare*, the passport that would enable them to avoid the endless formalities of the customhouse. The consul was also requested to arrange apartments for them in Rome.

In some ways everything was much simpler than it had been when he set off on his own travels. People fell over themselves to be helpful to a marquess, especially one who was an important and respected figure in the House of Lords, and—even more especially— one who was one of the wealthiest men in England.

On the other hand, not much had to be arranged for a young man traveling on his own, one who avoided mentioning his title and enjoyed the anonymity this provided. Nobody paid much attention to Harry de Vaux, who had far more freedom that Viscount Tunbury could ever have. However, that sort of travel also presented certain dangers, and more than once he had occasion to be grateful for his size and strength. Lady Penworth and Lady Elinor were entitled to all the safety and comfort that could be provided. Except...

Norrie would enjoy traveling the way he had. She would love the freedom of it, and he would be all the protection she needed. Together they could...

No.

He clamped down on that thought, determined to dismiss Lady Elinor from his mind. He had obligations, obligations he had neglected for far too long. He had two sisters.

&

The springs on the hired gig should have been replaced years ago, and the padding had almost completely disappeared from the seat. As good a way as any to do penance, Tunbury decided. Did he qualify as a prodigal son? Could one be a prodigal son if one's parents were prodigals themselves? The right wheel hit a bump and he went up in the air, landing on his hip and putting an end to meaningless speculations.

He was a bit late for a visit to his sisters, wasn't he? He should have come the minute he returned to England. He snorted. What rot. Late wasn't the half of it. What he should have done was talk to them before he left in the first place. Maybe he should even have taken them with him. No, that was impossible. They were only children. He couldn't have told them the truth, of course. But he could have told them something.

Instead, he had run away. There was no other way to put it. And he was planning to run away again after this visit.

The self-reproach was veering dangerously close to self-pity by the time he found himself in the blue drawing room of Bradenham Abbey, pacing nervously while he awaited his sisters. Shouldn't the room seem more familiar? This was his home, in theory at least, no matter that he'd spent little time here in the past fifteen years. Still, had it always been this smothered in heavy draperies? He would surely have remembered all these badly painted landscapes on the walls with their anatomically bizarre deer. But if they were new, what blind man had chosen them?

He paused to stare out the window, trying to decide if there had been any changes in the landscape. Perhaps it just looked gloomy because it was February and the weak sun had almost set.

"Harry!"

He turned in time to catch the bundle that hurtled into him. It wrapped its arms around him, and he looked down into brown eyes and a glowing smile under a mop of blond curls. He hugged it back. "Hullo, Olivia." He managed to squeeze the words out around the lump in his throat.

He looked up to see his other sister standing just inside the door, hands folded at her waist, face impassive. "Hello, Julia."

She gave him a brief nod of acknowledgment.

"You remember our names. I stand amazed. I had thought that you had quite forgotten our existence."

He flinched at the sting, deserved as it was. Had she polished that speech, preparing for this scene? All the words he had rehearsed had vanished from his mind.

"Oh no," Olivia protested. "I knew you were coming back. When we found out you had left, Mama said you would not come back, but I was sure you would. We had your letters."

"Your letters." Julia's voice was flat. "Let me see. You wrote to us from Greece and told us there were ruins. Then came India. You said it was hot. And America. You said the Great Plains were flat and empty."

He forced himself to meet her eyes. "I'm sorry. That sounds ridiculously inadequate, I know. I can't explain, but I had to leave. I simply had to."

"Sorry? Sorry that you left?" she asked incredulously.

"No. Sorry that I had to leave you and Olivia here on your own."

They stared at each other in silence. Finally, she turned away and flopped down in a chair. The haughty young lady had been replaced by a sulky child. "You might as well sit down," she said. "I'm not really angry." She thought for a moment. "Well, yes, I am. But it's mostly envy. I'd run away too if I could."

He sat down on a sofa cautiously, with Olivia beside him clinging to his hand. He had no idea what he ought to say. It was as if his sisters were strangers.

Well, of course they seemed like strangers. They'd been little more than babies when he went off to school, and since then he had never been at the

Abbey for more than a few days at a time. But they were his sisters. He felt that he ought to know them. Pip knew his sisters.

In fact, he knew Pip's sisters too. Far better than he knew his own. He squirmed uncomfortably. He wasn't even sure how old Julia was, though she certainly wasn't a child anymore. In fact, she was really quite pretty, and her hair was up. That meant she was grown up, didn't it? He thought for a moment. She was seventeen, he was sure of it. Unless she was eighteen. No, seventeen. "Have you come out yet?"

The abrupt question won him a glare. "No, I haven't. Nor will I be coming out this season. Something else I have to thank you for."

He blinked. "How can that be my fault?"

"Without you about, Mama was trying to pretend she was not much older than thirty. That fiction will be harder to maintain once I am out."

"That's ludicrous." He had to laugh. "You can't be serious."

She shrugged, the look on her face far too cynical for a young girl.

"Are you going to be staying now?" Olivia was looking up at him with those big brown eyes.

"Don't be foolish, Livvy," said Julia. "Why would he want to stay?"

"It's not that," he said, the guilt piling up. "I'm going to Italy in a week or so with the Tremaines."

"Oh, of course," said Julia. "With the Tremaines. It's always been the Tremaines. For as long as I can remember, you've stopped off to see us only on your way to the Tremaines. They're your real family. Not us."

The protest died in his throat. The Tremaines weren't his real family. He knew that all too well. But he had always wished they were, and he had been able to find a refuge with them for all those years. Did his sisters have such a choice? "Do you have some friends you can stay with? Some neighbors?"

Julia gave a short, bitter laugh. "Respectable people wish to have nothing to do with us. We might bring the contagion of the notorious Lady Doncaster with us."

What an idiot he had been. He should have realized that it would be even worse for them as girls than it had been for him. He had been able to fight, and after he had bloodied enough noses, the other boys left him alone. Girls couldn't do that. They would be surrounded by whispers and slights, and they would have no way to fight back.

The stigma of bad blood would color everyone's thinking. Decent people would avoid any contact with them, fearing they would turn out just like their mother. It wouldn't be long before there would be others who sought their company, hoping they would indeed be just like their mother. He would have to deal with that problem, but he could not at the moment. Not yet.

"This trip to Italy—I have to go." He lifted his hand in a hopeless gesture.

"Really?" Julia managed to invest that single word with a remarkable amount of scorn.

"I owe them so much, and I gave my word. But I promise that when I get back, I will take care of you. I will find some way."

"Really?" said Olivia. There was no scorn in her voice, but the hope in her face was heartbreaking.

"Really," he said. "Have I ever broken a promise?"

Olivia stopped and frowned in thought. "I don't think you've ever made one," she said at last.

No, he didn't suppose he ever had. "Well, I'm making one now."

❦

For Lady Elinor, preparations for the trip were centered on the dressmaker. Her mother shared her concern. What were they to wear while exploring ruins and descending into tombs? Crinolines were out of the question.

Long hours in conference with the dressmaker were required, then days when Elinor and her mother spent a good deal of time with a sketchbook, followed by more hours with the dressmaker. When the final product was tried on, Mrs. Packer looked at her clients in surprise. She walked slowly around them, examining the outfits from all angles. "Well," she said at last, "I doubt I will find any other clients willing to dress in this fashion, but I do believe you two will be able to pull it off. I only hope Lord Penworth won't demand my head for it."

Elinor laughed and spun around. "You know he will not do anything of the sort. I only wish I could wear something like this all the time."

"In London you would either be pelted with eggs or arrested on the spot," said her mother dryly. "But the outfit definitely seems practical."

It was more than practical, thought Elinor. It was

wonderfully flattering. The color, a deep blue with hints of green, deepened the color of her eyes. The sturdy poplin jacket, with its corded seams running from the shoulders to the vee at the center of the waist, made her waist look tiny even without tight lacing. The ruffles at the wrists and neck of the blouse looked as soft and frivolous as lace without being nearly so fragile. As for the skirt, they had taken a leaf from Mrs. Bloomer and improved on her design. It was a divided skirt, far narrower than anything that had been seen in decades, coming down below the knee, over loose trousers that tucked into boots.

Elinor smiled at her reflection, a devilish smile. She looked ready for adventure. Harry would not be able to dismiss her as a child when he saw her in this. He would finally see her as an adventurer like him, as an equal, as a worthy partner.

She would make him see it.

Five

THE *LADY ANNE* ROSE AND FELL AS SHE PROCEEDED across the Channel. She was no leaking sieve, no indeed. At more than a hundred feet, the *Lady Anne* was one of the finest steam yachts designed by Robert Napier, elegant enough to carry the Penworth party in style, practical enough to serve the multitudinous Penworth interests. The party had embarked in London in the early evening, and the highly competent and experienced captain had assured them that by the time they awoke in the morning they would be safe and sound in Calais.

The Channel apparently took offense at such hubris.

There was not a storm, precisely, but winds and tides and currents all decided to play a game of tag, tossing the yacht about as if it were nothing more than a dinghy.

Lady Penworth crouched over a chamber pot and moaned that she was going to die. Her husband held her gently, emptying the chamber pot and wiping her face with a damp cloth as needed, and made soothing noises.

Rycote lay collapsed in his bunk, an arm covering his eyes, regretting that he would not live to see the newly planted apple and pear trees in his orchards bear fruit. There were more regrets, but he always tried to ignore foolish dreams.

The three servants huddled on the floor of the main cabin, clinging to the legs of the dining table, which was firmly bolted to the floor. They could not imagine what on earth had ever possessed them to leave dry land.

Lady Elinor stood on deck, holding firmly onto the rail to maintain her balance, and took deep breaths of the salty wind. It was wonderful, spectacular, fantastic, exhilarating—she did not know enough superlatives to describe the way she felt. She was beginning an adventure, and she reveled in a freedom she had never known.

It was not that she had grown up in a stifling atmosphere. Neither of her parents considered ignorance and stupidity to be virtues, even for women, so she had always been encouraged to learn, to examine, to question—at least, in private. But she had always been protected, she knew. While standing here on the deck of the ship was not actually dangerous, it was possible to pretend that it was, that she was riding a storm-tossed sea that could wash her up on the shores of some fantastic land where dragons and dangers awaited, prepared to test her courage.

"Norrie, what in God's name do you think you are doing?"

She looked up to see Tunbury running toward her, skidding a bit on the wet deck as he came to a halt beside her. His hair was blown every which way, and he was fighting the wind in an effort to button his coat.

"Hullo, Harry. Isn't it grand?" She grinned up at him, not commenting on the skid. Even though he had broken her mood, her heart gave a surprisingly familiar thump. To her confusion, that seemed to happen every time she saw him. "We're surrounded by darkness. You can't see a thing. We could have sailed off the ends of the earth, be traveling through space, for all we know."

"And when you get washed overboard, we won't have a prayer of finding you because no one will be able to see you, you ninny." He had to shout over the noise of the waves. He probably would have shouted anyway.

She turned away slightly. He was talking to her as if she were still a child, the way he always seemed to talk to her these days. Honestly, he had treated her with more respect when she was ten and he was showing her how to bait a hook. Couldn't he get it through his head that she was an adult? And entitled to be treated as one?

"You have no sense," he said, still shouting.

Just then the ship lifted and sent her lurching into him. He put an arm around her waist to steady her, and she found herself leaning against him, her hands on his chest. There was a frozen moment when the world seemed to go silent. She could swear she heard her own heart beating, and his as well.

Something strange was happening. That much she knew, though she could not say what it was. Men had put their hands on her waist and held her before. It happened every time she danced at a ball. But that felt no different from her brother's touch.

This was different.

This felt nothing like having her brother hold her.

She wanted Harry to hold her closer. She wanted to wrap her arms around him and melt right into him. She felt her bones dissolving. If he hadn't been holding her up, she would be a little puddle on the deck. She wanted…she wasn't sure what she wanted, but there was something, and it was important. A little moan escaped her throat.

Then the wind and the waves regained their voices and he jumped back, snatching his hand away.

"You aren't wearing a corset." He sounded a bit hoarse, and she might have thought he was making an accusation if she hadn't recalled the tremor she had felt when his arm was wrapped around her waist. Of course, she probably would not have been able to feel the tremor if she had been wearing a corset. Then again, if she had been wearing a corset, he might not have trembled. A puzzlement.

But he had been trembling. It wasn't just her own trembling that she had felt. And she could still feel the heat of him where he had touched her. She wouldn't have been able to feel that through a corset, at least not as well.

How dare he scold, as if she had done something wrong, when he was the one who was making her feel—well, all these things. If anyone was at fault, he was. She put up her chin and snapped at him. "That's right. I'm not wearing a corset, nor am I wearing crinolines or a half-dozen petticoats. The way we are tossing about, I wouldn't be able to move about on deck if I were, so I left them off."

They both glanced down. The wind was blowing her skirts against her in a way that made it obvious that she had left off her petticoats. That she had legs. It was quite liberating. He made an odd sort of growling sound. Then the ship did its dip-and-rise thing again. She wasn't holding the rail any longer so she went tumbling against him again.

She didn't make any effort to keep on her feet because—she wasn't quite sure why—she wanted to lean against him. Her hands were pressed against his chest, where the rough wool of his jacket was lightly covered with damp. She could feel it right through her gloves. Would it be too forward to put her hands on his shoulders?

Apparently he thought so. He grabbed hold of her arm just above the elbow and held her away from him. Half leading and half dragging her back toward the cabins, he spoke without looking at her. "You will get inside and stay inside until your mother tells you that you may come out on deck. And that will be when it is safe to come out properly dressed."

He sounded absolutely furious, but she was now feeling quite furious herself. "I am not a child, Harcourt de Vaux, and I am quite sensibly dressed even if I do not live up to your standards of what is proper." She pulled her arm from his grip and stumbled to the door. "I came outside for some fresh air because, in case you had not noticed, it is quite stuffy in the cabins, to say nothing of the unpleasant smells. And I was perfectly safe until you

came along and began hauling me about and acting
like a bear."

She pulled open the door on the passage to the
cabins and marched through. How could he manage
to be so utterly infuriating? So stupidly male? Her only
regret was that the wind prevented her from giving the
door a satisfactory slam.

&ho;

Acting like a bear, was he? Well, that seemed reasonable, since all he wanted to do was crush her in his
arms. Did she have no notion of the effect she had,
walking around like that? Not just on him. She would
have the same effect on any man.

He closed his eyes and leaned against the door. No,
the problem was him. She was right. The way she had
dressed was perfectly sensible if she wanted to come
out on deck, and it was perfectly sensible to want to
come out on deck. The cabins were filled with people
moaning and retching. She could do nothing to help
them and the fresh air was welcome. He had come out
for the same reason.

After all, it wasn't as if this were a public steamer.
It was, practically speaking, her own home. This was
her father's steam yacht, and the only passengers were
her own family.

And him.

He thumped his head against the door. He had
behaved like an idiot. She had every right to be
annoyed. It was hardly her fault that the realization
that she was not wearing a corset and a dozen petticoats had given him an overwhelming desire to rip off

whatever she was wearing and make love to her right there on the tossing deck.

He was a beast.

She was an innocent. She was part of a decent, loving family. A young girl like her knew nothing of the passions raging in him. If it seemed that he always ended up scolding her like some elderly pompous uncle, it was because as long as he scolded, he was in no danger of saying the things he must not say. He dragged her about by the arm because as long as he did that, he was not pulling her into an embrace, crushing her to him.

Self-disgust welled up in him. He had no right even to be in the same room with her. His very existence could contaminate her. His father—the earl—was a useless drunkard and his mother was no better than a whore. How could he even put a hand on her?

How could he not put a hand on her when she stood beside him, looking so innocent?

He had to keep his distance, make certain he was never alone with her. Surely it would be easier once they were on dry land again. There would be steamers on the Saône and the Rhone, and another to take them from Marseilles to Civita Vecchia, but those were not likely to be difficult journeys, not like the Channel. The others would always be around.

As long as they were all in a group, he would be able to manage. He was sure of it.

∽

They spent a day in a hotel in Calais while Lady Penworth recuperated. Lady Elinor took care of her mother, and Rycote and the servants huddled in their own rooms to recuperate, while Tunbury and Lord Penworth took a long walk and spoke of nothing more personal than politics.

The drive to Paris took place under a gray and gloomy sky, which in no way managed to dampen Lady Elinor's spirits. She was enchanted by the rows of poplars lining the road and by the signs in French on buildings—"It's so much more thrilling to stop at an *auberge* than at an inn!"

She was slightly less enthusiastic about staying at the British Embassy on the rue du Faubourg Saint-Honoré. Lord and Lady Cowley, the ambassador and his wife, were perfectly gracious in welcoming the marquess and his family, but she had not come to the continent to visit Englishmen, especially Englishmen of the sort she saw every day at home.

Even the meals were the same. Breakfasts of sausages and eggs and tea, when what she wanted were croissants and café au lait. Afternoon tea, when she wanted to sip an *apéritif* in a café surrounded by artists and writers—which was precisely what Pip and Harry had done, curse them.

Nonetheless, she behaved herself. She smiled sweetly and thanked Lady Cowley prettily and didn't scream with frustration. Nor did she snap at Lord Cowley when he chuckled and apologized for boring her when he realized that she had been listening to the conversation he was having with Papa about the best way to handle Louis Napoleon and his dreams of glory. She even managed a sugary simper. Fortunately, Harry came along and drew her away. At least she supposed it was fortunate.

"It is so infuriating." She strode across the room, fists clenched, and plopped herself down on a settee. "Why do men assume that women are featherbrained idiots with no interest in anything other than fashion and frivolity?"

Harry had followed her and sat down beside her, a bit more relaxed. "Um, perhaps because you just simpered at him like a featherbrained idiot?"

That earned him a glare. "Of course I did. If I had done anything else, he would have been horrified. Poor Papa has to deal with these ignorant, bigoted fools, and I don't want to make things any more difficult for him than they already are. I do have some common sense, you know."

Harry looked dubious.

"Papa actually finds me quite useful."

"Useful? What do you do, charm people into supporting him?"

"Don't be silly. That would never work. What I do is ask them to explain something to me, like the public libraries or the coal mine inspection proposals. They naturally explain in a way that makes their view sound like the only sensible one. Then I can tell Papa what they really think even if they have been waffling in public."

He stared at her and then burst into laughter. "Why, you conniving little minx!"

"Oh, stop it." She started to grin. "I only do that sort of thing when I have to."

"When you have to," he agreed.

"And I only have to when gentlemen assume that I am a brainless ninny." The grin faded. "It really isn't fair, you know. You were able to go off wherever you wanted and do whatever you wanted, and I can't even go for a walk around London by myself. Here we are in Paris, wonderful, glamorous, exciting Paris, and here I am shut up in the embassy, smiling politely at the same kind of stuffy, pompous Englishmen who used to come to Papa's political dinners at home."

Lady Penworth appeared before Harry could say anything. There was an excited gleam in her eye. "Elinor, Lady Cowley has promised to take us shopping tomorrow. There is an Englishman at Maison Gagelin, a Mr. Worth, who is said to design the most marvelous gowns."

Elinor perked up instantly. "Wonderful!"

"Fashion and frivolity?" Harry murmured.

Elinor sniffed. "I never said I didn't like fashion. I love clothes. I just resent it when people assume I can't possibly be interested in anything else."

❧

One of Mr. Worth's gowns was finished just in time for a visit to the opera—a deep rose taffeta. Elinor loved the slithery rustle it made when she moved and the way the lace ruffles of the sleeves lightly tickled her arms. With some of the new silk flowers twined around the elaborate chignon her maid, Martha, had fashioned in her hair, she felt quite pleased with her appearance.

She felt even more pleased when she heard Harry's sharp intake of breath when she entered the hall and saw the look in his eye. He definitely was not thinking of her as a child.

More pleasure awaited her when they reached the building on the Rue le Peletier that housed the Théatre Impérial de l'Opéra—the official name of the Paris Opera. Although the building had been intended merely as a temporary home for the opera company and was built of wood rather than stone, Elinor decided it was quite decorative enough.

The ambassador had an excellent box in the first of the four tiers of boxes, providing a good view of other boxes as well as the stage. The gilded pillars and arches, to say nothing of the patrons' jewels, glittered under the gaslit chandeliers and sconces. A quick glance around told her that although she and Mama might not be the most spectacularly dressed women in the audience, they were probably among the top dozen.

Elinor allowed Harry to seat her in the front row, sent a dazzling smile in his direction, and prepared to be admired.

Even after the lights dimmed and the opera began—something by Donizetti or Rossini, she thought, given the elaborate trills the soprano indulged in—Elinor maintained a graceful pose, lifting her fan to her cheek on occasion without ever being so rude as to fidget and distract other patrons. When the lights went up again for the interval, there was an expression of delight on her face, which changed to innocent surprise as a stream of elegant young Frenchmen flowed into the box to ask the Cowleys for an introduction.

❧

By the time they were ready to leave, Harry thought he was going to go mad. What in God's name did

Norrie think she was playing at, encouraging these clowns? They might call themselves *comte* or baron or whatever, but they were obviously cads, each and every one. The way that cretin with the curling moustache—he had to be wearing a corset to fit into that wasp-waisted frock coat—had bent over her shoulder, he was obviously trying to peer down her bodice.

And then there was that pair right beside him discussing her *attributes!* When he spun around in fury and they realized that he spoke French, the speaker had blanched. "*Pardon, monsieur.* I intended no disrespect, I assure you." If the fellow hadn't been such a namby-pamby, Harry would have challenged him on the spot.

The minute the final curtain fell, while the applause was still going on, he had wanted to grab hold of Norrie and drag her out of the theater and into the carriage. But no, the ambassador had insisted that they wait until the crowd thinned out so that the ladies wouldn't be crushed. As they waited, Lady Penworth and Lady Cowley stood to one side chatting while Norrie stood at the front of the box, looking out over the sea of departing Frenchmen, half of them stumbling into each other because they were looking at her instead of watching where they were going.

With a muttered curse, Harry grabbed Norrie's hand and pulled her to the side, out of sight of those idiots.

"Ouch!" She pulled her hand loose and rubbed it.

"Sorry." He doubted he sounded sorry. He certainly didn't feel particularly sorry. He snarled at her. "Don't you think you've put yourself on display sufficiently for one evening?"

"What on earth are you talking about? I was only watching the audience. The gentlemen are remarkably elegant, aren't they?"

"Is that what you call it? They were practically drooling over you at the interval."

"Yes." She beamed at him. "Wasn't it delightful?"

"Delightful? They almost came to blows trying to retrieve your program when you dropped it. And the things they were saying. Don't pretend you didn't understand. I know how fluent you are in French, for all you were pretending to understand not more than one word in ten and sounding like a schoolgirl at her first lesson."

"That was fun. You hear so much more when people think you don't understand them—you hear all the interesting things."

"Well, you shouldn't understand them. Damnation, Norrie, it wasn't decent. You ought to be spanked."

"Don't be such a prig, Harry." She smoothed her glove over her wrist. "They should use me at the peace conference. I could eavesdrop and then tell them what the French are really thinking."

Too angry to say anything coherent, he snatched up her cloak and wrapped it around her. At least sandwiched between her parents and the Cowleys, she was cut off from her slavering admirers.

❧

The coming peace conference to end the Crimean conflict was threatening to ensnare Lord Penworth. After a dinner with the emperor, he spent the day locked in conference with the ambassador, the special envoy, and assorted aides. This was not at all what Lady Penworth had in mind when they left London. Her husband had, she felt, been distressed enough by the war in the Crimea. This trip was intended to distract him from it, not to draw him in deeper.

It was time, she decided, to leave Paris.

What Lady Penworth wanted was generally what came to pass. A few days later, they were on the road to Lyon. The weather was still cold and gloomy, the post horses were sorry plodders, the roads were indifferent, and Lord Penworth worried that his wife and daughter were uncomfortable, a worry Tunbury and Rycote shared. The ladies bounced around in the coach and laughed at the discomforts.

After a day-long trip down the Saône in a cheerful red steamboat, they arrived at Lyon and settled in. This inn was comfortable, with a dining parlor that looked out on the river, which was sparkling under a cloudless sky. After tasting the croissants served for breakfast, hot and flaky and accompanied by fresh butter and fragrant honey, Lady Penworth suggested that they remain for another day and see the sights.

Rycote looked about sadly, but neither eggs nor ham nor any other sort of meat appeared. It was just as it had been at every other inn. The world outside England seemed sadly deficient in its understanding of a proper breakfast. It could not be helped, so he joined the others in agreeing to his mother's suggestion. After all, it was not as if they did not always agree with his mother's suggestions.

By pure chance, they arrived at the Cathedral just before the clock struck noon, unaware that the clock was one of the wonders of the town. It was an astronomical clock, some thirty feet high. When the noon hour struck, a rooster atop the edifice beat its wings, raised its head, and crowed three times. An angel with an hourglass turned it over while other angels played a hymn on the bells. In a small oratory, a dove descended while the Angel Gabriel appeared to Mary for the Annunciation.

The first bell caught their attention and they watched in fascination. Lady Elinor darted around the clock to try to see all its wonders. The sacristan, a little gnome of a man in a dusty cassock, was delighted by the attention and gladly began answering all the questions that were thrown at him.

The clock was indeed of great antiquity, being first mentioned in the fourteenth century. The wicked Calvinists had almost destroyed it in 1562, and the evil Jacobins attacked it again during the Revolution, but it was always repaired and new figures were added over the centuries.

Rycote had begun by viewing it with his English distrust of things not only foreign but papist. However, the mechanics of the thing caught his interest, and he turned to Tunbury. "Can you ask him to explain the dials?"

The sacristan was happy to do so. An oval dial represented the minutes, with the hand lengthening and shortening as required. On the west side of the tower was a perpetual calendar, and above it an astrolabe showing the stars with a round ball gilded on one side to show the phases of the moon.

While Rycote was absorbed in the mechanics of the thing, Elinor succumbed to its enchantment and grabbed Tunbury's arm. "Harry, just look. Isn't it wonderful?"

He could not look away from her face. Most people leave that eager enthusiasm behind with childhood. Not Norrie. She was staring wide-eyed, pulling him around to see the different figures move.

He had forgotten how much fun everything was with Norrie.

Six

A CONFUSED LADY ELINOR LAY ON HER BUNK AS THE engine of the steamer carrying them from Marseilles to Civita Vecchia chugged in time to her thoughts. He *has* come *back*, he *has* come *back*. Her friend Harry had come back. He was treating her as a friendly companion now, just as he always had. She could be herself with him. There was no need to pretend. He knew her, faults and all, just as she knew him. They understood each other. That was what she wanted, wasn't it? His friendship?

Well, yes, she wanted that. At least, it was what she had thought she wanted when he first returned.

Now she wasn't sure.

She had come to think that she wanted far more than friendship from Harry, but she wasn't at all sure she knew what Harry wanted.

Her confusion had started on the Channel crossing. Something had happened to her then, and she thought something had happened to Harry as well. She was sure of it. Well, almost sure. There had been some sort of spark between them. She thought so, but he had kept away from her after that and had just been brotherly.

On the other hand, when he had gotten so angry at the opera in Paris, he hadn't sounded exactly brotherly. After all, Pip hadn't pounced on her to bawl her out for flirting, and when it came to his sisters, Pip was about as stuffy as a young man could possibly be. But the way Harry had reacted—she couldn't help thinking that it seemed a lot like jealousy. Her body arched and twisted slightly, and she smiled at the memory. Very well, it probably hadn't been the most virtuous way to behave, but she had enjoyed it.

Her smile broadened. She had felt powerful. Harry's reaction had been exciting. No one else had ever made her feel excited that way. Certainly not those silly fellows hanging over her at the opera. How foolish of Harry not to realize that in comparison to him, all those fellows were nothing, barely real.

She stopped to examine that thought. Had she just had a revelation? Compared to Harry, every young man she met was simply…nothing. Was that why all her suitors in London had seemed so boring? Had she been comparing them to Harry all along, without even realizing it?

Why would she have done that?

Was she in love with Harry? She rolled the notion around in her mind, tried to dismiss it, but no. It refused to be dismissed. She had somehow fallen in love with Harry. When on earth had that happened? Had it always been true, ever since they were children?

That was silly. Children don't fall in love, not that way. But there might be something in the idea because she could see now that no one had ever measured up to Harry.

All through her childhood, he had been the one who understood her, who never expected her to be timid or insipid, the brother who was always there to protect her, to make sure she never ran into real danger. She was not a fool and thought it unlikely that she ever would run carelessly into danger, but the feeling of safety he gave her was…comforting. It had been comforting then, and it was comforting now.

He had always been her friend. Her brotherly friend.

But she was no longer a child, and she found that she wanted him to be far more than a friend. Her thoughts turned back to that evening at the opera. It had been exciting. Just the memory of the way Harry had looked at her, had grabbed her arm to pull her out of sight, gave her a warm feeling deep inside. She could almost feel his hand on her arm, the warmth of it, the strength of it.

There was no point in trying to hide it from herself. She wanted him to love her, and not in some platonic way.

She ached to have him touch her, hold her, and—she was not certain what else she wanted, but she knew there was more, much more.

This yearning could not be just on her part. Of that she was certain. Almost certain. Whenever she brushed against him accidentally, she could swear she felt a current running between them. Every now and then she caught him staring at her with a hungry look before he drew a curtain over his expression. She really did not think this was all her imagination. It could not all be wishful thinking.

But if he felt this same yearning, what was holding him back? Whatever it was, she needed to do something about it. She was not going to just sit back and wait. This was much too important.

The dark shapes in the cabin were beginning to grow clear in the gray predawn light. She could make out her mantelet hanging on a hook. The sun would be up soon. They had none of them undressed for the night, since they would be landing early, but she wanted to see the sun rise on her first glimpse of Italy. She slipped her feet into her boots, snatched up her mantelet, and tiptoed out into the hall.

The world was still a hazy gray when she came out on deck, but Harry was there waiting for her with a lazy grin on his face. Did hearts really jump? She could have sworn hers did when she saw him.

"I knew you would never be able to resist getting up to catch the earliest possible glimpse of Italy," he said.

"And how did you know that?" She took a deep breath and tucked her hand around his arm as they walked to the rail.

"I did the same thing the first time I came."

"And you would have done it again even if I weren't here."

He grinned again. "True enough. But it's even more fun with company. Watch over there."

She followed his pointing finger and gasped when she saw the sharp edge of land appear against the sudden brilliance of the rising sun. "Do you know where that is?" she asked.

"Part of the Maremma, I think. It's a marshy area and will be pretty unhealthy in a couple of months."

"It's beautiful."

"You can't even see it, ninny." He laughed and put an arm around her shoulders.

It was a perfectly acceptable brotherly gesture, not something you could call an embrace, really. But his hand felt warm and his arm around her made her feel sheltered and something more. She leaned against his chest and rested her head against his shoulder. This was so right, so perfect. For a long moment they stood there, united in their enjoyment of the scene, where every moment the rising sun revealed more details of the landscape, and she gave a little sigh of pleasure.

She should have kept quiet because the sound obviously disturbed him. He jumped away, pushing her from him abruptly. His voice sounded strained when he spoke again. "That's Civita Vecchia off to the south. That's where we land."

Impossible man. She had to ask. "What's the matter, Harry?"

"Nothing, nothing at all. What makes you think anything is wrong?" He turned to look at her with shuttered eyes. "But you had probably best get back to your cabin now. We should be landing in an hour or so, and you and your mother will want to have some breakfast and freshen up before that."

She allowed him to lead her back to her cabin, but it was frustrating. Very frustrating.

❧

The scene at the docks in Civita Vecchia was chaotic. Her brother was looking ridiculously stiff and pompous, which meant, Elinor knew, that he had no idea what to do. Even her father seemed taken aback by the number of people hurrying about looking either worried or officious. Lord Penworth was standing slightly in front of Elinor and her mother, one arm outstretched and resting on the knob of his walking stick as if to create a barrier between them and the world. Lady Penworth bestowed a loving smile on him before she turned to watch the turmoil with interest.

Tunbury had gone off to see if anyone from the bank was there to meet them, preferably with a carriage and all necessary documents. He returned smiling with a tall, elderly man, thin—almost cadaverous—but meticulously dressed in a black frock coat and a silk hat that he promptly doffed as he bowed to the ladies while Tunbury performed the introductions.

The gentleman was Mr. John Freeborn, who served as both the British consul and the head of Freeborn's bank. After welcoming Lord Penworth and his family to Italy, he gestured at the two smiling men following him, dressed as servants. "I have a carriage and a baggage cart waiting. These fellows will carry your trunks and anything else you have, but I am afraid they understand very little English. If you could tell your servants to point out to them what needs to be taken…?"

It needed nothing more than a nod from the marquess to have Millie, Martha, and Crispin waving the Italians onward. "They will take everything to the customs shed?" Penworth asked.

"No need for that." Freeborn smiled. "I may not be His Holiness's favorite Englishman, but even in the Papal States an English marquess is not subjected to tiresome formalities. If you will come with me, I think we can have you settled in Rome well before sunset."

No one was inclined to object to that forecast, and Penworth insisted that Freeborn share the carriage.

Once they were settled and on their way, Lady Penworth could not restrain her curiosity. "Surely it must be difficult for you as British consul to be out of favor with Pope Pius. In what way have you offended him?"

Mr. Freeborn smiled. "I fear I was a bit too obvious in my support of the Roman Republic a few years ago. As an Englishman, and accustomed to the freedoms Englishmen enjoy, I cannot regret it, but neither can it be denied that the followers of Mazzini and Garibaldi were determined to limit the pope's power. His temporal power, at least. His Holiness objected, understandably, I suppose."

Rycote was frowning. "But surely that is all in the past. I thought the rebels were thoroughly routed when the French came to the pope's support and they all ran off."

"Well, yes, they did run off, as you put it." Mr. Freeborn was still smiling. "But I do not believe they consider the matter settled. Garibaldi has returned, you know, and there is considerable support for unification in Rome itself, even among the nobility."

He turned to Penworth. "Indeed, the apartments I have found for you are in the palazzo of the Crescenzi family. If you find them acceptable, you will be occupying the *piano nobile*, the main floor, while the family retains the ground floor. The marchese himself is an invalid, cared for by his wife and daughter. The son was a somewhat hot-headed follower of Garibaldi. He fled, of course, but his family has found things somewhat difficult since then."

"How very unfair! The rest of the family should not be punished for what the son did." Elinor could not manage to keep silent.

Her mother put a restraining hand on her arm. "I hope it will not be too distressing for the Crescenzis to have strangers living in their home."

"On the contrary," Freeborn said. "To put it bluntly, the rent will lift a burden of care from Donna Lucia and her daughter, and since your rank, Lord Penworth, is equal to his, the marchese has convinced himself that he is simply offering hospitality to a fellow nobleman. He thinks of you as his guests."

Lord Penworth exchanged smiling glances with his wife before turning to Freeborn. "We would be honored to be the guests of the marchese," he said.

Rycote frowned again. "You might want to see the place first," he muttered.

Freeborn turned to the young man. "I think you will find they are probably the finest apartments available in Rome. The palazzo dates to the sixteenth century and has been reasonably well maintained. It is off the Corso and perhaps a little distant from the English quarter, though within easy walking distance. A carriage house and stabling are also available if you wish."

Elinor grinned. "Well, I hope we didn't come all this way to spend our time with Englishmen."

Tunbury grinned back at her. "Never fear. You'll encounter all the Italians you like."

"Remembering your position, of course," Rycote said. He had never quite left off frowning.

Elinor made a face at her brother. "I shall obviously have to insist on Harry's company, rather than yours, if you are going to be impossibly stuffy."

Lady Penworth raised a brow at them and turned to her husband. "Dear me. I thought we had left the squabbling little ones back at school."

&c&

They were all weary by the time the carriage rolled into Rome, weary and sore. Even Elinor could barely turn her head to look around her at the shuttered buildings of ochre stucco lining the narrow streets, so very different from the gray stone of London. When the carriage stopped, they all raised their heads enough to see a pair of heavy wooden gates set into walls of rusticated stone instead of stucco. Before they could see any more, the gates had opened and they rolled into a cobbled courtyard edged with huge pots of unfamiliar flowering plants.

Rycote and Tunbury stepped out first and helped the others down. Lady Penworth seemed to revive the moment her feet touched the ground. She shook her skirts out and looked about her with lively interest. Even in the fading light it was clear that those plants made the courtyard a place of vibrant color.

Freeborn unfolded himself and straightened up with a smile for the visitors. "My lord, my lady, the marchesa thought you might well be too weary for introductions this evening, so she suggested that I conduct you to the apartments."

Penworth looked a bit surprised, but his wife took his arm and explained. "That way, if we take one look at the rooms and flee in horror to the nearest hotel, as Pip half suspects, there will be no embarrassment for any of us."

Rycote flushed. "Now, Mother, I never said any such thing."

"You don't need to," said his sister. "We all know what you are thinking all the time." When he glared at her, she simply laughed. "And you will never get away with strangling me."

"Enough," said Penworth. "Suppose we simply follow Mr. Freeborn."

The consul led them through an arch to a wide marble staircase that divided into two semicircles to reach the upper floor. The entrance hall was covered with frescoes. Clouds and cherubs floated on the high dome of the ceiling, while a quattrocento hunting party circled the walls, moving through idyllic woods in pursuit of a fleeing stag. The party heaved a collective sigh of pleasure.

"The marchesa had bedchambers prepared for you, of course, and the servants can bring up hot water for bathing as soon as you wish," Freeborn said as he led them into the next room, a salon covered with more frescoes, this time of pastoral scenes set into carved frames, and furnished with a plethora of chairs and settees covered in velvet. Numerous small tables, draped in fringed cloths, bore lamps, vases of flowers, and crowds of porcelain figures. The consul kept going, leading them on to a library, this room paneled in dark wood, and a dining room, the table set for five with an array of covered dishes on the sideboard and several bottles of wine, opened and breathing.

Waving a hand at the sideboard, he said, "Donna Crescenzi thought you might prefer a light supper, but if you would like anything more, you need only ring. And the maids will show you to your chambers."

Two girls stood giggling beside a stern older woman dressed in black, a bit of iron-gray hair visible under her cap. "Signora Albani," she introduced herself, and all three of them curtsied. "*Se permetti.*" She waved them further on.

Freeborn looked questioningly at Lord and Lady Penworth, who exchanged an amused glance. "Mr. Freeborn, you need have no worries about the apartments. I assure you my wife and I find them more than adequate. I can only be grateful that you achieved such perfection for total strangers."

A slight blush stained Freeborn's cheeks. "In that case, if you do not object, I will stop by tomorrow to introduce you to the Crescenzis?"

"We would be delighted," said Lady Penworth. "I don't know about the young people, but I think I will need the morning to recover myself. Shall we say about two tomorrow?"

"I am entirely at your service, my lady." Freeborn gave an elegant bow and departed.

Seven

WITH GREAT SOLEMNITY, THE ELDERLY SERVITOR ushered the Penworth party into the salon where the Marchese di Crescenzi and his family waited. Lady Elinor wasn't quite sure what position the servitor held. He was not dressed in black, like a butler, but in some elaborate costume of a previous century, and he carried a staff a good ten feet long that was elaborately carved and painted and—she stole another glance at it—entwined with ribbons. Was he perhaps a major-domo? That did not seem quite important enough. There was surely a title from some medieval office that would be more appropriate.

The solemnity continued in the salon, a room whose dark green walls were covered with portraits from the past five centuries. The marchese himself was sitting as still as any portrait in a throne-like chair of carved and gilded wood. His stiff posture may have been caused by the carving. It looked to Lady Elinor to be an extremely uncomfortable chair. Then again, Mr. Freeborn had said that the marchese was an invalid, so the lines of pain on his face may have been etched there by illness.

To his right stood a lady—his wife, to judge by the richness of her black velvet gown—whose expression of welcome seemed tempered by worry. On his left was a very beautiful girl of about Lady Elinor's own age. She had golden curls, brown eyes, and fair skin that made her look more English than the English visitors. She looked at them with a frank interest that, Lady Elinor realized, was probably the mirror image of her own. They smiled at each other.

Mr. Freeborn, dressed formally in a black morning coat with striped trousers, stood slightly to the side and, in excellent Italian, presented the Marquess of Penworth to the Marchese di Crescenzi.

Penworth bowed.

The marchese bowed his head in acknowledgment and spoke in Italian, pausing to allow Freeborn to translate. "You must forgive me for not rising to greet you, but old age and illness have conspired against me."

"Not at all," replied Penworth. "You are graciousness itself in welcoming me and my family into your home."

The marchese waved a hand. "My family has always prided itself on its traditions of liberality and hospitality. I consider it only fitting to open my home to a nobleman such as yourself."

Lady Elinor and Tunbury shared an amused glance over all this formality, but when she turned to include her brother in the joke, she was startled to see him staring poleaxed at the marchese's daughter, who was in turn looking down, blushing, and twisting her fingers. This sight so delighted Lady Elinor that she missed some of the exchange of courtesies. When she returned to the conversation, her father was speaking.

"You are all kindness," Penworth said.

"Not at all. When I myself was a young man, I visited London and was welcomed into the homes of some of your most noble families. Perhaps you were acquainted with the late Earl of Flyte?"

Penworth blinked, and then smiled. "I fear I never met the late earl, though I have often heard him spoken of. I am, of course, acquainted with the current holder of the title."

"A noble family." The marchese smiled his approval.

Lady Elinor's eyes widened at that. She had met Lord Flyte. Then she had the misfortune to catch Tunbury's eye, and they both promptly looked down and stared at the floor in an effort to maintain their composure. Lord Flyte was known to all as Lord Flighty for his inability to hold a thought in his head for more than ten seconds.

Finally introductions were made—Lady Penworth, Lady Elinor, Viscount Rycote, and Viscount Tunbury on the one hand, Donna Lucia Crescenzi and Donna Lissandra on the other—and bows and curtsies were exchanged. The marchese's son, Messer Pietro Crescenzi, was unfortunately traveling out of the country at the moment. Since by now the marchese was looking visibly tired, Donna Lucia invited the visitors to partake of some refreshments in the other room while the marchese excused himself.

Once they had reached the next room, the atmosphere lightened considerably. Donna Lucia, leaning in apparent relief on Mr. Freeborn's arm, offered them a genuine smile of welcome, along with coffee, tea, and wine. Donna Lissandra, still blushing, explained that, unlike her parents, she spoke some English. As both Lady Elinor and Tunbury spoke Italian, communication among the young people was greatly facilitated, and friendship seemed likely to bloom.

Her initial shyness vanishing rapidly, Donna Lissandra was eager to show the visitors her city. Donna Lucia had difficulty refusing, insisting only that Lissandra's maid accompany them. A carriage was sent for and, in a flurry of capes and gloves, they were soon out the door.

~~

It was an elderly carriage, practically an antique. Rycote scowled at it. A creature as ethereally beautiful as Donna Lissandra should ride in a coach of gold, drawn by snow-white horses. Well, that was idiotically fanciful. But she certainly deserved something better than this. He opened the door of the landau and frowned at the faded fabric of the seats. The nap had been worn almost entirely off the brown velvet and the cushions were none too plump. It suited the witch-like maid scuttling behind her, but not the smiling goddess who was allowing him to hand her into the carriage.

With a few words of rapid Italian, Donna Lissandra dispatched the scowling maid to sit beside the driver and collapsed next to Lady Elinor with a delighted laugh. The others looked at her with a bit of confusion, so she made an apologetic face. "You must forgive me. It is just that I do not often go anywhere simply for pleasure these days. My father, well, you could see, he is not well these days, and my mother does not like to leave him, even to pay calls." She gave a shrug.

"And, of course, the daughter of the marchese cannot possibly go for a walk by herself. Oh, no, no, no! Not even with my dragon Maria glowering at me every moment." She gestured at the maid, enveloped in black, who seemed to radiate disapproval even while sitting with her back to the young people. "And we must speak only English, because she does not understand."

"We are, of course, delighted to be of service to you," said Rycote with as much of a bow as he could manage while seated in a landau. She smiled at him. He wished he had read more poetry. If he had, he might have been able to describe that smile and the way it turned his insides into mush.

"The avoidance of dragon-like chaperones is a particular specialty of mine," said his sister. She grinned at Lissandra.

Lissandra grinned back. "Ah, I knew the moment I saw you that we would be friends."

"That's what we need. Two of them," Tunbury said to Rycote in an undertone.

"As if anyone had ever been able to make my sister behave. But it's really too bad of her to be trying to lead a young lady like Donna Lissandra astray." He scowled at Elinor.

"Now, I have told the driver first to take us to the quarter where all the English go," said Lissandra.

Elinor looked disappointed. "But we did not come to Italy to see Englishmen."

That won raised eyebrows from Lissandra. "Ah, that is what all the English say. But sooner or later they all go to the Caffè Greco and talk and talk. All the artists and the poets, that is where they go." She looked at Rycote intently, then turned to Elinor. "Your brother, he is a poet?"

Rycote felt himself turned red while the other two burst out laughing.

"Heavens, no," said Elinor when she could talk again. "Whatever gave you that idea?"

Lissandra was still looking at Rycote. She lifted a shoulder. "He has the air that all the young men who fancy themselves poets attempt. Like your Lord Byron. Only your brother is more handsome, no?"

While his sister went off into further gales of laughter, Rycote turned to glare at a grinning Tunbury. "The least you could do is stop enjoying this!"

Getting himself under control, Tunbury said, "Alas, Donna Lissandra, I fear that when Rycote has that distant look in his eye, he is not contemplating a new epic. He is merely considering crop rotation or thinking of ways to improve his dairy herd."

"Ah, a farmer. *Bene.* That is good." Lissandra looked at him with genuine approval. "Farmers are always needed. They do some good in this world instead of always making trouble. There are far too many useless dreamers in this world, dreamers who do nothing but sit in their *caffès* and talk all night."

They rode past several caffès in addition to the famous Greco, and Lady Elinor looked at them wistfully. "Could we go to one, do you suppose?"

"Hah! The men in the caffès, they talk of *important*

things." Lissandra held up a hand and shook her dangling fingers. "They cannot allow women to enter. They might hear some sense!"

"Sorry, Norrie," said Tunbury. "They're just like the clubs in London. And probably just as dull and stuffy."

Lady Elinor did not look convinced.

Lissandra, on the other hand, looked pensive. "We cannot go to a caffè, you understand, but perhaps… perhaps you would like to go to a trattoria? It is like a restaurant, only not elegant, not for fine ladies and gentlemen. But we could have coffee and talk, and pretend we are in a caffè."

Rycote frowned slightly. "Are you sure this place is quite proper?"

"Do you never do anything but frown, Signor Viscount? Del Falcone is most assuredly 'proper'! My old nurse and her husband, who was once our chef, it is they who run this trattoria. My father and my mother, they have themselves visited and even dined there. Bah!" She sat back, folded her arms, and scowled at Rycote.

He flushed with embarrassment. "I do beg your pardon most sincerely, Donna Lissandra. I should never have questioned your judgment. It is only that in my ignorance of the customs here…"

At this point Elinor broke in with a laugh. "I fear it is only that my brother is accustomed to my fits and starts. I am always wanting to do something that he thinks is 'not proper,' so now he is worried about anything new. And as you can see," she said with a wave, "it requires two of them to keep me in my place."

"To keep you even a little bit safe, you mean." Tunbury was half laughing, half frowning.

Lissandra looked at both young men, then smiled at Elinor. "Brothers. They are always so concerned that we be proper, until they get themselves into trouble. Then they want us to get them out of trouble, and there is no thought of the trouble they make for us, eh?" She reached over to prod the driver with her parasol and gave him an order in Italian too rapid for the others to follow. Nor could they understand the words—in an unfamiliar dialect—that followed when the maid turned around with an angry scowl and began to scold her mistress, who ordered her to be silent. The old woman subsided, but not until she had sent angry glares at the Englishmen.

With an apologetic smile, Lissandra said, "I must beg you to excuse her. She trusts no one but the priests, and thinks I should be locked up behind convent walls." She shrugged. "What is there to do? She is old, and she lost a brother and a nephew in the fighting."

"The fighting?" Rycote came to attention. "What fighting?"

"When the French came to drive out Mazzini and Garibaldi. You did not know of it?"

"Yes, of course. But that was years ago."

She smiled sadly. "Not so many years ago for us in Rome."

Rycote flushed again. "I apologize. I seem to keep speaking without thinking. It must have been quite terrifying for you."

That won him another of her shrugs.

He tried again. "Your maid is a republican, then."

"Maria?" Her eyes widened in mock horror. "Never say such blasphemy! Her brother and uncle were fighting with the French against the impious devils who dared raise a hand against the Holy Father."

Rycote looked thoroughly confused. "But I thought Mr. Freeborn said that your brother…"

"Very true. My brother was one of those impious devils. It is most terrible for poor Maria. She has always been with our family and now, when she would like to pile coals of scorn on our heads, she has nowhere else to go." She sighed. "Poor Maria."

Just then the carriage entered the Piazza Navona, where the late-afternoon sun struck the three fountains, casting dramatic shadows across the wide space. Elinor's gasp of pure delight startled Lissandra, who looked around at her surroundings, cocked her head, and smiled.

"Yes, it is good, is it not? One forgets to see the place where one lives sometimes. But look. We have arrived." She gestured at the building that proclaimed *Del Falcone* in red script on a green background. Behind the windows, baskets of bread and platters of sausage were displayed to entice passersby.

Lissandra led the way, with Elinor and Tunbury close behind and Rycote still looking uncertain. The rear was brought up by Maria, muttering angrily. Once inside, Lissandra was promptly greeted with cries of enthusiasm by a middle-aged couple, both of them plump, rosy-cheeked, and enveloped in aprons. Introductions revealed them to be Amelia and Eduardo Falcone, who proclaimed themselves ecstatic to welcome the English visitors and ushered the party upstairs to a table where they could look out onto the piazza.

As Amelia led the way, chatting enthusiastically to Elinor and Tunbury, Rycote was far enough behind to notice that Eduardo had drawn Lissandra apart to say something to her that seemed to distress her. He also noticed that Maria seemed to be edging over in an effort to overhear, so he stumbled into the old woman and began to apologize loudly.

Lissandra spun about, startled, and took in the scene. With a murmur to Eduardo, she went over to Rycote and took his arm. "I see you are a gallant knight, my lord. I thank you." She directed a glacial frown at the maid, who retreated, muttering to herself yet again.

Rycote started to lead Lissandra to join the others, and she gave him one of her brilliant smiles. This time, however, it did not seem to reach her eyes. "Something seems to be worrying you," he said abruptly. "If there is anything I can do, you need only ask."

Surprise flickered in her eyes. "No, no, my lord. Eduardo wanted only to tell me about someone from his village. It is nothing."

Rycote nodded as if satisfied. He could hardly accuse her of lying, and after all, why should she confide in him? He was a stranger.

By the time they were all seated by the window and supplied with small cups of bitter coffee, she had recovered her aplomb. Eduardo and Amelia covered the table with plates of pastries, bread, sausages, and cheeses, and Lissandra entertained them all with a stream of comments about the people in the piazza, spinning fantastic histories for them.

Her gaiety seemed to drop from her when a group of French officers came into sight. She muttered something in Italian, almost certainly a curse from her tone of voice, and pulled back, but not before one of them caught sight of her.

At the sight of Lissandra's pale face, Elinor reached over to her and asked what was wrong. Lissandra just shook her head, but was still clutching Elinor's hand when one of the Frenchmen strode into the room. He was reasonably tall for a Frenchman, and his uniform fit him well. All that gold braid and tassels would look impressive onstage. The fellow had a moustache, twirling up at the ends, and probably thought himself quite the ladies' man. Rycote scowled at him.

The officer swept off his plumed shako, clicked his heels, bowed, and spoke in French. "Donna Lissandra, I would not have expected to find you in such humble surroundings. Had I realized your parents were now permitting such outings, I would have offered to escort you myself."

Lissandra held up a hand to her companions to tell them to remain seated and looked somewhere off to the side of the officer. "Any such offer would be refused, as you have doubtless surmised." Her voice dripped ice.

A flush of anger crossed his face, and he glared at the others. "You will perhaps introduce me to your companions?"

Her lips tightened, but she relented and waved a hand in his direction as she turned to her companions. "This is Lieutenant Girard. He is one of the French troops here to protect us, they tell us."

When it appeared she intended to say nothing more, he ground out, "And your friends?" He made the word sound like an insult.

Rycote stood up, towering several inches over Girard, and smiled thinly. His French was adequate to understand Lissandra's exchange with the Frenchman, but he preferred to speak English himself. "Allow me, Lieutenant. I am Viscount Rycote. This is my sister, Lady Elinor Tremaine, and our friend, Viscount Tunbury. We and my parents, the Marquess and Marchioness of Penworth, are staying with the Crescenzis. Her parents consider us acceptable companions for Donna Lissandra. I trust you have no objection?" He was pleased to see that the lieutenant looked taken aback.

"I assure you, no insult was intended." Girard clicked his heels again. "But as you are English, you may not realize that the protection Donna Lissandra dismisses so casually is indeed needed." A slight stiffening of his posture was the only indication that he heard the contemptuous noise Lissandra made. "The rabble who were driven out of Rome only by the arrival of the French troops have begun to creep back. We are ever vigilant and will root out all these rebels, even the misguided fools who are betraying their noble families." He shot a venomous glare at Lissandra with that last comment.

Lady Elinor decided to break in at this point with a sunny smile. "Really, Lieutenant, I don't think there is any need for you to be afraid. I am sure that if there were any danger, the emperor would have mentioned it to Papa when we stopped in Paris on our way."

Girard goggled at her. "The emperor... your father..."

She continued to smile. "It would have been rude not to call on him while we were there. Especially with the peace conference going on."

The heels clicked once more. His moustache quivering, Girard gave a short bow before he turned and marched out.

Rycote brushed his own moustache with the side of his finger. He decided to shave it off.

Eight

EARLY IN THE MORNING ON THE DAY OF THEIR FIRST trip to view the ruins of Etruria, the mysterious civilization that was old when Rome was new, Lady Penworth and Elinor came down the wide marble staircase to the courtyard. Penworth and Tunbury turned to greet them and, after a moment of stunned silence, Penworth began to laugh. Rycote, who had been looking out the gate to see if their carriage had arrived, turned at the sound.

"Good God, Mother. Elinor. You're mad, both of you." He looked as shocked as he sounded. "You can't go out in public dressed like that."

"Don't be silly, Pip," said his mother. "You can hardly expect us to be exploring tombs underground in crinolines or hoops." She looked down complacently at her divided skirt of deep red wool, short enough to show the riding boots on her feet. "Besides, no one will see us in the carriage, and I doubt there will be many others wandering around the Etruscan cemeteries."

"Or did you think we would just sit under a tree,

twirling our parasols, while you gentlemen had all the fun?" Elinor tossed her head and turned aside to ignore her brother and smile at Tunbury.

He smiled back. He couldn't help it. But it was a weak smile, and his mouth was too dry for him to say anything. He should have known she would do something like this, and he should have known her mother would join her. It was just as it had been crossing the Channel. She hadn't worn a corset then, either. Her reasoning had been perfectly sensible, and it was perfectly sensible now as well. Of course they couldn't go climbing around tombs with their skirts sticking out six feet in every direction. But this...

It wasn't that he could actually see anything. There was more of her skin exposed when she wore a ball gown, almost baring her shoulders and cut low enough to give a hint of bosom. But now—it was what he *knew*. She was within reach. Without those petticoats he knew that if he slid his hands down from her waist he would be able to feel the swell of her hips, the curve of her derrière...

"Anne, my dear, you look enchanting." Lord Penworth swept into a courtly bow and kissed his wife's hand. "And I am exceedingly grateful that you do not intend to parade about the city in this costume, delightful though it is."

"You know I would never embarrass you, Philip."

"You could not." He tucked his wife's hand into the crook of his arm and patted it fondly. "But I fear you might drive the gentlemen of Rome to distraction, and I am getting too old to be fighting duels."

Tunbury watched the exchange with a stab of envy. The marquess and his wife loved each other. Even after all these years of marriage. What he would not give to have had a family like that. Rycote might grumble and blush at his parents' displays of affection, but he had no idea how fortunate he was to have always lived surrounded by love.

Tunbury's parents had barely been able to tolerate being under the same roof. On the rare occasions when they were, the vicious sneers at each other, the shouts of "Whore!" and "Drunkard!" poisoned the atmosphere and drove him from the house. Rycote and Norrie had no idea how vile the world could be. Norrie had to marry someone who could protect her and keep her safe in that world of love.

Not someone who carried with him a heritage of shame and dishonor.

Not someone with bad blood.

Not someone like him.

He gave himself a mental shake and went to join Rycote in watching for the arrival of the carriage. By the time it arrived and the ladies were safely hidden inside, he had managed to inure himself to Norrie's appearance. He prided himself that his voice sounded perfectly normal, at least so long as he kept his eyes on her face, not her body.

There was a slight setback when they reached La Storta where they had arranged to have saddle horses awaiting them. The horses were there, and perfectly acceptable mounts—neither slugs nor overly excitable. Unfortunately, Lady Penworth had arranged that she and Elinor would be riding astride.

Elinor took exception to the expression on Tunbury's face. "Oh, for heaven's sake, Harry. You know perfectly well that Mama and I always ride astride when we are at Penworth. I will put up with a sidesaddle when I am trotting along the manicured paths of the park, but this is obviously much safer when exploring unknown wilderness."

He couldn't deny it, so he shut his mouth and helped her to mount. How did she manage to make the most outrageous things she did seem perfectly sensible? He gritted his teeth. At least, he consoled himself, he was handling it better than Rycote, who had protested so vehemently that his father had to reprimand him.

As they rode along, everyone grew calmer. The gently rolling plain, almost treeless, seemed utterly deserted. They might have been in a different world. When they reached the top of a small rise, they could see a steep cliff about a mile off with some buildings atop it—whether ruins or hovels could not be discerned from this distance.

"According to Mr. Dennis's book, at the foot of that cliff lie the remains of the city of Veii, perhaps the most important of the cities of Etruria," said Penworth.

They looked out at it in silence. From a distance, there seemed to be nothing to see, just a slightly bumpy plain fringed with trees. Finally, Tunbury broke the silence and suggested that they at least ride over and see the place. Even so, they remained as quiet as trespassers as they crossed a glen separating the cliff from the ancient city. They forded a small stream and followed a path that led up to what had once been a city gate. Of the ancient walls, all that remained were some small rectangular stones.

There was an atmosphere to the place. Not frightening, precisely. Just odd. Tunbury was not given to imaginative flights, but he felt impelled to pull his horse up so that he was riding close to Norrie. Whatever it was about this place, she seemed to feel it too, because she gave him a quick smile and seemed to relax slightly, as if she was grateful for his nearness.

Eventually they came to the Arx, the city's ancient citadel, a sort of plateau with sides dropping sharply to the streams that ran through the glens. Only a narrow ridge, rather like a causeway, connected it to the rest of the city. A few stones near the edge of the plateau could be the remains of a temple, or perhaps the towers that defended the citadel. Did anyone know, or was that one of the mysteries surrounding the Etruscans?

Penworth dismounted and the others followed. An eerie hush hung over the area, with the wind carrying mournful whispers. There were no birds; that was it. Harry took Norrie's hand and tucked it under his arm, pulling her close to him. She offered no objection. In fact, she was almost clinging to him.

"Do you feel it?" she said softly. "There is something about this place. It's as if some ancient sorrow still clings to the ground here."

He knew what she meant. He could not identify it precisely, but he knew there was something, some memory, some emotion, still lingering.

"Legend has it that the people of Veii held out here against the Romans for ten years," Penworth said, turning slowly in a circle. "Finally the Roman commander Camillus had his men dig a tunnel under the citadel through which he led them. According to Livy, they burst into the temple of Juno just as the priest conducting a sacrifice declared that he who completed the sacrifice would be victorious. The priest was about to hand the entrails to the Etruscan king, but Camillus snatched the entrails from him and offered them to the goddess himself." He sighed. "And that was the end of Veii."

Elinor shivered. "It seems so sad."

"Sad? Perhaps," her father said. "But a reminder to us that every victory is a defeat for someone, and that eventually enough time will pass to ease both the pride and the pain. All our victories and defeats will be forgotten."

"There is no need to be quite so gloomy, Philip," said Lady Penworth sharply. "One might equally well think of it as a reminder not to take ourselves too seriously."

Penworth's sudden laugh echoed around them. "Quite right, my dear. And indeed the Etruscans are probably the last people who should be giving rise to gloomy thoughts. By all accounts, they were a cheerful lot. Come, let us leave the place of defeat and see if we can find something happier. I understand that there is not much left to discover here—the antiquities dealers have been ransacking it for the past twenty years, at least. However, there is a painted tomb of which much has been made."

They found it without too much difficulty and discovered that it was not just interesting but delightful.

The earthy colors of the frescoes retained much of their freshness, but it was the design that intrigued them all, the painted doorway in the middle with two horizontal panels on either side depicting people and bizarre animals in hierarchical sizes.

"Everything—the people, the animals—they look almost playful," said Elinor. "How strange to think of a tomb being cheerful, but it is. No mournful faces, no tears and cries. Just this, this exuberance."

"Fascinating," Harry agreed, though whether he meant Norrie's enthusiasm or the paintings was uncertain.

"They're not just strange, they're bizarre," Rycote said, frowning. "They're all in different colors and patterns. Look at that horse. Its forequarters are red and its hindquarters are gray. And it's speckled. Preposterous."

His sister glared at him. "You are the most unimaginative *clod,* Pip."

Their parents paid their offspring no heed.

"Is that a sphinx underneath?" Lady Penworth peered at the painting closely.

"Yes," said Lord Penworth slowly, bending over beside her. "Remarkable."

Harry stepped back and looked slowly over the whole wall. "It's a tomb painting, I know, but what's really strange about it is that it's so…so happy."

Elinor nodded in agreement. "I can imagine living in a house with a wall like this. Is that what it means, do you suppose? They seem to have had a very cheerful view of the afterlife."

"I'm not sure about the colors, though," said her brother. "They'd get a bit monotonous." He grinned when she aimed a swat at his shoulder.

"The colors are one way they know this is one of the earlier tombs, the colors and the fantastic creatures," said Penworth meditatively. "From the seventh century BC, they say. More than two thousand five hundred years ago. We have no way of knowing who painted this wall, but he speaks to us across all those centuries. Veii may have been defeated, but the spirit of these people speaks to us and triumphs over time."

He was still studying the wall when his wife suggested that perhaps they should leave if they intended to get back to Rome before nightfall. On the ride back, he was unusually quiet and took out a small notebook in which he wrote from time to time. He quite ignored the lively chatter of his children and Tunbury.

That evening, as they were preparing for bed, he said to his wife, "I think I shall ask Freeborn if he knows of anyone who is conducting excavations. I would dearly like to see a tomb before it has been disturbed by looters."

Nine

Rycote was feeling at loose ends. His mother and sister had gone off shopping, Tunbury had headed for the Caffè Greco to meet some writer friend of his, and his father had gone to call on Freeborn. None of those activities appealed to him. What he really wanted to do was go for a long walk along the cliffs at Penworth or through his own woods at Rycote. He wanted to check on his apple trees. The ones on the south slope should be blooming soon if they weren't already. He wanted to breathe the sweet-scented air of home.

Sweet-scented was not how he would describe the air of Rome. It was every bit as malodorous as London, though the scent was not quite the same. Precisely what constituted the difference was not something he cared to think about. He glared out the window at the street. At least London had the occasional tree visible. Here everything was either gray stone or endless streets of stucco, painted in that brownish yellow or brownish red. The same colors as that Etruscan wall they were all making such a fuss about.

In fact, this street might as well be a tomb for all the life on it. Things were busy enough over on the Corso, he supposed, but here every window was shuttered, every door was barred. Anyone would think the city were under perpetual siege.

No, there was some life on the street. Not particularly lively life, however. Down toward the end of the street, on the shadowed side, there was a doorway, and he could just make out someone in its depths. He would never have noticed him if he hadn't moved to adjust his position. What was he doing there? He looked furtive enough to be hiding, but from what, Rycote couldn't imagine. There was no one else about.

Well, well, well. The world was getting livelier. The small door in the corner of the palazzo was opening very slowly. As he watched, he could see a head covered in black move out to peer around the edge of the door, checking the street. One of the Crescenzi servants on a private errand?

She stepped out and Rycote received a jolt. Not a servant. That was Donna Lissandra. He didn't have to see her face, and that black shawl was no disguise at all. He would recognize the way she walked, the way she moved, anywhere. All thoughts of home vanished in an instant. What the devil was she up to, sneaking out without even that blasted maid to accompany her? His protective instincts were outraged.

As she started down the street in the direction of the Piazza Navona, another movement caught his eye. The figure at the other end of the street came out of the doorway. It was that damned bounder Girard. Rycote muttered an oath and ran to snatch up his hat and coat. He was down on the street before he had even finished pulling on his gloves. Why Girard was spying on Lissandra he didn't know, but he didn't like it.

He didn't like it at all.

Lissandra must have turned a corner because she was not in sight. Girard was, however. He was easy to spot in his uniform. If he was going to spy on Lissandra, you would think he'd have the sense to at least put a cloak over it.

As if he could read Rycote's thoughts, Girard shook out the bundle under his arm and swung it around himself. It was a long cloak, complete with hood.

Well, at least he would be uncomfortably hot, wrapped up that way. Rycote took some satisfaction in that thought as he hurried to catch up.

It was not long before he caught sight of Donna Lissandra. She was glancing back often enough to force Girard to keep his head down. One time she stared hard at him, and he stepped around a corner. Fortunately, she had not noticed Rycote, whose long legs were rapidly cutting down the distance between them. When one of her backward glances sent the Frenchman ducking into a doorway, Rycote strode right past him and called out, "Donna Lissandra!"

She noticed him then and stumbled to a halt. By the time he reached her, she was wrapped in anger as well as that shabby black shawl. "How dare you call out my name that way on a public street? Do you think I am some sort of…" She waved her hand around. "I don't know what you call them in English."

Rycote frowned, took her hand firmly, and tucked it under his arm as he began slowly walking her in the direction she had been headed. "Now listen to me before you erupt any further. This is important. Did you know that Lieutenant Girard is following you?"

She stopped abruptly. Whatever imprecations she had been about to rain down on him faded from her lips. "Are you certain?" She started to turn, but he stopped her.

"Don't look back," he commanded. "Keep walking. Yes, I am certain. He was across the street from the palazzo, waiting for you to come out."

"*Maledizione*," she whispered. Her hand trembled on his arm as they walked ahead slowly, and she was biting her lip.

He gave her a minute to absorb his news before he spoke. "We seem to be going in the direction of your friends' trattoria. Is that where you are meeting him?"

"Him?"

He glared at her. "Do not take me for a fool."

She had the grace to blush. "No, no, meeting him there would be foolish. That is the first place they will look if they know he is here."

"They? Your parents as well as the lieutenant?"

"My parents? They might be annoyed, but they will hardly betray him."

"Really? I believe my parents would be more than annoyed if my sister were sneaking out to meet a lover." He sounded stiff and priggish. He knew it, but he couldn't help it. Did she expect his approval?

"A lover?" She pulled away from him. Now it was her turn to glare. "You think I was sneaking out to meet a lover? How dare you suggest such a thing!"

He shot a quick look over his shoulder. "Keep

your voice down. There are people about, and Girard is close enough to hear." He took hold of her arm and began walking again. She tossed her head and kept her eyes turned away from him. He could feel the injured pride radiating from her. After several minutes of silence, he finally asked, "If you weren't going to meet a lover, who were you going to meet?"

"My brother, of course, *cretino*!"

He stumbled slightly. It was surprising how much lighter he suddenly felt. "We need..." He cleared his throat and began again. "We need to talk. Can we speak privately at that trattoria?"

She nodded, and then she began to smile. "That will be perfect. We must let Girard see us. Then he will think that I came out to meet you somewhere away from our families. He will think you are my lover." She laughed with delight.

Rycote smiled, though he was not sure he liked her thinking the notion comic. He did, however, enjoy the way she now walked beside him, hanging on his arm and smiling up at him.

"I just realized," she said, coming to a sudden stop, "you have shaved off your moustache. Let me see." She stood in front of him and put up a finger to turn his face first one way and then the other. "Yes, you are far more handsome this way. You have a most excellent mouth. Moustaches should be left to those with something to hide."

Rycote could feel himself turning red.

"That was to pay you for calling out to me in the street and for thinking that I was a bad woman going to meet a lover." She grinned at him. "But you are a beautiful man, and I think you must know it."

He could think of absolutely no reply to make to anything she had said. Nothing, at least, that wouldn't make him sound like even more of an idiot than he already felt himself to be. So they proceeded with him walking in silence while she occasionally hummed a cheerful tune until they reached Del Falcone.

As he held the door open for Lissandra, he looked around as if casually admiring the fountain in the middle of the piazza. A hooded figure that he was almost certain was Girard lurked in the shadows. He hoped the lieutenant was gnashing his teeth.

Seated at a table—not by the window this time— and served with coffee, cakes, and suspicious glares by Amelia, he settled down to hear Lissandra's story.

It took her a while to get started. Amelia had placed three little jewel-like tarts in front of Lissandra, and she sat there poking them with a fork. First she arranged them one way on the plate and studied them. Apparently she disliked the arrangement, because then she set the tarts in a different order, studied them, and turned her attention to the coffee. After putting three spoonfuls of sugar in it, she stirred it carefully, took a sip, and made a face.

"Donna Lissandra," he said patiently.

She looked across at him and her mouth quirked up at one side. "My brother is not always the most sensible of men."

There was a pause, so he nodded in what he hoped was an understanding, reassuring way.

"He is full of—enthusiasm. He does not lack

courage, you understand. He is very brave. But he is not always sensible." She looked at him uncertainly, so he nodded again. "And he does not always see what will happen, the problems that will come. He lacks…"

"Foresight?" he suggested.

Her smile beamed at him. She should always smile that way. She should never be worried.

"Foresight," she repeated. "Yes, that is it. That is what he lacks. He admires Garibaldi, he believes in a united Italy. These are wonderful ideas, and many agree with him. But he never thought about what would happen to us when he fled Rome. Our father is old, he is ill, and he did not know how to deal with problems. French soldiers march into our home looking for Pietro, and Papa cannot say his son has run off. No, no, Papa is too proud. He must defy them, call them names, and so they smash things, they fine him, they confiscate things." She shrugged.

He hated to see the sadness in her eyes. "It seems to me that they are very much alike, your father and your brother."

"Alike? But no, they argue all the time. Or they did when Pietro was here."

"I don't mean they have the same ideas. I mean that they both think they are right all the time and never consider how their actions will affect other people."

She stared at him in surprise, but slowly the surprise turned to admiration. "But you are right! That is precisely how they are. How very clever you are."

He shifted uncomfortably in his seat. "But you said you were going to meet him. Is he back in Rome?"

"Yes, and that is the same sort of thing." Her

shoulders slumped and she leaned back. "He comes back to Rome thinking to discover the attitude of the people here now that Garibaldi has come back to Italy. But he forgets that Rome is full of people who know him, people who are his enemies. He cannot walk about the streets freely. Many people would be glad to sell him to the French, who would shoot him."

He raised a hand in protest, but she spoke vehemently. "Yes, yes, they would. That Lieutenant Girard would be only too happy to capture my brother, and we would never see him again. And the lieutenant must have some suspicion, he must have heard something. Why else would he be following me?"

Was she really that foolish? All she had to do was look in a mirror to know why Girard would be following her. Rycote had deduced that the first time he saw the bounder. That presumptuous little Frenchman would do just about anything to get close to Donna Lissandra.

"I cannot help thinking that it would be wiser for you to have taken a servant with you," he said carefully.

"No, no, no. Anyone I took with me would have to tell my parents, and they would have forbidden me to come."

Very wisely, to his way of thinking. "But how did you know your brother is in Rome?"

"Eduardo brings a message with the pastries in the morning. But I have to wait until now, when everyone is resting, to be able to leave the house."

"But still you were followed."

She nodded. "It was good of you to warn me about Girard." Then an idea struck her—he could almost see it arrive—and her brilliant smile returned. "And it is even better because he has already seen you. He will think that you are courting me, and that the reason I came out alone was to meet you."

"Yes, he will." *And he will be quite right that I am courting you, though you don't seem to have realized it yet.*

"And so he will not be watching so carefully now. If I leave by the back, he will not see me, and I can go to meet Pietro."

Rycote, who had been watching her fondly, amused by her naïveté, looked at her in shock. "Don't be ridiculous," he snapped. "You will do nothing of the sort."

Her smile vanished and she looked at him with a regal chill. "I do not recall asking your permission."

"It is not a question of my permission. It is a matter of common sense. I cannot believe that Rome is so different from London that it is considered acceptable for a young lady to wander about the streets on her own. If it were, you would not have needed to sneak out of the house." No sooner were the words out of his mouth than he knew he shouldn't have said that. It sounded pompous even to him. He didn't need to see the look of outrage on her face.

"What you think about it is a matter of indifference to me. I will do what I must do, and you have nothing to say about it." She sat stiffly, looking somewhere over his shoulder.

Rycote was feeling a bit stiff himself. "I cannot believe that your brother would wish you to go about by yourself at the mercy of blackguards like Girard."

She made a dismissive noise that sounded somehow sad. "My brother has far more to think about than the fate of one woman. He works for the future of all Italy."

The future of all Italy. Oh Lord, her brother was one of those idiots out to save the world. He probably planned assassinations and threw bombs instead of protecting the people he was supposed to protect. Like his sister.

Rycote had to say something, do something, and obviously common sense and reason were not going to serve his purpose. This was like trying to argue with his sister when she wanted to do something outrageous. "Please, Donna Lissandra, do not be offended." He thought that came out rather well. His voice sounded calm. "I know I have no right to tell you what to do. It is simply my concern for you. I would not be able to live with myself, were anything to happen to you while you were off on your own." He tried to look plaintive.

She tilted her head and looked at him now. Finally she smiled again, to his relief. But then she said, "Very well. I accept. You may accompany me. Come. We must hurry. Eduardo will let us leave through the back, just in case Girard is still watching."

She was on her feet and heading toward the kitchen before he could even begin to think of a reply. That was not at all what he had meant. Unfortunately he now had no choice but to hurry after her on her mad errand.

They went through a maze of narrow streets. Rycote had absolutely no idea where they were, or even in what direction they were heading. This was clearly an old part of Rome, the medieval city, where streets were laid out without rhyme or reason. All the buildings looked alike, drab and run-down, peeling stucco on the walls, and heavy shutters covering all the windows. They walked in silence. He had no idea why she did not speak, but he was too angry to frame a coherent sentence.

At last they stopped before a door. How she knew it was the right one, he could not imagine. It looked exactly like a dozen doors they had already passed. She knocked in what he realized was an odd rhythm. That was all that was needed in this ridiculous melodrama—secret signals.

The door opened a crack. Then a hand reached out and pulled Lissandra in. The door began to close, but Rycote slammed it open and pushed his way in.

A young man was still holding Lissandra's arm, but pushed her behind him and let loose a stream of utterly incomprehensible Italian. He was no doubt the brother. He had her delicate features, a bit too pretty on him, and light hair, though darker than hers. The idiot was wearing a red shirt with a scarf wrapped around his waist from which he pulled a dagger.

More melodrama, thought Rycote in disgust. He bowed slightly and said, "Messer Pietro Crescenzi, I presume. I am Rycote."

The young man half stumbled as he was halted in his attack by Lissandra, who had grabbed hold of his arm and was pulling him back, her own stream of incomprehensible Italian mingling with his in some bizarre contrapuntal duet. Rycote could not help but smile.

"He is a friend, Pietro, you idiot." She finally switched to English so Rycote could understand her.

"He came with me to protect me. He and his family are staying at the palazzo."

Pietro eyed him dubiously but put away the dagger before he spat out a few more sentences, less aggressive perhaps, but still incomprehensibly in Italian.

"I'm afraid I do not speak Italian," Rycote said.

Pietro looked confused for a moment and then broke out in smiles. "Ah, English. You are a sympathizer, then."

"I'm afraid I have no interest whatsoever in your politics one way or another. I wanted to accompany Donna Lissandra for an entirely different reason. This." He drew back his right fist and delivered a punch to the jaw that sent Pietro flying back to land on the floor.

"Stop!" Lissandra jumped between them before Pietro recovered enough to pull out his knife again, but turned from one to the other, not certain which one required protection.

Before Pietro could speak, Rycote said, "That was for putting your sister in danger."

"What danger?" Pietro looked confused.

"You think it is safe for Donna Lissandra to go wandering around Rome by herself, with no protection?"

"No, no, I thought..." He turned to his sister. "I know you could not tell our parents, but why did you not at least have a maid with you? Maria?"

She looked at him in amazement. "Maria? Are you mad? The moment she so much as suspects that you are back in Rome, she will be running to the police or to the French." She stopped, worry shadowing her face. "Perhaps she did suspect. Perhaps that is why Girard was watching."

"A gentleman protects his sister," said Rycote

stiffly. "He does not put her in a position where she is prey to creatures like Girard."

"Girard? Who is this Girard?"

"He is nobody of importance, I am sure. He is a French lieutenant. He probably thinks that to capture someone like you would win him notice." Lissandra gave a careless shrug. Too careless to be convincing.

Rycote shook his head at her and turned to Pietro. "He may be interested in you, but I think he is far more interested in your sister. You simply provide him with an excuse to put pressure on her."

"Ah." Pietro looked thoughtful and turned away from them to pace around the room. He stopped at one point to look at Rycote. "Your family stays at the palazzo? How is this?"

Lissandra sighed and said, "Mr. Freeborn arranged it. You know we need the money. And Lord Rycote's father is an English marchese, so Papa considers it hospitality and is not shamed."

Pietro looked at Rycote appraisingly. "A marchese. That is good." He smiled. "Then you will be watching out for my sister. You are perfectly correct. She should not be involved in this."

"What do you mean, I should not be involved? Do I not get to decide such things?"

"Such things are not for ladies," said Pietro loftily. "I need to send a message, but there must be another way."

"You think me incapable of delivering a simple message?" Lissandra was sounding quite outraged.

"Not this one. It is to a waiter at the Caffè Greco and it must be delivered there. You know they would never let you enter, and you can hardly stand around the door without attracting suspicion. But perhaps…" He looked at Rycote as if an idea had suddenly struck him. "Perhaps *you* could deliver it. No one would be surprised if you were to go there. All the English do. And there would be no need for Lissandra to endanger herself." He smiled. It was not a particularly friendly smile.

Rycote knew blackmail when he heard it. He smiled back with his teeth clenched. "I would be delighted to be of service in this small matter. Simply tell me which waiter."

"Of course. It is Giovanni. He is the small one, very young, with a nose that is crooked. He works during the day—they send him home at night. I am sure you will be able to recognize him with no difficulty." He went over to a small table, scribbled out the note, and handed it to Rycote. Just before he let it go, he said, "And I am sure I can trust you to see that no danger befalls my sister, is that not so?"

"It is most assuredly so. I have a sister of my own, so I know precisely how you must feel."

Lissandra stamped her foot. "Bah! You will stop talking over me as if I am some sort of imbecile. Both of you with your silly plots and protections, you are the infants." She flung her scarf about her and headed for the door.

Rycote and Pietro exchanged what was probably their first look of real understanding.

❧

Lissandra marched down the street, not bothering to wait for Lord Rycote. She knew he would be following because that was what they did, these honorable gentlemen. That was what they thought courtesy meant—making certain that a woman did not take two steps unescorted. Did they ever stop to ask if the woman wished to be escorted? Did they bother to ask if the destination to which they took her was the destination she desired?

Of course not!

She would like to smash something over his head, the idiot. He was just like her brother. Because a woman was not strong enough to knock him down the way he had knocked Pietro down, she must be a mindless ninny, incapable of understanding anything.

He had caught up with her and was walking beside her. She sneaked a sideways glance at him. He was looking straight ahead with a martyred air about him, as if he was the one who had been insulted back there. His mouth—his beautiful mouth—was set in a sulky pout.

It was not fair for him to be so handsome. Everything about him, not just his face. He was tall and strong but not bulging with muscles. No, he was all lean grace, like a leopard. Why did he have to be stupid, like her brother?

She sneaked another look at him. No, that was not fair. He was not entirely like her brother. Pietro sent her to run his errands because he thought she was too stupid to see the danger and refuse. Lord Rycote wanted to protect her because he thought she was too foolish to see the danger for herself.

He was wrong, but it was not so terrible to have someone wanting to protect you. Not terrible at all. In fact, it gave her a warm feeling inside.

She reached over and tucked her hand around his arm. He almost jumped, he was so startled, and looked down at her as if he could not quite believe it. She smiled, and he smiled back, not a courteous smile, but a glorious smile that lit up his face, a smile full of joy. He put his hand over hers to hold it in place, and they walked home in silence.

There was no need to say anything.

❦

"We'll be dining with Freeborn and his wife on Thursday," Lord Penworth told his wife with a smile.

She looked at him curiously. There were few people at whose homes Penworth actually enjoyed dining, and they were all either close friends or relations. "Is this some special occasion?"

"Not precisely." He looked a trifle embarrassed. "I asked Freeborn if he knew anyone conducting excavations who might be willing to let me observe. It seems there is a Prince Savelli who is an expert on the Etruscans. And not just an expert. He's actually an experienced archaeologist himself. He and some friends are establishing an Etruscan museum here in Rome. In addition, he has what seems to be a large Etruscan necropolis on one of his estates and is in the process of excavating it. Freeborn knows him well and thought to introduce us."

"What an excellent idea." She beamed at him. This trip had been a good idea. An interest in ancient tombs was far better for him than constantly worrying about the messes the fools in the government were creating.

Ten

THE CONSUL'S HOUSE, ON THE VIA CONDOTTI, WAS not as splendid at the Crescenzi palazzo. It lacked the centuries of history, the ancient frescoes. The chairs were upholstered in plush, not faded brocades. One did not walk through the rooms thinking that perhaps an assassin had hidden behind those tapestries, a lady had fled with her lover through that portal. It lacked, somehow, the romance that permeated the palazzo. However, as they were welcomed by the Freeborns in a most proper drawing room, Lady Elinor could not deny that it was all in much better condition.

In fact, it was much like home. Penworth Castle might be centuries old, but it also had windows that fit properly, fireplaces that did not smoke, gas lighting, and proper plumbing. There were days when she would have traded the romance of Italy for a nice hot bath.

The treacherous thought did not last long, because she truly was looking forward to meeting an Italian prince and his family. An Italian prince, or a Roman prince, was not the same as an English prince. He wasn't a member of the royal family or anything like that. He was more like a duke, Papa had said. She hoped the prince would not be as old and dull as the dukes she knew in England. At least this one was interested in Etruscans. That was a major improvement over the last duke who had been her dinner partner. He had spent most of the evening telling her about his gout and the treatments he had tried, all of which had failed.

Mr. Freeborn was as meticulously dressed as ever and seemed even more cadaverous next to his wife, a sweet dumpling of a woman with rosy cheeks and gray hair worn in a simple bun. Her dress, of pale gray velvet trimmed with bands of satin, was precisely right both for the lady and the occasion. Elinor was pleased that her own dress of changeable blue-green taffeta with a bertha of cream-colored lace did not clash with her hostess's gown and wondered momentarily whether that was one of the things a consul's wife had to consider. Perhaps that was the reason for the choice of gray.

No sooner had they greeted the Freeborns than the other guests arrived. Prince Savelli did not disappoint. Although not particularly tall, he held himself well and looked most dramatically handsome and distinguished, with a head of thick iron-gray hair that he wore slightly long. He was accompanied by a lady of a certain age who was quite breathtakingly glamorous and moved with languid grace. She had black hair, perhaps a little too black, worn in a madonna style, and pale skin that reminded Elinor of thick cream. Her dark eyes were half covered by eyelids that seemed too heavy to stay quite open, so she looked sleepily out at the world. A full mouth just hinted at a smile. Her dress of crimson velvet was trimmed with black, and an extraordinary necklace of rubies circled her throat.

Elinor felt her mother stiffen and saw her lay her hand on her husband's arm. He looked down at his wife with amusement.

By far the most interesting member of the party was not the glamorous lady but the handsome young man beside her. Handsome was a most inadequate word for him. He was tall, almost as tall as her brother, and he had either broad shoulders or an excellent tailor who understood padding. His hair, as black as the woman's, curled around a high forehead, and his black eyes seemed to focus directly on Elinor the moment he entered the room. He smiled, and white teeth gleamed against his olive skin. He looked just slightly wicked.

Her breath caught and she was very glad that her gown was so becoming.

Introductions were made. The lady was the prince's cousin, the Contessa Landi, and the young man was her son, the Cavaliere Armando Landi. The prince made a fuss over Lady Penworth and Elinor. Lord Penworth made a fuss over Mrs. Freeborn and the *contessa*. The contessa made no fuss over anyone but looked at Rycote as if he were a particularly appetizing morsel. Rycote looked as if he would like to vanish. The cavaliere smiled at Elinor and held her eye just a little too long, then he and Tunbury looked at each other, not quite antagonistic but definitely wary, sizing each other up.

Despite this bit of awkward mistrust at the

introductions, dinner proceeded quite pleasantly for the most part. The contessa commiserated with the absent Crescenzis on the poverty caused by their foolish son's radicalism—"So much of their property was confiscated, you know"—prompting Lady Penworth to expatiate on the family's kindness and generosity to visitors. The cavaliere covered an awkward moment by turning the subject to opera, and managed to be both knowledgeable and amusing as he discussed the recent premiere of Verdi's *Il Trovatore* at the Teatro Apollo.

"Do you know Verdi's work?" Landi was sitting beside Elinor and she received the full blast of his eyes, looking into hers with a surprising hint of passion. Not really offensive, but still surprising, to her at least. He was, after all, a stranger.

"I've never seen the appeal of opera," Tunbury interrupted from across the table. "All those squawking sopranos with their silly trills, going on and on about dying before they finally get around to it."

"Ah, then you have not heard Signor Verdi's works." The cavaliere turned his back to Tunbury and concentrated on Elinor. "In his operas you will hear true passion. The count loves a lady, but she loves another, a troubadour. For him she will sacrifice everything, just as he will for her."

He was leaning toward her. Actually he was leaning a little closer than was quite proper, uncomfortably close. He was wearing a heavy, musky scent that seemed to overpower her. She was about to lean back when she saw Harry scowling and decided to stay where she was. Perhaps a bit of prodding was what

Harry needed. She smiled at Landi. "Why, Cavaliere, you make it sound truly exciting."

Since the group was small, the conversation was general, ranging from opera and music to a comparison of garden styles to the acknowledgment of a fondness for macaroni on the part of all. There was one moment of confusion when Rycote suddenly leaped back from the table, almost overturning his chair. Conversation came to a halt while everyone stared at him, but he mumbled a confused apology and subsided into his seat.

Landi proved himself skilled in the art of offering graceful compliments—not just to Lady Elinor but also to Mrs. Freeborn on the gracefulness of her hands and to Lady Penworth on the elegance of her posture. The ladies rewarded him with smiles. Tunbury regarded him with narrowed eyes.

After dinner things were a bit strained in the drawing room where the ladies waited for the gentlemen to join them. The contessa seemed to find the effort at conversation so exhausting that she found it necessary to lean back in an armchair with her eyes barely opened. Whenever Mrs. Freeborn offered a topic of conversation, the contessa would open her eyes slightly, raise her brows, and resume her semi-somnolent pose. She came to life only when Lady Penworth admired her rubies, at which point she embarked upon a loving description of jewels she owned, jewels she had seen, jewels she coveted.

Finally, as she was winding to a close, she focused on the brooch nestled in the lace of Lady Penworth's bodice. It was a large sapphire, a very fine one, surrounded by a filigree of delicate gold set with small diamonds. It was also the only jewelry Lady Penworth wore, other than her wedding ring. The contessa looked puzzled. "You do not greatly care for jewelry?" she asked.

"I do not care to take much jewelry with me when I travel."

Lady Penworth's tone was not encouraging, but the contessa did not seem to notice. She nodded understandingly. "That is very wise. One never knows what sort of people one may encounter."

Lady Elinor turned away. Had she met the eye of either her mother or Mrs. Freeborn, she was not sure that she could have restrained her laughter.

⤟⤞

Things went a bit better among the gentlemen, who were enjoying Freeborn's excellent port, an English habit of which Savelli heartily approved. While the others discussed Etruscans with considerable erudition, Tunbury drew Rycote aside.

"What the devil was going on at dinner? You jumped up so fast I thought you were going to hit the ceiling."

Rycote turned uncomfortably red. "It was that... that *woman*. She put her hand on my leg."

"Oh for goodness sake, Pip. You aren't carrying on because a woman's hand brushed you."

"She didn't brush me," he said in outrage. "She put her hand right on my thigh, and then, and then she *moved* it."

Tunbury had all he could do to keep from howling

with laughter. "It's those damned Byronic looks of yours, Pip. You get that faraway look in your eyes and women think it's passion smoldering in you when what you are really doing is deciding which varieties of apples to plant."

"I'm glad I amuse you," Rycote said stiffly, "but how am I supposed to look that woman in the face when we rejoin the ladies? She's old enough to be my mother!"

As it turned out, there was no need for him to worry. When the gentlemen reached the drawing room, the contessa ignored Rycote and concentrated on Penworth. Then, when Lady Penworth joined them, she smiled and withdrew to offer her charms to Freeborn. Tunbury watched them for a minute, fearing he might have to go to the older man's rescue, but he concluded that the consul was accustomed to the lady. He handled her with admirably polished courtesy that warded off anything even slightly warm.

Tunbury was less approving when he turned around and realized that Landi had managed to seat himself next to Norrie and seemed to be making himself agreeable. Too agreeable. Norrie was enjoying his company far too much. Not that Harry didn't want her to enjoy herself, but Landi was a stranger. He might not realize that Norrie was just a friendly person. Landi might think she was actually interested in him. She really needed to learn to be more distant with strangers. He went over to them.

"May I join you, Norrie?" He didn't bother waiting for an answer but sat down, even closer to her than Landi was sitting.

"Hello, Harry. Cavaliere Landi has been telling me about a wonderful Etruscan amphora his uncle discovered with a painting of Admetus and Alcestis between two demons."

"Oh?" Tunbury looked at Landi coldly. "Alcestis belongs in one of those Greek myths, doesn't she? If it's a Greek subject, how do you know it isn't a Greek amphora?"

Landi smiled, showing too many white teeth. "In this case, because the writing is Etruscan. But you are correct. There is much Greek influence to be seen." He paused and looked at Norrie quizzically. "The viscount calls you Norrie? Is this a name?"

She glared at Tunbury before she turned to smile at Landi. "It's a nickname. When I was a baby, my brother couldn't say Elinor and called me Norrie. The name stuck, and as a child I was always called Norrie by my family. It seems that some people have trouble realizing that I am no longer a child."

"I see." Landi smiled happily. "Then Lord Tunbury is a member of your family."

"Not at all. Just an old friend." Tunbury smiled back.

"Yes. Harry and my brother went to school together, and he's been around our family for years and years."

"How nice for him," said Landi, his smile a bit cooler. "I would have liked to see you as a child. You must have been a delightful little girl. Did you have tea parties for your dolls?"

"Actually, she was a dreadful little hoyden, climbing trees, fishing, swimming in the sea." Tunbury grinned. "She was forever escaping from her governess to join Pip and me in our games."

Landi smiled at her warmly. "That is an even more enchanting picture. You are a woman of spirit, not one to be bound by silly rules."

She smiled at Landi and was pleased to see that Tunbury's grin faded.

⁂

In the carriage on their way home, Landi shook his head at his mother. "You are really too bad. You greatly shocked poor Rycote."

She shrugged. "These English are impossible to understand. He is so beautiful. Who would have expected him to be so cold?"

"You will have to behave yourself. His Excellency seems likely to take them up, and you must not cause trouble. You saw the girl, did you not?"

She sighed and leaned back. "Yes, yes, I will be good. What of the girl? Her father has a title, but titles are of no use."

His smile gleamed in the darkness. "They are rich, these English."

"What makes you think that? They wore no jewels, the women. One paltry brooch the marchesa had on. It was a good stone, but still."

"They may not wear their wealth, but I made some inquiries. The father is one of the richest men in England."

"Ahh." The contessa sat up and peered at her son. "Then you must make haste. Capture her interest."

"That should be no problem. She already smiles at me."

"The other young man is not a rival?"

"Bah. He growls and glowers when I am near her, but he has no idea how to woo her himself. It never occurs to him to give her a compliment, to show his admiration."

"You will have to move quickly. You are not likely to find another girl so rich."

"Both rich and pretty. Do not fear. I have no intention of allowing her to escape." His teeth flashed once more in a smile.

Eleven

A COMMON INTEREST IN THE ETRUSCANS HAD CREATED an immediate rapport between the English marquess and the Roman prince. That in turn led to an invitation for the English party to visit the Palazzo Savelli to view the prince's collection of antiquities.

Lady Elinor looked about her and decided that the palazzo itself was more than worthy of a visit. Like the Crescenzi palazzo, it had walls and ceilings covered with frescos and floors covered with tiles. Unlike the Crescenzi palazzo, it showed no signs of faded glory. Everything here was beautifully maintained. The marble floors gleamed with wax and were covered with thick carpets from Persia and India.

Far from flaking, the frescoes looked as fresh as the day they had been painted. In the enormous reception room where they awaited the prince, one wall was devoted to a landscape of the Roman countryside that seemed to quadruple the size of the room. On another wall, windows opened into a garden, letting in the spicy scent of wisteria, already blooming in April. And something else. Something sweeter.

"What is that?' Elinor asked Tunbury quietly.

"What is what?"

"That sweet smell from the garden."

He sniffed. "Lemon blossoms. The lemon trees are blooming."

"Oh," she breathed out on a contented sigh.

"Why are we whispering?"

She looked at him impatiently. "Because I don't want to sound like an ignorant foreigner."

He bit back a smile. "But you are a foreigner. In case you hadn't noticed, we're in Rome. The fact that everyone here speaks Italian might have given you a hint."

"You're just being difficult. You know perfectly well what I mean. And don't think I haven't noticed how you pride yourself on your Italian accent. I saw you preening the other day when the waiter asked if you were from Florence. You like to think you fit in."

He had the grace to blush slightly. "Point to you. And I do know what you mean. But you needn't worry, you know. People never get upset when you are admiring their country, only when you are sneering at it."

"How could anyone sneer at Rome? At Italy? Just look around." She waved a hand at the room. "Everywhere you look there are treasures from the past. The very stones are ancient."

There was a gentle laugh behind her, and she turned to see Prince Savelli smiling at her. He was really quite handsome despite his age, she thought. Not at all portly, as so many elderly gentlemen were, but slim and standing straight, and he had a full head of hair, even if it was graying. She didn't generally care for aquiline noses, but on the prince it looked appropriate. Especially when, as now, a smile softened his fierce features. Elinor smiled back at him.

"I am pleased indeed that you admire my city," he said. "And the very stones of which this building was constructed are indeed ancient. My ancestors—who were, perhaps, not as respectful of the past as we are today—found it convenient to build this palazzo on the ruins of an ancient theater. Fortunately, the Romans were not careless, and the arches they built provide us today with a firm foundation. You will see them in the rooms below that house my Etruscan collection."

"We are looking forward to that, Your Excellency," Tunbury said, taking Elinor's hand and putting it on his arm.

Savelli turned his eyes from Elinor and stared at the younger man briefly before smiling again. "It will be my pleasure."

As the prince stepped away, Armando Landi appeared at Elinor's side. Tunbury tightened his arm against his side, firmly trapping Elinor's hand. She ignored this and greeted Landi with a smile.

"Lady Elinor, your smile brings new life to these old stones." The cavaliere lifted her free hand, brushed a kiss over her knuckles without ever taking his eyes from her face, and kept her hand in his just a fraction too long for her comfort.

She would have said something discouraging, but Tunbury's derisive snort was too audible. Instead, she made herself look flattered by the flowery welcome. "It is delightful to be invited to the prince's beautiful home."

Just beside them, Rycote looked around nervously. "Is your mother joining us as well?"

"Not just yet." Landi smiled at Rycote's obvious relief. "She is still preparing herself for dinner and will join us later. I suspect that her real reason for delay is that she does not wish to disturb her costume in these underground chambers. I fear she cares little about the past. Her home, her family—it is there that her interests lie. Someone like the beautiful Lady Elinor, who takes an interest in the history of our country, is most unusual and delightful." He sent a flashing smile, accompanied by a bow and a flourish, in Elinor's direction.

Rycote may have looked relieved, but Tunbury did not. He continued to glower, and Elinor wanted to shake him. Did he really think she was flattered by the sort of drivel Armando spouted?

"Do not monopolize our guests, Armando." The prince spoke sharply to his cousin, who flinched at the tone. Then, with a smile, Savelli suggested that the tour begin.

They proceeded down a broad stone staircase, accompanied by servants carrying lamps to illuminate the way. Although the rough stone of the walls and arches was a warm gold in tone, there was a chill to the place as they descended. Elinor was glad to hold on to Tunbury's arm, finding comfort in his nearness.

"I apologize for the inadequacy of the lighting," said the prince with a rueful smile. "Gaslights have come to the cities of Lombardy, but here in Rome we seem to prefer the dimness of the past. Change is very slow here."

"But change is coming," said Landi, sounding a bit angry, thought Elinor. Or resentful.

Savelli looked at him in silence, no expression on his face, and then gave a quick smile. "Is it?" he said softly. "Perhaps. We shall see."

"I notice that you speak of Rome and of Lombardy, but not of Italy," observed Penworth. "Do you disapprove of the efforts at unification?"

"Disapprove? No, I neither approve nor disapprove. If it happens, it happens. Will it change anything? That I doubt. Mazzini, Garibaldi, they seem to think that unification will somehow transform us into a great nation of honorable and virtuous men. I fear that most of their followers want only to benefit themselves." Savelli was looking at Landi in a way that seemed half amused, half contemptuous.

Whatever that look meant, it caused Landi to flush. "If you will excuse me, I will see if my mother is in need of anything."

His departing footsteps echoed in the uncomfortable silence.

"I apologize if my question ruffled feelings," said Penworth. "I did not intend to provoke. I was simply curious."

"That is quite all right, my friend. You see, my young cousin is somewhat embarrassed by the knowledge that he joined himself with the Garibaldini during the early days of the Roman Republic."

"And you disapproved?"

"No, I would not say I disapproved," Savelli said slowly. "I was surprised, I confess it, but rather pleased to think that he had some ideals, however foolish they might be. Unfortunately, he drew back as soon as it appeared that the Republic might be crushed. It seems he was as self-seeking as I always suspected. I would have preferred to be wrong."

There was not much one could say to that, so Lady Penworth turned to examine a statue of a reclining couple. "This pair looks remarkably cheerful," she said.

"Indeed," said Savelli, smiling once more. "I believe that is why the Etruscans give me so much pleasure. They are, to our eyes, most remarkably cheerful. They were defeated by the Romans, their cities destroyed, their language lost. All we have left of them are their tombs, and yet what we find in those tombs is a testament to the joy of life. Look at these two, carved for their sarcophagus. They look at each other and smile. They hold hands. Who they are, what they did, we do not know. But we can see the love and happiness they shared, and that is enough."

Nodding in agreement, Penworth said, "We know the Etruscans must have been great warriors. They held off the Romans for centuries, after all. They probably worried about war and politics, affairs of state, just as we do. Their great gift to us, however, is their recognition that joy and happiness, music and feasting—these things deserve celebration. We may know nothing else about them, but that is enough."

Tunbury had left Elinor to examine a beautifully chased bronze mirror and was circling a black-figured amphora. "What we don't know is perhaps part of the appeal," he said. "We can use our imaginations." He turned back to the sarcophagus. "That pair over there. Was he a warrior? A merchant? Did he bring home this amphora to please his wife, or did she choose it? Did she bring that mirror with her when they were married, or was it his gift to her?"

Elinor looked at him in surprise. She had never thought of him as so imaginative, so romantic. The realization made her happy, and she smiled.

"That is part of both the appeal and the problem," said Savelli, also giving Tunbury a smile of approval. "In the case of these three items, they are of the same period, but from the same tomb? It is possible, but we can never know because I purchased all of them from antiquities dealers, and they rarely even know where the things they sell were discovered."

"But isn't that foolish?" asked Penworth. "Aside from the importance for scholars of knowing about what things belong together, would the items not be more valuable if their origin were known?"

Savelli shrugged. "More valuable to scholars, certainly, but more valuable to the finders? That depends. If a shepherd tumbles into a tomb and discovers that mirror there, he can tell his master, who thanks him and gives him a few *baiocchi*, a few coins. If instead he takes the mirror, he can sell it to a merchant, who gives him a bit more, perhaps a few *scudi*, more than he earns in a year. Then the merchant takes it to an antiquities dealer, who gives him a few hundred *scudi*. Then the dealer sells it to me for a few thousand *scudi*."

"Thousands?" Rycote sounded shocked.

"Oh, yes indeed. And if that shepherd is enterprising, he will discover where the merchant sells the mirror. Then he goes back to the tomb and gradually empties it out, selling to the antiquities dealer for enough to buy himself a house in town and spend the rest of his life sitting in a caffè. It is a sore temptation for a poor man. That is why we rarely find an untouched tomb. Even on my own estates, tomb robbers and thieves are a constant problem."

"The temptation must be great," said Elinor, looking again at the mirror. The back of it had an engraved picture of a woman with a winged boy—Cupid, perhaps? It was quite lovely.

She turned to Savelli. "May I touch it?"

He smiled with delight. "Certainly. After being buried for thousands of years, it will no doubt appreciate the touch of a lovely woman."

She held it out at arm's length and discovered that she could see herself in the polished bronze surface. "Oh, goodness!" She turned to Tunbury, smiling with delight. "I can see myself in a mirror that belonged to a woman thousands of years ago. Thousands of years. Can you believe it?"

He smiled back, and she knew he understood exactly how she felt.

She was having a wonderful time. She had been having a wonderful time for weeks now, for months even. Ever since Harry came back. He was the only man she knew, outside her family, who didn't assume she was an idiot, who didn't *expect* her to be an idiot. He was never surprised when she was interested in something or even knew about something that was generally considered the sort of thing only a man could understand. He gave her such an incredible sense of freedom.

That's what love was, she realized. The freedom to be yourself.

Tunbury drifted back to the sarcophagus. The couple haunted him. The woman was smiling up at the man, and he was looking tenderly at her. His arm rested on her shoulder protectively. They seemed complete, in and of themselves. They needed no one else. Love, trust, faith, certainty—these were all there in this one carving.

He closed his eyes. He must be going mad. Here he was feeling jealous of a couple who had died more than two thousand years ago.

But he longed for the happiness they had had, the happiness he feared he could never have. He wanted Norrie to smile up at him that way, with a smile full of love and trust. He wanted to be able to put his arm around her. He wanted to be the one to protect her. He wanted her in his arms, melting with passion.

He wanted… God, how he wanted!

Rycote settled into the blue chair across from Marchese Crescenzi. He was beginning to think of it as his chair, since he had been sitting in it practically every day for the past two weeks. They were, as always, in the marchese's hot, stuffy room, surrounded by little tables covered with miniatures, while Crescenzi ancestors glowered at them from the dark portraits on the walls. The marchese had greeted him with what he now knew were the accustomed courteous phrases, and he had responded with the equally courteous phrases Lissandra had taught him.

It was strange, really. He had always hated trying to

speak French because he knew his pronunciation was all wrong and he felt like such a fool. But he didn't mind at all that Lissandra was teaching him Italian. He didn't even mind when she laughed at his pronunciation. He sometimes mispronounced things just to hear her laugh.

He loved her laugh. If he could, he would see to it that she always laughed, that she never had to worry about her parents or her fool of a brother. If she allowed it, he would protect her always.

The formalities completed, the marchese began one of his stories about Rome, or rather, one of his stories about the importance of the Crescenzi family in Rome. Rycote didn't mind. The stories were interesting enough and Lissandra sat on a low stool beside her father to translate. That meant Rycote could feast his eyes on her without seeming in the least rude or impertinent.

This story sounded a bit familiar, however. He was reasonably certain that he had been told once before how, four hundred years ago, a Crescenzi, Ser Rinaldo, got the better of an Orsini, Ser Bruno, a member of another important Roman family. He looked quizzically at Lissandra, who gave an amused shrug.

He made admiring comments whenever a pause seemed to indicate that they were needed. Then Lissandra began making her own interpolations. Ser Rinaldo hatched his plan in the marchese's tale. "Of course, it was not really his plan, for everyone knew Ser Rinaldo was a fool," she said. "It was the plan of his clever daughter."

Ser Bruno fell right into the trap, according to the marchese.

"Which would never have happened had he not been as big a fool as Ser Rinaldo, and a greedy fool as well," Lissandra added, maintaining an innocent look.

He thought he was going to choke. She seemed determined to make him laugh, and he was equally determined to school his features to the serious interest her father expected. Fortunately for him, the marchese was more fatigued than usual today and sent them off early to join Donna Lucia for refreshments.

Rycote managed to last until the door had closed behind them before he collapsed in helpless laughter. "Oh, that was too bad of you," he said when he finally caught his breath. "You should not tease so. You know I would not want to insult your father."

"You looked so very proper and stuffy that I could not resist."

She was laughing like a happy child. He did not mind in the least if she made him feel foolish so long as she had that happy look. It meant she felt safe.

He wanted to think that his presence was making her feel safe.

Unfortunately, he was about to be absent.

"Donna Lissandra," he began, and he could see the formality of his tone drive the laughter from her face. He tried again. "Donna Lissandra, my family has received an invitation to visit Prince Savelli at his estate north of Rome. He is conducting excavations there, and my father is eager to see them."

"I see," she said. "Well, that is easy to understand. I know that your father is greatly interested in the Etruscans. I am sure my parents join me in wishing you well." She held herself stiffly and did not look at him.

The sudden frost was alarming. "No, you don't understand. We are going for a week or so. It's just a short visit. Then we will be back."

She did look at him then, though uncertainly.

"I was worried—I *am* worried—about leaving you here with Girard around and your brother." He probably looked as flustered as he felt. "I want you to know that you must send for me if there are any problems. It's only a few hours away. I can be back in no time. If you want me to come, of course. If you need me."

"Ah, my gallant knight." The frost was gone, and she was beaming her smile at him again. "Thank you. You need not worry about Girard. He cannot harm me."

He was not so sure about that, but he had to be satisfied with her promise to call on him if she needed help, and the conversation degenerated into various indirect assurances that each would miss the other and looked forward to his return.

Returning to his family's apartments, he consoled himself that at least he had paid another visit to Pietro, this time without Lissandra. The numskull had finally gotten it through his head that a gentleman did not put his sister in danger, especially for his political games. It simply was not done. More than that, it was dishonorable, even cowardly. A man should protect, not endanger, a woman. He had made Pietro understand.

At least, he hoped he had made him understand.

Twelve

THE CARRIAGE LEFT THE FLAT, RATHER UNINTERESTING
wheat fields on the plain along the coast and followed
a road that wound through woodlands, rising gradually. The shade of the oak and chestnut trees was a
pleasant respite from the harsh glare of the noonday
sun on the plain, but that did not seem to make a
significant impact on the uneasy spirits of the travelers.

Lord Penworth was the only one who seemed to
be looking forward to the visit to Savelli's villa with
complete enthusiasm. His wife was enjoying his cheerful anticipation of viewing and even taking part in
tomb excavations, but she wished Italian roads were a
bit smoother. A particularly deep rut in the road sent
her up in the air to land with a thud on the hard seat,
and she had to clench her teeth to keep from saying
something that would distress her husband.

Rycote worried that he should have remained in
Rome. He was not convinced that, despite his assurances, Pietro would not get his sister involved in his
schemes. And they all seemed to underestimate Girard.
The Frenchman looked the sort to make himself a

serious nuisance. Lissandra, and her parents as well, needed someone to protect them. He wished he were back in Rome.

Tunbury also looked worried. He would have been looking forward to seeing the excavations with as much enthusiasm as Penworth if he thought it could be done in the absence of Cavaliere Landi. Unfortunately, he was almost certain the bounder would be there, drooling over Norrie. He had been calling on her in Rome far too frequently, and if he was staying at Savelli's villa too… Tunbury couldn't understand why Norrie kept encouraging him. She was intelligent enough to see what a snake the fellow was. Nor was he particularly happy about the way the prince was always flattering Norrie. She might laugh and say it was just the way old men enjoyed flirting with their granddaughters' friends, but Savelli wasn't that old.

Lady Elinor was uncertain about the trip. She was always pleased at the thought of seeing something new, and she was looking forward to the Castello Savelli. An Italian castle sounded very Gothic and ought to come complete with haunted towers and dungeons. The tombs, she supposed, were probably interesting too. But then there was Armando Landi. He was handsome, of course, and she should probably think it pleasant to be treated with such flattering admiration.

Much more pleasant than having Harry blowing hot and cold all the time, one minute so close that they seemed to have one mind between them and then pulling back and glaring at her for no reason at all. It was maddening. She had been trying to lead him gently into greater intimacy, but he would never take that step over the border of friendliness. She'd tried using the cavaliere to prod Harry with a bit of jealousy, but all that had produced so far was a mixture of glares and scoldings. What was she to do? She was beginning to think that he really wasn't interested in her except in a brotherly fashion.

In addition, Landi's attentions were just a bit too smooth, and he had begun pressing a bit too hard. When she tried to be politely discouraging, he didn't seem to notice. Perhaps it was just the difference between English manners and Italian manners. Whatever it was, he made her uncomfortable, and the discomfort was getting worse.

It was not long before they came out of the shade onto a graveled drive that led past a trim lawn to the porte cochere of a large and elegant neoclassical building of pristine white trimmed with beige. Servants materialized to usher them into the guest wing, where there were bedchambers, bathing rooms, sitting rooms, rooms for their servants, and a library, with huge bowls of flowers and trays of tea and fruit juices delivered without even a request.

But no towers for ghosts. And no dungeons.

It was all lovely but, Elinor couldn't deny, just a bit of a disappointment.

❧

A few hours later, Elinor stepped out of the French doors in her sitting room onto a wide terrace overlooking a formal garden. This, at least, was no disappointment. Stone urns at regular intervals along the wall held blossoming lemon trees. She had recognized the scent the moment she opened the windows, which, for some unknown reason, Italians kept closed all the time. The contrast of the thick white blossoms, the glossy leaves, and the rough urns was irresistible, and her fingers slipped lightly over each element.

"What a lovely picture you make, my lady. *Bellissima*." Landi appeared beside her, caught her hand, and bent over to kiss it. "Do you steal the perfume of the lemon blossoms, or do you lend your perfume to them?"

"There is no need to be quite so poetic, Cavaliere." She gave a tug to try and free her hand, which he was holding far too long, to her way of thinking.

"Cavaliere?" He smiled at her, wrapping her hand in both of his. "Will you not call me Armando?"

"I do not think that would be at all proper." She gave her hand a firm pull and succeeded in freeing it at last.

"How so? You call Lord Tunbury Harry, do you not? Why not the same kindness for me?" He placed a hand over his heart and looked plaintive.

"I have known Harry since we were children. It is not at all the same thing."

"No, I do not wish it to be the same thing. He is like a brother, you said. I do not desire to be a brother to you." He was close enough to her now to be breathing in her ear. "I think you know this. I think you understand that my desires are very different."

Elinor backed up as far as she could and found herself against the wall. This was getting awkward. "Please, Cavaliere…"

.

His hands slammed against the wall on either side of her, trapping her. "Armando," he whispered. "My name is Armando."

His mouth was descending toward hers. Oh dear, he did not seem willing to take *no* for an answer. She was going to have to do something unpleasant, and they had only just arrived. How awkward.

She ducked away from him and, to her enormous relief, saw Prince Savelli approaching. "Good afternoon, Your Excellency," she called out. "I was just admiring your lemon trees. The terrace, the gardens—it is all so lovely."

Landi stepped away from her with a mutter that sounded very much like a curse.

The prince approached, smiling. "No, Lady Elinor, it is you who bring loveliness to the scene." He also bowed to kiss her hand, but from him the gesture seemed pleasantly gallant, not suggestive. "Armando, the men are crating up the fragments we found last week. Make sure they don't lose any of the pieces and that they know where to take them. And you might remind your mother that we have guests. She will not wish to sleep through dinner."

"Certainly, cousin." Landi spoke with offended formality. "You will excuse me, Lady Elinor."

Savelli watched him stride off and shook his head with a sigh. Then he smiled at Elinor. "I see you have quite recovered from the rigors of the journey. Will you permit me to show you my garden? There is a fountain of which I am very fond."

"I would be delighted, Excellency." She took his arm, thinking it surprising that the older man could be so much more attractive than the younger, more obviously handsome one. Giving way to curiosity, she asked, "Do your cousin and her son live here with you?"

They had reached the end of the terrace and were descending the curved steps leading to the garden before he spoke. "Here, yes, but with me? Not precisely. I have several other homes where I often stay. It allows them to think of this as their home." He shrugged. "They have nowhere else to go. My cousin's husband was…profligate. At his death there was nothing for his widow or his son." He noted her look of surprise and nodded. "You are thinking of her jewels. I fear my cousin is very fond of jewels. She sometimes accepts gifts from admirers."

Elinor did blush at that, and they walked on in silence until they arrived at a circular pool in which a pair of playful stone dolphins chased each other under a spray of water.

"What a delightfully happy fountain!" Elinor smiled with pleasure.

"It is, is it not?" Savelli smiled back at her. "It always makes me smile to come here. It is not Etruscan, of course, but I think it shares their spirit." He turned and looked back at the house, his smile fading. "It is hard on a young man, knowing he is dependent on the goodwill of others. He could find employment, of course." A rueful shrug. "If he finds that unpalatable, he must marry a rich wife."

Elinor smiled. "Your Excellency, are you by any chance warning me about fortune hunters?"

He patted her hand. "I like your father very much.

He is a most honorable and intelligent man. It would distress me greatly were I to be the occasion of bringing unhappiness to him and his family."

"You need have no fear. Your cousin is a very handsome young man, but I am in no danger of losing my heart to him."

"*Bene*. I thought it as well to make certain you were aware of Armando's situation. But I see someone else seems concerned." He looked amused.

❧

Tunbury was hurrying across the terrace. He slowed a bit when he reached the path and saw that it was Savelli who was walking with Norrie. He did not, however, stop scowling even when he reached them. "Excellency. Lady Elinor." He bowed rather curtly.

In return, Savelli beamed at him. "Lord Tunbury. I trust you found your chambers satisfactory."

"Chambers? Oh, yes, of course. Most comfortable." He wanted to snarl. Savelli's hand was covering Norrie's. What was she thinking? She was in no need of support to walk. In fact, he would wager she could walk the old man into the ground.

"Isn't this a lovely garden? His Excellency has been showing me about, and there is the most delightful fountain." She looked quite happy to be walking on the old man's arm.

"I fear I must return to my affairs, but perhaps, my dear, you would care to show the fountain to Lord Tunbury? If, of course, young men are interested in such things." Savelli looked at Tunbury in inquiry.

Tunbury smiled back, baring his teeth only slightly.

"I would be delighted to have Lady Elinor show me the beauties of your garden, Excellency."

They parted with a flurry of bows and curtsies, after which Savelli strolled back to the house while Tunbury spun Lady Elinor around and marched her rapidly away.

"Stop that!" She pulled back and yanked her arm free. "Will you stop dragging me around like a…like a…"

"Like a what?" he snarled.

"Like a badly trained dog." She was rubbing her arm where he had been holding her.

"Oh God, Norrie, I'm sorry." He felt sick, disgusted with himself. "Did I hurt you?"

She shook her head impatiently. "I just don't understand. Why on earth are you angry? You keep having these…these *fits* where you're suddenly snarling and snapping."

"Ah, Norrie." He turned away to collect himself before he looked back at her. "I'm sorry. One of the servants told me Landi was out here with you."

"Well, he was, before His Excellency sent him away."

"Good. I don't trust him. He's much too…too *oily*. But I'm not sure Savelli is much of an improvement."

"Really, Harry, the prince is perfectly charming and perfectly proper," said Norrie in exasperation.

"Don't you see? He's an old man, much too old for you."

"Too old? Prince Savelli? Too old for me?" She started to laugh so hard that she had to lean against a tree. "Oh, Harry, you are so ridiculous. Whatever gave you the idea that he was interested in me?"

"There's nothing ridiculous about it," he said truculently. "He takes you wandering down garden paths and I saw him patting your hand."

"In a very fatherly fashion. For goodness' sake, he and my father are friends. Besides, he just wanted to warn me that his cousin is a fortune hunter. As if that wasn't obvious." She took Tunbury's arm. "Come, let me show you that fountain."

He let her lead him away, but did not feel reassured. She was too naïve. She did not realize what a prize she was for any man, even one who did not covet her dowry.

❦

That evening, while they were gathered in the salon before dinner, Prince Savelli drew Elinor's attention to a small Etruscan bronze, not more than seven inches high. Even to her inexpert eye, it was clearly a late work, with all the grace one might find in a Greek statue, and beautifully rendered. There was nothing archaic about this Hercules. He stood there frowning, hand on hip, in all his strength and power, wearing nothing but his lion-skin cape.

He was naked. Quite naked. Quite gloriously naked.

She ought, she knew, to be admiring it as a work of art. She should say something about the pose, the exquisite workmanship, something. Unfortunately, her mouth was so dry she could say nothing. All she could do was stare at the miniature but still arrogant male displaying his perfectly muscled form. His perfect form.

"Do look at his face. Does he remind you of

anyone?" The prince's voice penetrated her fog. He sounded amused. Embarrassingly amused.

She managed to lick her lips and swallow before reaching out carefully to tilt the statue for a better look at his features. The face was remarkably individual, despite the small size. This Hercules was frowning. He was frowning just like... He looked just like...

She turned to face the prince. "Good heavens, it's Harry. It's just like him."

Savelli smiled. "I am delighted that it was not simply my imagination. I thought there was something familiar about him when we met in Rome, but it was not until I saw this statue again that I realized what it was. Young Lord Tunbury must have had an ancestor wandering around Etruria thousands of years ago."

Her own delight had not evaporated when Harry came up to them, scowling again. He took one look at the statue and turned on Savelli furiously. "That is hardly the sort of thing you should be displaying to Lady Elinor."

"Do calm down, Harry," she said. "We were just discussing your ancestry."

Harry turned to her, his face white. He made a strangled sound of horror, and she felt quite frightened. "My ancestry?" His voice was barely audible.

"Yes," said Savelli. "This statue bears a remarkable resemblance to you. I commented that you must be descended from an ancient Etruscan. I assure you, no insult was intended."

Harry took a deep breath and nodded slowly. His color was returning. "An Etruscan ancestor," he said softly. "How very interesting. You will excuse me."

He walked quickly from the room. Elinor was about to follow him, but the prince caught her arm.

"No," he said. "I do not know what has upset him, but he will want to recover himself in private." When she tried to protest, he said, "Trust me. I know better than you how young men feel."

Thirteen

ON THE EVENING OF THE FOURTH DAY OF THEIR VISIT, Savelli and Penworth came back to the villa in great excitement. The workmen had uncovered what appeared to be the entrance to a tomb, and the two noblemen seemed to have left their dignity behind with the shovels. Savelli was almost beside himself with enthusiasm, his florid gesticulations in wild contrast to his usual dignified manner.

"You understand, we have found many tombs, but all too often, someone has found them first. The thieves seem to smell them out, I swear it. By the time we reach a tomb, we find broken pottery, little clay figures, but nothing of real value. But this one is different. There is something of real importance in there. I can almost smell it!"

"It's extraordinary, the way he found the place. A remarkable piece of deduction," Penworth said. When Savelli tried to dismiss it modestly, the marquess insisted, "No, it really is." He turned to his wife. "He noticed the trees. That part of the cliff has just a shallow layer of earth over the travertine rock, so only a few scraggly plants can grow. But in one place, there are real trees growing. If the soil is deep enough for trees to grow, something must have excavated the rock. And sure enough, he found an opening filled with rubble. The workmen have been digging out the rubble, and today we found it. A tomb marker with an Etruscan inscription!"

"It was growing too dark to see much," said Savelli, breaking in, "but I could feel the letters. I touched them."

Penworth beamed at Savelli, and the prince tried unsuccessfully to hide his delight. His joy was infectious. Delighted laughter filled the room.

"This one is different," Savelli said. "I know it. For one thing, it is on the other side of the river. All the tombs we have found before have been on this side, caves dug into the walls of the ravines. But this one is on the far side, across the bridge, and it is an underground tomb. That will make it much later, I think." He broke off his exposition. "Ah, my friend, you have brought me luck." Savelli threw his arms around Penworth, who was too excited to object and returned the embrace with laughter.

Everyone else joined in the excitement. Contessa Landi managed to lift a languid hand in acknowledgment. Even the young people, whose interest in the Etruscans ranged from moderate on the part of Tunbury to indifferent on the part of Rycote, were infected by their elders' enthusiasm and vowed to be present early the next morning.

◦◦

Not long after sunrise, with the grass still damp with dew and wisps of mist lingering about, they rode across the ancient bridge that spanned the river separating the *castello* from the plateau on which the ancient city once stood. The sun would be strong soon enough. Elinor was glad her mother had agreed that they would wear their exploring outfits today. Poplin, sturdy though it might be, was far cooler and more comfortable than layers of petticoats. The men were also dressed practically, with broad-brimmed hats, loose jackets, and shirts open at the neck. Except, of course, for Landi, who rode with his mother in a landau at the rear of the party, both of them dressed in their usual fashionable finery.

Here on the empty plateau, a desolate moor for the most part, the grove of trees that had drawn Savelli's attention was immediately noticeable. At least, thought Elinor, it was noticeable now that he had pointed it out.

Turning back in his saddle to address the party, Savelli said, "You must not be disappointed if we cannot immediately enter the tomb. Even though the entrances are not deliberately blocked, as was the Egyptian practice, tunnels often collapse, and we must proceed very carefully."

"We quite understand, Your Excellency," said Lady Penworth cheerfully, "and we will be quite willing to watch and wait. Staying away, however, would make the suspense unbearable."

The contessa, riding in the landau at the end of the procession, turned and glared at her son sitting beside her. "You did not mention this when you said I must arise at this ungodly hour."

Landi patted her hand in its soft kid glove. "Now you know you would not have wished to miss an event such as this." Then as the others pulled ahead out of earshot, "Behave yourself. The prince may not be willing to put up with your fits of pique indefinitely."

As the road curved, the contessa tilted her parasol to keep the sun from her face. "He knows I have no interest in this, this grave digging. I am not a peasant to admire a man when he is covered in dirt."

"But perhaps he begins to find you tiresome. Do you not see him there, chatting with Lady Penworth, who shows a flattering interest in his activities?"

"Bah. You cannot think he is falling in love with that woman."

Landi took a deep breath. "Do not be stupid. But she does not bore him. He admires her. And the more he admires her, the less patience he has with you."

She narrowed her eyes at her son. "And the less patience he has with you?"

He smiled bleakly in acknowledgment. "And with me."

"So why are you here with me? Why are you not up there with the girl? If you intend to marry her, you need to make her fall in love with you soon," she snapped. "Entertain her. She is probably bored."

"Our cousin does not approve. I must *entertain* her when he is not present." He looked at the three Englishmen, dressed no better than ordinary workmen. He sneered slightly and brushed an invisible speck from the sleeve of his immaculate black frock coat.

The workmen were already at the site when they arrived, and had swept away the remaining debris at the entrance. Savelli dismounted and strode over. Reaching out a hand, he delicately traced the inscription carved in the tomb marker, *Ravnthu Seitithi*.

"A woman's name," he said softly. "This must be your family tomb. Please forgive us for disturbing you after all this time." With a pickax, he carefully loosened the stone sealing the entrance until, with the help of his foreman, he could remove it. They laid it to the side, and he peered into the darkness.

His shoulders slumped.

Turning to the others with a rueful smile, he said, "As I feared, at least part of the passage has collapsed. It appears there will be a delay in the proceedings. I apologize for having taken you from your beds at such an unseemly hour." He waved a hand at the tomb. "It will take some time, perhaps even days, to clear a passage. And the rubble must be carefully examined. Who knows what may have been buried by the collapse?"

"Well, we can help with that," Elinor said cheerfully. "If your men can bring the debris out, we can sift through it."

"We can?" Rycote looked startled.

"Certainly," said Lady Penworth. "I may not have any expertise, but I can tell a piece of pottery from a pebble. If we are uncertain about anything, we can set it aside to be examined later."

Prince Savelli looked at them, and a trace of his buoyant optimism returned. "It is good to have friends."

By noon, the volunteers were no longer so enthusiastic. The rubble was not greatly compacted, so the workmen made rapid progress. That prompted Savelli to think that the collapse had not happened too long ago. That also meant that the piles of rubble grew quickly. More quickly than Elinor and the others might have liked.

Sitting on the ground soon became uncomfortable, and there was a dreary monotony in picking up a pebble from one bucket and putting it into another one. Had Lord Penworth not been so obviously committed to the task, Lady Penworth might have given in to a desire to return to the castello for a nap. And had Lady Penworth not skewered her children with a glare whenever they showed an inclination to flag, they might have found a way to sneak off after their alfresco luncheon of bread, cheese, and wine.

But they kept at it until Tunbury made a weird sound, something between a shout and a gurgle. He held up an object about three inches wide and slightly rounded. Elinor looked at him and began to feel alive again, no longer weighed down. Something was actually happening.

Savelli hurried over and took the fragment reverently from the younger man. With a soft brush, he delicately removed some of the dirt, until it was possible to see that part of the shard was dark and a lighter section curved into it.

"Red-figure pottery," he said, looking up with a grin. "They learned that technique from the Greeks, but rather late. Perhaps the fourth century BC. I cannot clean this here—that will have to wait for my workroom—but we may find more fragments. Perhaps enough to give us an idea of the whole piece."

Suddenly, the entire party revived, and by late

afternoon a respectable pile of shards had been collected. Enough enthusiasm had been generated to ensure everyone's return.

Unfortunately, no further bits of broken pottery appeared on the next day. The workmen had progressed far enough in clearing the passage to have gone beyond the area where the pot may have been. Hours passed in what they were all beginning to think was futile labor. Even Lord Penworth began hinting that perhaps his wife might wish to return to the castello for a rest. Elinor was about to say that sounded like an excellent idea when she reached into her bucket and made a new discovery. However, this one was far less encouraging than Tunbury's pottery shard had been.

"Cloth?" she said, pulling out what seemed to be a filthy rag. "I would never have thought it would survive all these centuries."

The chatter gradually faded away. The workmen had spent enough time on the prince's excavations to know how unlikely a piece of cloth was. They turned to watch as the prince walked over to her and took the cloth from her hand. A muscle twitched in his cheek as he examined it.

"You are quite right," he said eventually. "This would not have survived. It is of no great age at all." Without another word, he returned to his post, supervising the workers clearing out the passage. Lord Penworth watched for a minute and then went to stand silently beside him. A moment later, Lady Penworth joined them.

Elinor looked at the others in confusion. "I don't understand. Why is the prince so upset?"

"It means someone has been in the tomb," Tunbury said. "Thieves, for certain, and not very long ago." He thought for a minute. "Most likely during the night after Prince Savelli's men uncovered the entrance. They could have sealed up the tomb easily enough when they were finished, and they probably caused the collapse to cover their traces. If you hadn't found that piece of cloth, no one would have suspected."

"But surely there was a guard set," Rycote protested. "The prince is hardly careless."

Tunbury shrugged. "The guard could have been bribed. Or given some drugged wine. In which case he would not want to admit he was asleep all night when he should have been on watch."

They sat there rather glumly watching the progress at the tunnel until Elinor spoke.

"Really, Harry," she said, "you seem to know a great deal about underhand dealings. I shall have to remember to ask your advice, should I ever decide to turn to a life of crime." She smiled, and the gloom lifted a bit.

A shout from the tomb entrance brought them to their feet. The despondency brought upon everyone by the discovery of the cloth dissipated and the workmen began chattering excitedly. By the time they got there, Savelli had disappeared. The workmen had cleared a passage big enough for a man to crawl through, and Savelli had gone in, Lord Penworth told them.

They waited. And waited.

Elinor realized she was clutching Harry's hand so tightly that it must be causing him pain. She loosened her grip a fraction, but he turned and smiled at her. Then he squeezed her hand, so she decided it was all right.

At last, with a small fall of gravel, Savelli crawled out of the passage, his appearance transformed. It was not simply that the normally immaculate prince was covered with dust and grime, his jacket discarded and his shirtsleeves rolled up, a tear in his trousers. It was that his face bore an expression of awe mixed with fear. He set the workmen to finish clearing the passage and then came over to Penworth.

He shook his head and gave a short nervous laugh. "I do not know… I dare not say…" He shook his head again. "I cannot believe I saw what I think I saw. I cannot describe it. You will have to see. Then you can tell me if I have lost my mind and am seeing things."

"We will wait with you," Penworth said. "It cannot be long now."

And so they waited once more. At least this time there was a bit of noise from the workmen as they dug out the rest of the rubble. It would have been less tense, Elinor thought, if people would at least say something, but since no one did, she felt obliged to be quiet as well. Not only quiet, but almost motionless. They were all too intent on the tomb entrance as workmen carried out basket after basket of rubble.

Finally the foreman appeared with a broad smile on his face. Savelli gave him a quick nod of acknowledgment, then turned to Penworth. "Lanterns. We will need lanterns."

This was quickly arranged and they entered the

tomb, Savelli in the lead. The beginning passage was narrow but soon opened into a small room carved out of the rock and perhaps nine feet high. That, in turn, opened into a larger room, perhaps twelve feet high, with seven doorways leading from it. They stepped in and stood, staring, in silence.

"My God, Savelli. It's incredible." Penworth barely managed a whisper.

The prince turned slowly in a circle. "I was not dreaming then."

The walls were covered in frescoes, vivid, almost alive. Life-sized figures in realistic colors and natural poses, nothing like the stylized paintings they had first seen. These were war scenes, for the most part, some of men fighting furiously, some of slaughter. And above these, one wall had a frieze of animals and birds, while another had complicated geometric decoration.

"Have you ever seen anything like this before?" asked Tunbury.

The prince shook his head. "No, never." Then he threw his head back and laughed. "Those fool–ish thieves. Whatever they stole, it cannot have a tiny fraction of the value, of the importance of these murals. They will perhaps peddle a pair of earrings or a gold brooch. Merely an annoyance. But these paintings, through them the Etruscans will speak to us. They will reveal themselves. They will tell us something of their history."

Elinor stood in front of a painting that showed a bearded man holding a woman by her hair and threat–ening her with a sword. She shivered. "But who are they, all these people?"

"Something is written next to them," said Tunbury, "probably their names, but I can't read it."

Savelli came over and held up his lantern. "The letters are Etruscan. Aich by the man and Cas'ntra by the woman. That would be Ajax capturing Cassandra, part of the story of the Trojan War. But we will decipher them all. We know that the Etruscans adopted many of the Greek myths. With luck, not all of these pictures will be of Greek heroes. I hope, I am certain, that some of the stories told here will be of Etruscan history." With a smile he began to make a slow circuit of the walls.

"Will you want to set up a guard on the tomb?" asked Rycote, a bit hesitantly.

"My foreman, Lorenzo, will take care of that." The prince spoke absently. Then he stopped and a shadow passed over his face. "Ah, you are thinking of my foolishness in not setting up better protection when we first found the tomb. Yes, I thought no one knew of the discovery so a single guard would do. I will not make that mistake again."

✺

In the morning, Savelli and Penworth had already gone off to the tomb when the others sat down to breakfast. Lady Penworth had a decidedly smug look on her face as she sipped her coffee. "This trip was definitely one of my better ideas," she told her children. "Your father looks ten years younger and he has lost that worried look."

No one was inclined to argue with her, though it is doubtful that Contessa Landi even heard her. Looking dreamily off into the distance, the contessa said, "A ball. I shall hold a ball in four days' time. It will be to honor my cousin's discovery. That will please him, I think. Should it be a costume ball? With everyone in Etruscan garb?"

She tilted her head and considered. Then she shook her head decisively. "No. They wore ugly things, tunics. Not at all becoming. No. We will be elegant. Everyone will come." She smiled at the guests. "You will wear your finest jewels, and the men will wear their decorations. It will be magnificent." She tossed aside her napkin. "I must confer with the majordomo."

She rose and glided from the room in a cloud of lace.

Her son looked after her with exasperation. "Be warned. The villa will be impossible for the next four days. All the servants will be running about at her beck and call, and she will change her plans every few hours. Myself, I plan to keep out of sight." With a graceful bow, he too departed.

The visitors looked at each other in amusement.

"Ought we go back to Rome?" Rycote sounded a bit hopeful.

Lady Penworth promptly dismissed that notion. "We could hardly leave without your father, and we could not possibly drag him away from the tomb at this point."

"We will just have to do some exploring of our own," said Elinor. She looked at her brother and Tunbury. "I'll meet you at the stables in half an hour."

"Half an hour?" jeered her brother. "You'll never be changed in less than forty-five minutes."

"I can change in less time than it takes you to pull on your silly boots," she retorted.

"A bob says I beat the pair of you," said Tunbury, pushing away from the table.

In no time at all, Lady Penworth was alone. "Children," she murmured fondly.

Fourteen

Savelli went off to Rome to find an artist to do detailed drawings of the frescoes before exposure to air and light could damage them. Carlo Ruspi would be the man for the job, he said, and would be eager to do it the moment he heard of the discovery. Penworth was in the library organizing their notes and sketches, and Lady Penworth was helping him. Contessa Landi had sent her son off with a list of purchases to make for the ball that evening while she lay in her room recuperating from the exertion of giving orders. Rycote, Tunbury, and Lady Elinor had gone off riding yet again, but Rycote's horse came up lame, and horse and rider were forced to limp back to the stables.

After a good gallop, the other two riders slowed the horses to a walk as they went down a lane beside yet another row of tombs that had been uncovered by Savelli over the years and dismissed as of little interest. Had anyone asked her, Elinor would have been perfectly willing to admit that her interest in Etruscan tombs was fading rapidly. Besides, she was feeling uncomfortable. May in Italy was much warmer than

May in England, and they had been riding over a flat plain without any shade.

In deference to the possible prejudices of her hosts, she was wearing a conventional riding habit rather than her tomb-exploring outfit. It was her favorite habit, a bright blue wool with a skirted jacket reminiscent of a more flamboyant era. Its wide sleeves and lapels were of dark blue velvet trimmed with loops of gold braid, and the matching hat, with its low crown and curved brim, perched forward over one eye while a plume swept back and curved down around her ear. Whenever she wore it, it brought back memories of her childhood, when she had ridden over the fields at Penworth with Harry and Pip, pretending they were Cavaliers off to defend the castle from the Roundheads.

At the moment she had no interest in adventures, imaginary or not. She was simply hot. They rode into a glen that seemed to be an ancient road between two rows of tombs. Spying a tree large enough to offer some shade, she rode over to it and dismounted by unhooking her leg from the horn of her sidesaddle and sliding to the ground.

"You're supposed to wait for me to help you. Don't you ever remember to be helpless?" Tunbury dismounted beside her and took the reins from her hand. "At least let me tie the horses up."

She was more than willing to let him take care of the horses, and while he led them off, she removed her jacket and tried using her hat as a fan. Even in the shade it was hot. The air was utterly still, and the only sounds came from Tunbury and the horses clomping around and a few insects making insect noises. The whole world smelled dusty. She sat down on a rock and pulled out a handkerchief to blot the sweat that was probably making muddy tunnels in the dust on her face.

She was bored.

It was unreasonable. She knew that. After all, she hadn't been bored when they were in Rome. But here, even though the villa was beautiful and strange and all those things that people travel to see, she had nothing to do. Her father and the prince were busy with their excavations, and her mother was busy transcribing their notes for them, while she was told to keep out of the way so she didn't disturb anything.

The contessa didn't seem to do anything except sleep and change her clothes. Armando paid attention to her, but it was in the form of ridiculously florid compliments, and his increasing intensity made her uncomfortable. Pip and Harry talked to each other and treated her like a pesky little sister trailing along after them. She wanted to smack Harry over the head and shout, "Look at me! I'm all grown up!"

She heaved a sigh. It wasn't Harry's fault that she couldn't win his interest. It was her own fault. She had mistaken his feelings. Although she was in love with him, his feelings were only brotherly. No passion. She had no right to complain. She wasn't just being unreasonable. She was acting like a spoiled brat. Knowing it did not make her feel any better.

"Catch."

She turned and put up her hands just in time to catch the object Harry had sent flying in her direction.

It almost splattered in her hands. "An orange. Lovely." She smiled in delight and started peeling it immediately.

Harry had tossed aside his coat and neck cloth too, and unbuttoned his waistcoat. He plopped down on the ground beside her and grinned. "There's another orange for you and some rolls. I remember how cranky you get when you haven't been fed for a while."

She slipped the first of the orange segments into her mouth, holding a hand under her chin to catch the drips. She held the morsel against the roof of her mouth with her tongue, letting the juices wash away the feeling of dust while the sweet-sharp scent of it cleaned the air she breathed. She swallowed and turned to him with a dreamy smile. "I forgive you."

"Forgive me?" The grin disappeared and he looked startled. "What did I do?"

"Well, if you don't know…" She turned away and shrugged.

There was a brief silence, and then they both began to laugh.

"Idiot!" she said affectionately.

"Ninny!" he replied.

By the time they had demolished the crusty rolls and licked up the last drop of juice from the oranges, Norrie's mood had improved mightily. She stood up and stretched before looking around. Harry was lying back and seemed to have fallen asleep. She picked up his jacket and began checking the pockets to see if he had anything else to eat. Preferably something sweet.

❦

Harry had been half dozing when he heard her stand and watched through half-opened eyes as she stretched. Did she have any idea what she looked like? A woman might stretch in that cat-like way as she rose from her lover's bed. Norrie should have more sense. It didn't matter that she obviously thought him asleep. A glimpse of her with her head arched back like that would wake any man. It had certainly awakened his male organ.

This had to stop. He closed his eyes, concentrated on keeping his breathing slow and even, and thought about cold porridge.

"Harry!" It was half a shriek, half a demand.

He jumped up wide awake, his heart thumping. What had frightened her?

But she didn't look frightened. Confused, perhaps. Nervous, even. She was holding his jacket in her lap, and then lifted her hand.

It was his Colt. She had found his revolver and was holding it by the barrel, dangling over her lap.

He gave a short laugh, shaky with relief. "I thought something had happened to you."

"Well, it looks as if you were expecting something to happen. What on earth is this?"

"It's a handgun."

She gave him the look that idiotic reply deserved. "I know it's a handgun. What is it doing in your pocket?"

He started to relax. "Well, it isn't just a handgun. It's a revolver. A Colt pocket revolver." He took it from her, checking to make sure she hadn't accidentally cocked it. "It shoots five rounds without reloading. I bought it when I was in America. They're very popular over there."

She was still staring at it. "All right, it's in your

pocket because it's a pocket revolver. But why do you have it with you at all?"

He shrugged, feeling a bit embarrassed. "Habit, I suppose. I grew accustomed to carrying it with me all the time when I was traveling. And we are in a strange place here. There could be bandits. Or snakes."

Now she was looking dubious. "Snakes," she said flatly. "Could you even hit a snake with that thing?"

"I will have you know that I am an excellent shot." He was offended.

She looked even more dubious.

"I'll show you. Do you see that bush over there?" He pointed at a wilting shrub on the far side of the glen.

"I could hardly fail to see it. It must be ten feet high—quite as big as a barn door. I won't be impressed if you hit that."

He gave her a look of disgust. "Do you see the branch in the middle that sticks off at right angles to the main branch?"

She considered. "Yes, I see it."

"All right then." He took aim and fired.

The branch was severed just where it joined the main branch. There was a moment of silence—the shot seemed to have silenced the nearby insects—followed by a growing rumble. The wall of the glen behind the shrub trembled and then broke loose and began to roll down. With an oath, Harry pulled Norrie out of the path of the boulder that came crashing through the shrub and down the hillside to land not far from where they had been sitting.

They stared at the large slab that came to rest in a cloud of dust at their feet.

She pulled slightly away from him, though not quite out of his encircling arm, and leaned over to examine it. "Harry, I think you killed a stone."

He snorted and released her. She might be perfectly calm, but his hands were shaking. "Aren't you supposed to be distressed or impressed or something when a boulder lands at your feet? A mild swoon might even be in order." He looked at the spot where the shrub had been before the stone rolled over it. There was an opening there, and she was already climbing up to it. "It's probably just another tomb," he called up to her. "Haven't you seen enough of them by now?"

She stood beside it and threw an impatient look down at him. "I know it's just another tomb. But someone has left candles and a lantern inside this one. Why would anyone do that?"

He joined her and frowned. Why indeed? There should be no need for candles in a tomb that had been already excavated, a tomb that was one of the ones Savelli said contained nothing of interest. He peered inside, but it was too dark to see anything.

"We'll need to light the candles to see in there," she said.

He looked at Norrie and smiled slightly. Here she was, faced with a mysterious cave on her host's land, a cave no one had mentioned but which was obviously being used for some purpose, some secret purpose, which probably meant some illicit purpose. Given all that, what would she want to do? Explore it, of course.

"I have some matches in my coat pocket," he said. "I'll be right back."

She had collected all the candles, some half dozen,

by the time he returned. He was about to protest that they would be able to hold only one apiece when he realized that if they found anything worth examining, they might need more for illumination. Fortunately, he hadn't opened his mouth and said something foolish before she tucked the extra candles into the pocket of her riding skirt and handed him the lantern.

Once it was lit, she was about to charge into the tomb, but he caught hold of her arm. "Norrie, pretend you are a timid, fragile damsel and let me go first."

She rolled her eyes, but stepped back.

"Thank you."

It was cool in the cave, almost chilly after the heat outside. He should have realized that it would be and fetched Norrie's jacket as well as the matches. He glanced back to ask if she was cold, but she was busily examining the walls with her fingertips as if there might be some secret hidden in them. With a soft sigh he continued ahead, hoping they would find something to justify her interest.

They were in a tunnel, a common enough feature of the tombs they had visited. But as he moved ahead cautiously, he realized that this one was unusual. The floor seemed to have been swept clean. No crumbling bits of rubble lay about to trip the unwary. No broken walls narrowed the passage to make progress difficult. There was no need to tread cautiously. On the contrary, progress was so easy that he didn't like it. Something about this worried him. He wished he could send Norrie back.

He stopped so abruptly when the entrance tunnel opened into the central chamber that Norrie crashed right into him. Under other circumstances he might have enjoyed that.

"What on earth…?" She peered around him. "Oh." It came out on a long, awed breath.

Oh indeed. He took a deep breath himself and let it out slowly. The light of the lantern was enough to show a flat slab of stone serving as a table to display objects that glittered like gold.

Only gold glittered like gold.

They approached slowly, cautiously, stepping silently as if there were someone or something here that could be disturbed.

The central object was something that looked like a breastplate, more than a foot wide, shaped to curve around the neck. The embossed designs were difficult to make out, but there seemed to be a variety of winged creatures as well as strips of spirals. They lit the extra candles, dripping wax onto the stone to set them in place.

Brighter light did nothing to chase away his uneasiness, the feeling that something was wrong here. Very wrong. In other tombs he had sometimes felt awe at the age of the relics, even sadness at his inability to understand the inscriptions, but there had always been something almost welcoming. The Etruscans had filled their tombs with depictions of pleasure and happiness.

Not here.

Norrie reached out to touch a wide gold bracelet, its embossed figures of a woman surrounded by animals clearly visible. But she drew back. "Something is wrong here," she said.

So she felt it too. He stepped around the stone

to take a better look and halted abruptly. There was another table, this one of wood, against the wall. On and around it were several oil lamps, enough to make that area as bright as day. It was apparently a work table. On it was a large red-figure jar depicting a sacrifice. That jar was complete, and the piece of beeswax next to it suggested that its luster was being improved. Another jar was in the process of restoration. Some of the pieces had already been glued together while others were arranged about it. Pots of glue, paint, and gesso were all at hand along with containers of brushes.

Everything needed for the restoration of ancient pottery.

On the ground were several small wooden chests, two of them nailed shut, one partly filled, and one empty but lined with straw. More straw lay in a pile to the side.

Norrie came to join him, and her eyes widened. "Where did these things come from?"

"My guess would be the tomb Prince Savelli just discovered, and perhaps from earlier discoveries."

"His Excellency said nothing about this," she said.

"I doubt His Excellency knew anything about this."

"Then who?"

He shrugged. "I don't know."

They both turned back to contemplate the artifacts in silence.

"If the prince were here, we could simply tell him about this," Norrie said.

"But he isn't. He may not be back for days. Since the packing seems to be almost done, we can't wait until he returns."

"We'll have to move these things ourselves. But we'll have to finish the packing before we can take them back to the villa." Norrie picked up the breastplate and laid it carefully at the bottom of the open chest, covering it with straw. Harry grinned and went to help her.

Packing didn't stop him from thinking. By the time they finished he had come to a conclusion. "While I agree that we need to move these things, I think it unwise to take them back to the villa."

Norrie stopped and considered. "You think someone in the prince's household is responsible? I cannot imagine the contessa or Armando actually soiling their hands." She smiled and wiped her grubby hands on her equally grubby skirt.

"Or someone among the servants. Or one of the workmen on the excavation. But it has to be someone closely connected to the prince. No one knew about the tomb before Savelli and your father told us."

She nodded slowly. "But where shall we put these things?"

Harry grinned. "How many tombs do you suppose there are hereabouts? As long as we stay on Savelli's land, we can take our pick. And imagine the thieves trying to figure out what happened to their treasure."

Fifteen

By the time they returned to the villa, filthy and exhausted, shadows were lengthening and a breeze was carrying the evening chill. Reaching their rooms without attracting attention turned out to be surprisingly easy. All the servants were scurrying about taking care of the last-minute preparations for the ball, while the guests and members of the household were in their own rooms resting in preparation for the coming exertions.

While Tunbury went off to tell Lord Penworth and Rycote about their discovery, Elinor made it into her room, closed her eyes, and leaned against the door in a combination of relief and weariness. She had never thought of herself as a pampered, fragile flower, but she had never before engaged in actual physical labor. Her arms and shoulders and legs and back all ached. She felt sweaty and grimy. She was certain that she absolutely stank.

She heard a shriek.

She opened her eyes and saw her maid looking at her in horror. Apparently she looked as awful as she felt. She managed a smile. "I would like a bath, Martha. Right away."

Martha put her hands on her hips and glowered. "Do not go anywhere near your dress. I just laid it out on the bed. Stay right where you are until we get those filthy...*things*...off you." The maid opened the door enough to call out to a nearby footman and demand a bath and hot water *subito*! Right away. Martha had mastered that much Italian.

In no time at all Elinor was soaking in a deep tub of steaming water, breathing in the perfume from the rose oil Martha had poured in with a lavish hand. Her head leaned back as the maid brushed her hair, muttering about foolish madcaps who get their hair all dusty and dirty when there's no time to wash it before a ball.

"We washed it just yesterday, Martha," she murmured in mild protest.

"And it was still damp this morning, wasn't it?" Martha brushed harder. "You know how long it takes to dry."

Elinor smiled to herself. She had heard Martha bragging more than once about how nice and thick Lady Elinor's hair was. The scoldings were so familiar, so normal after the afternoon's upheavals. It was an exciting adventure, of course, to have discovered a theft, especially when she shared that adventure with Harry. It was also very nice that she and Harry could do something to repay their host for all his kindness. But still...there was something unpleasant about the thought that someone she knew, or at least someone she had seen, was a thief. She was not sure what the penalty for thieves was in Rome, but she doubted it was much more pleasant than the penalty in England.

The realization was uncomfortable.

She didn't want to think about penalties and punishments. To wash the thought away, she lifted the sponge and wiped it over her face, and then wiped it again. She closed her eyes and thought about dancing. There would be waltzing this evening, she was sure of that. Balls were filled with waltzes and she had never waltzed with Harry. Would there also be mazurkas? Polkas? She loved to whirl with her partner in a polka. She began to hum a polka. That would surely drive all other thoughts from her mind.

❧

Since no guests were invited to dinner before the ball, and since the duke had not returned from Rome, the contessa had decreed that all would be served a light meal in their rooms. Although such an arrangement had seemed decidedly odd to the English visitors, Elinor was grateful for it. It meant there had been time for a nap. That, in turn, meant that by the time she was dressed she had completely recovered both her spirits and her energy.

Her dress was one she had ordered in Paris. The ivory Pointe Duchesse lace on the wide bertha collar and trimming the sleeves was even more beautiful than she remembered, and the aquamarine silk played up the color of her eyes. Martha arranged a wreath of flowers and ribbon around the chignon of her hair, and three ringlets curled down to touch the nape of her neck. Her kid gloves were the precise ivory color of the lace, and her fan was an antique silk painted with a rococo design of shepherds and shepherdesses. The only jewelry she wore was a single strand of pearls.

She felt beautiful. Harry could not fail to notice that she was a woman.

She stood at the top of the stairs. Harry was standing below talking to Pip. It was funny, really. Pip looked so poetically handsome, with those curls that wouldn't be kept down and those dark eyes like Papa's. If you didn't know he was such a stuffy old stick, you could imagine him as the hero of all sorts of dramatic adventures.

Then there was Harry. His evening clothes—of the finest cut and cloth—fit him perfectly, but they could not disguise the fact that he was far more muscled than a gentleman should be. And dear though he was, no one would be likely to call him really dashing. Yet he was the one who had gone adventuring around the globe while Pip wanted nothing more than to stay at home and farm.

And the mere sight of Harry made her heart stop.

She waited, watching them from the corner of her eye, her hand at her wrist as if she were still buttoning her glove. Harry turned and saw her. She could see his eyes widen. She could almost hear the sharp intake of breath. She allowed herself a small smile.

He had noticed.

"There you are, Elinor," Pip grumbled. "Come along. Mother and Father are already in the ballroom." As soon as she reached the bottom of the stairs, he grabbed her arm to shepherd her along. "Might as well get this over with."

The English party soon made a little island in the midst of the sea of gaily chattering Italians. The contessa, whose bodice was cut extremely low, presumably to allow room for the display of diamonds on her chest, greeted people as they arrived. However, she made no effort to introduce them to the English visitors, an omission that Lady Penworth clearly took amiss. That did not stop Elinor from insisting that her brother partner her for the opening quadrille—she was *not* going to ask Harry to dance with her—and their parents also joined in the dance.

When they returned to their place by the wall where Harry awaited them, Landi immediately appeared with many flowery compliments and asked Lady Elinor to honor him with a waltz. Before the music began, other young men appeared to beg for an introduction and in equally flowery phrases expressed their enchantment with the beautiful English lady who spoke their language so delightfully. Before Elinor knew it, her dance card was full—and not one of the names written there was Harry.

It didn't matter, she told herself. She loved to dance, and her partners were, almost without exception, excellent dancers. She whirled through waltzes, mazurkas, polkas, a varsouvienne, even a schottische, and flirted madly with handsome young men. If she occasionally caught a glimpse of Harry standing on the side and glaring at her, well, he had no right to do so. There had been nothing to stop him from putting his name on her dance card.

She had seen Landi too, talking intently to one of the servants and then staring equally intently at Harry.

When he arrived at her side to claim his waltz, before she had even returned to her family, there was a strange look about him, an almost hectic flush. It was not the result of dancing, for he had not danced the past few sets. She wondered if he had been drinking, but he did not smell of spirits. Only of his rather heavy perfume, which made her choke.

Before she could recover her breath, he spun her into the waltz with abandon, whirling her about so wildly that she could barely keep on her feet. When at last he slowed down and released her, she staggered for a few dizzy steps before she realized that he had whirled her right out of the ballroom and into the small library. He turned to close the door behind them. It closed with a loud click, like the sound of a lock closing.

Oh dear. This was beginning to look like an extremely tiresome end to a pleasant evening. She was not sure what he was planning, but she was quite sure it was not something she would like.

Hoops and crinolines made it difficult to maneuver, and she had not thought it necessary to bring a hatpin. A quick look around showed that the room was sorely lacking in potential weapons. The ornaments were all of the delicate china variety—not a sturdy bronze among them. And her fan was not only a fragile antique but one of her favorites.

Landi turned and smiled at her, holding out a hand. "*Cara*," he said in that unctuously caressing tone of his. Her stomach churned unpleasantly.

"This is a mistake, Cavaliere," she said, slipping behind a settee.

"No, *cara*, no mistake. You must know how much I admire you. I have never known anyone who could set my heart on fire as you do." He held one hand over his heart and the other out to her, with what she presumed was supposed to be a lovesick look on his face. It gave her indigestion.

She shook her head. "No, I am afraid you are definitely making a mistake."

He smiled again. Someone must have once told him that he had a charming smile, because he relied on it so much. "*Bella*, you are not cold like other English. I have seen you look at me. Together we will create such magic. You cannot imagine what magic."

"Really, I am afraid you are quite wrong. At the moment, magic does not interest me in the slightest, certainly none that we could make together. However, I would appreciate it to no end if you would open that door. At once." She edged toward the vase of flowers on the end table. It seemed to be the only available weapon.

"Do not be afraid, *bella*. My intentions are quite honorable. I seek nothing less than marriage." He was prowling closer.

"And I fear I cannot return your feelings and so must decline your proposal, Cavaliere." If he came around one side of the settee, she might be able to make a dash around the other side and get to the door.

He didn't go around the settee. He lunged over it and grabbed hold of her, pulling her into his arms and bringing his mouth down on hers, rather painfully crushing her lips against her teeth. She had hold of the vase, however, and brought it down on him. Not very effectively. She didn't have enough room for a good, hard swing. Still, she did manage to empty the water on him and she heard a surprisingly loud crash as the vase fell. That shocked him into giving her enough breathing space to pull back and throw a punch.

It never connected.

The crash she had heard had not been the vase falling but the door being kicked open. Harry came charging in and yanked Landi away before Elinor's punch could land. Harry failed to notice that he had frustrated Elinor's effort. He was too busy landing a few punches of his own. Quite a few.

In no time at all, Landi was curled up on the floor, one arm curved to protect his face.

"If you ever come anywhere near her again, I'll break you into a million pieces," Harry growled, not even breathing hard.

Not a terribly original threat, thought Elinor, but Landi clearly considered it effective. He spat out something in Italian, something Elinor did not understand but Harry clearly did, and he took a step forward. Landi scuttled backward before getting to his feet, straightening his coat, which was rather soggy, and leaving with as much dignity as was possible under the circumstances.

❧

She was shaking out her skirts as she came out from behind the settee and tending to the lace on her bodice. It had gotten torn, and there she was, tucking it into place, as if nothing had happened except a minor accident with her dress.

"You little idiot." He knew he shouldn't yell at her, but he couldn't help it. "Whatever possessed you to come in here with him?"

She held herself stiffly and didn't look at him. "I didn't precisely come in here so much as end up in here. He was spinning me in the waltz so quickly that I didn't realize we had left the ballroom. Besides, there was no need to make such a fuss. I had things perfectly under control."

"Under control," he jeered. "That is no doubt why you were cowering behind the furniture."

"I wasn't cowering! And I don't see why it's any concern of yours anyway. There is no need to act as if you are my brother. You can't even bring yourself to dance with me, so I can't believe you care who I kiss."

He was going to go mad. Oh God, there were tears starting in her eyes. She was upset with him now. She thought he didn't want to dance with her? She was impossible, infuriating. She was—he didn't know what to call her.

He swore furiously, grabbed her, and pulled her into his arms. One kiss he would have at least, even if she would never speak to him again. One kiss.

He pushed his hand into her hair to hold her head and brought his mouth down fiercely on hers. One kiss to last him a lifetime. For this moment at least, he would possess her. He coaxed her mouth open and slid his tongue in. He could feel her startled gasp, but he didn't care. He needed to taste her. She tasted of lemonade. For the rest of his life, lemonade would bring back this moment.

Her mouth had opened under his, and he slid his

tongue in to explore her. She gave a little moan, and then her tongue tentatively tangled with his.

He froze. Her tongue was…

He slowly became aware of other oddities.

She wasn't struggling. She wasn't pushing him away. In fact, her arms were around his neck and she was holding him almost as tightly as he was holding her.

He lifted his head enough to look at her. "Norrie?" He whispered her name uncertainly.

She smiled at him. Her eyes were dreamy and not quite focused, but she smiled up at him. He could see that.

He crushed her to him then. He kissed her eyes, her hair, her neck—every part of her he could reach with his mouth while standing just outside a ballroom full of people and murmuring between kisses. "Oh Norrie, I love you…I've loved you so long…I love you…I love you…" A piece of him knew that he should say something more, something poetic, but he couldn't think of anything. All he knew was that Norrie was in his arms and she was…

He groaned and pulled her hard against him again. He could feel her all along him, fitting perfectly against him despite all the corseting, all the petticoats between them. He slid his hand down her back, knowing she was there somewhere under all those layers.

❧

Yes…Yes…Yes… There was no thought at all. Just joy bubbling up in her. This was what she wanted, what she had been longing for. This. Being wrapped in his arms. Every inch of skin where his lips touched was burning, alive in a way she had never known before.

She pushed her hands under his coat, wanting to touch skin, but there were too many layers—the rough brocade of his waistcoat, the stiffly starched shirt. She made an impatient noise and returned to run her fingers over the skin of his face.

His lips were trailing down her throat, and she leaned back to give him easier access. When he reached the swell of her breast, she laughed aloud for the sheer joy of it.

❧

"Tunbury, get your hands off my sister!"

Harry lifted his head to see a furious Pip glaring at him, hands fisted. He smiled happily. "No," he said, "no, I don't think I will."

"No? What do you mean, *no*!"

Pip grabbed Harry's shoulder to pull him away, but Harry was still holding Norrie so tightly that she came right along with him. She was still laughing up at him and he grinned back. "No, I don't think I will," he repeated. "I don't think I will ever let go of her." He was looking at her, not her brother. "I'm going to marry her." He had a moment of hesitation. "You will marry me, won't you?"

"Hmm?" she said dreamily. "Oh yes, of course I will. You can propose properly later." She was smiling, looking as if she could see only him, so he laughed deep inside himself and began kissing her again, gentle kisses full of promise this time.

"Tunbury!" roared Pip. "There is a ball going on."

"Why on earth are you bellowing, Pip? What is going on?" said Lady Penworth, coming in followed by her husband and Landi. "Oh, I see." She smiled and turned to her husband.

Penworth's plaintive sigh was not good enough to cover his smile. "I confess, I am not entirely certain what I am supposed to say at this point. You will excuse me, my dear, but am I supposed to be stern or welcoming?"

Landi stepped forward and struck a pose. "You need not fear for your daughter's honor, my lord. I will marry her myself."

The others looked at him blankly.

"Whatever are you talking about, Landi?" said Penworth, sounding quite bewildered.

It was the Italian's turn to look confused. "The Lady Elinor, she is compromised, is she not? But even so I am willing to marry her."

Harry growled and started toward him, but Elinor kept her arms around his neck. "Don't be an ass, Cavaliere," she said. "I'm marrying Harry."

"Of course she is," said her mother. "We all knew that."

"We did?" Pip took his turn at confusion.

His mother looked at him pityingly. "Well, perhaps you didn't realize it. Brothers often don't."

Landi looked around angrily. The hectic look was back in his eye. He clenched his jaw and flung out of the room.

Lady Penworth looked after him. "Curious." She turned to her daughter. "Is there something I should know?"

Norrie was leaning happily on Harry's chest, his arm around her. "No, I don't think so."

Harry loved the feel of her leaning on him. He loved having his arm around her, moving his fingers ever so gently over the silk of her gown. He leaned his head just enough to have her hair tickle his cheek while he breathed in the scent of her. She was his. She was...she was Lady Elinor Tremaine. She was Rycote's sister. She was the Penworths' daughter. And he was nobody. Nothing. A fraud.

He could feel the color draining from his face and he straightened up, pulling away from Norrie so he was no longer touching her. He forced his hands to his sides.

He had to tell them. He had to tell them right away, before this went any further.

The old horror and disgust twisted in his stomach. He licked his lips. "My lord, I must speak with you." His voice sounded hoarse.

"Hmm?" Penworth smiled kindly. "It seems a bit late to be asking my permission. You two seem to have decided things for yourselves."

"No, my lord. I must speak to you, in private if you will." Penworth looked surprised, and Tunbury could see confusion on the faces of the others, but he stood his ground. He kept his face as expressionless as he could.

"If it's that urgent, I suppose we can find a private spot someplace." The marquess gestured for Tunbury to accompany him and they left the room.

After a few locked doors and an occupied room, Penworth opened the door on a sitting room, small

but adorned with frescoes depicting a remarkably energetic collection of amorous mythological creatures. He
raised his brows briefly at the sight, but then shrugged
and entered. Tunbury followed, and grimaced in turn
at the decor. The perfect setting, he thought.

"Well then, what seems to be the problem?"
Penworth sat in one of the green velvet chairs facing
the fireplace and gestured Tunbury to the other.

Tunbury shook his head and remained standing,
hands clasped behind him. He supposed he looked
rather like a schoolboy facing the headmaster. That
was what he felt like. No, he felt like a man facing the
firing squad. "I have to tell you about my family, my
lord." He looked at Penworth, who cocked his head
and listened. Tunbury licked his lips. His mouth was
so dry that his voice sounded hoarse. "You do not
know them, I think."

Penworth shrugged. "I have met your parents on
occasion. I cannot say I know them well."

"But you must know something of them by
reputation."

A hesitation, then a nod of acknowledgment.

"You must know, my lord, how much I admire and
esteem you and your whole family. Lady Elinor is, she
is… Well, no one could deserve her, but she deserves
someone who can at least approach her level."

Penworth smiled slightly. "She is the daughter of a
marquess, but you are the son of an earl, so that is not
a great step down, if that sort of thing worries you."

"Am I the son of an earl? I am his heir, but his
son?" He looked the marquess in the eye. "On my
twenty-first birthday, the earl told me that he has

no idea whether or not he is my father. Nor can my mother say. And the same is true of my sisters. We none of us can say with any certainty who our father is, and can only regret what we know of our mother. My father—the earl—did not seem to think that it mattered, since I was, after all, still his heir. He even laughed about it, said that for all he knew, some of his own get might be inheriting other titles."

He couldn't face Penworth any longer. He had to turn away. His childhood had been lonely enough when he thought his parents were simply too busy with their social life to care about their children. That was common enough. But when the realization was forced upon him that their social life involved little more than careening from bed to bed in God only knew how many adulterous liaisons or, in his father's case, careening from bottle to bottle…

He choked down the bile and forced himself to speak. "If you do not wish your daughter to wed a man of such uncertain and sordid parentage, I will understand. I had no right to even touch Norrie, much less ask her to marry me."

Instead of looking horrified or disgusted, Penworth looked somehow sympathetic. "Ah, so that is what has had you in a ferment and sent you off on your travels. We were worried about you, you see." Penworth looked kindly at him. "But that leaves the important question unanswered. Do you love my daughter?"

"Love her? Can you doubt it? I would die for her!"

"I suspect that she would prefer you to live." There was a suspicious twist to Penworth's lips as he waved the younger man to a chair once more. "That is

enough histrionics. Do sit down." This time Tunbury
did so. He had to. His knees were refusing to hold him
up any longer. Penworth smiled again. "Can I assume
that you have not yet told this to Elinor?"

"No, sir."

Penworth stretched out his legs and steepled his
fingers. "Then in exchange for your family secret, I
will be the one to tell you ours. The Tremaines have
not, in the past, been a family known for virtue. In
my father's and grandfather's generations, they were
known for little but vice. My father was the exception,
but he was the fourth son and had been disinherited.
When I unexpectedly came into the title, my grand-
mother informed me and my wife that I should not be
the marquess at all because my father had in actuality
been a bastard. His real father was a stable groom." He
was smiling when he raised his head to look at Harry.
"Do you know what Anne said?"

Harry shook his head.

"She said it was a great relief. Now she would
never have to worry that her children would take
after the Tremaines."

Harry sat there dumbfounded. He shook his head
again, in disbelief. "You don't mind…? It doesn't
bother you…?"

"I have known you since you were a boy, Harry.
I know you for a good and honorable young man. I
have no hesitation in entrusting my daughter's happiness to you. Now I suggest that you go and tell her
what you told me. I recommend that you arrange
things so that no sharp objects are within her reach."

❧

Elinor was fuming at her mother as she paced back and forth in the small library, waving her arms about theatrically. "He keeps doing that! Everything is going well, I think he is finally going to speak, and then he freezes up and turns into an iceberg. He kisses me, tells me he loves me, and then he acts as if he can't bear to touch me and leaves me. What on earth is the matter with the man?"

Lady Penworth tried to murmur consoling words, but in reality she was quite as confused by Tunbury's behavior as her daughter was. Rycote had vanished, to no one's surprise. He had never been one for emotional scenes.

Tunbury returned, looking both nervous and hopeful. There was no way he could fail to see that Norrie was upset. He offered a pitiable excuse for a smile. It did not suffice to placate her. She stood there, hands fisted at her waist, and glared at him. "Well? Are you planning to offer some explanation for your behavior?"

He darted a glance of appeal at Lady Penworth, who obviously had no intention of serving as protection for either one of them. Elinor's mother had long expressed her conviction that couples—married or not—needed to solve their own problems, and that included her children. Gathering herself together, she departed with a few murmured words about going to find her husband. Elinor continued to glare, but she allowed Harry to lead her to the settee and seat her beside him. He held her hands, a gesture she thought tender when he began to speak.

By the time he finished his confession, she had snatched her hands away and was trying to suck in enough air to enable her to shriek. He grew even paler and looked at her with pleading eyes.

She snatched up the first object at hand—one of the china figurines cluttering the tabletops—and sent it sailing at his head. It missed him by a foot, a clear sign that she was seriously upset. Her aim was rarely off.

"You blockhead!"

Another figurine flew over his head.

"You dolt!"

"Please, Norrie, don't hate me. I know I have no right—" He ducked and a third figurine almost nicked his ear.

"Cretin!" She was looking around but she seemed to have run out of throwable objects.

"I'll go away. You'll never have to see me again. Just please tell me you don't hate me."

She snatched up a pillow and began to beat him about the head. "You idiot!" Whack. "You fool!" Whack. "*That* is why you ran away?" Whack. "*That* is why you have been acting as if I am nothing but your sister, treating me like a child?" Whack. "You think that nonsense is *important*?" Whack. Whack. "I can't believe you could be so stupid!"

The idiot finally seemed to realize that it wasn't what he'd told her about his parents that was upsetting her but the importance he had given it. She was still angry, but at least he wasn't so dimwitted that he couldn't eventually understand. He stumbled back and landed on the sofa, fending off the blows with his hands, trying to placate her until at last he started to laugh. "Norrie, you're hitting me with a pillow."

She gave him one last whack with the pillow before

tossing it aside. "How could you ever have thought any of that would matter to me? Did you really think so poorly of me? You thought I was that superficial?" She felt tears begin to pool in her eyes and blinked to keep them back.

"No, Norrie, it wasn't you." He sat up abruptly. "Never think that. It was me. I was what was wrong. I didn't want to contaminate you."

The tears dried up and the anger returned. "Contaminate me? What sort of maggot do you have in your brain?"

"Look at me, Norrie." He stood up and stepped away from her. "Do I look like a gentleman? There's nothing elegant about me. I look like a bruiser. I could be a ploughman or a butcher or a blacksmith, and my father could be any one of those things. There is no reason to think that my mother limited her favors to members of society."

"And any one of those things could be considered an improvement on many of the drunken wastrels filling out the ranks of society, you saphead."

"But your family is so different, so wonderful, and mine is…" He shook his head.

She grabbed him by the shoulders, pushed him down so she could loom over him, and scowled. "You keep talking about my family. Harcourt de Vaux, do you want to marry me or my family?"

He looked at her, horrified. "Is that what you are thinking? No, oh no, Norrie. It's you, always and only you. I just have so little to offer."

She slowly began to smile. "You have yourself, you fool."

Sixteen

BREAKFAST THE NEXT MORNING WAS LATE, BUT EVEN so, it was a quiet meal. Savelli had not yet returned, though he was expected to arrive before evening. The contessa, of course, was sleeping the sleep of the exhausted hostess. Landi was nowhere in sight. This left the terrace and the morning sunshine to the English visitors.

They did not mind.

The two servants waiting on them managed to appear cheerful and energetic, even though they could have had little sleep themselves between ball and breakfast. They brought pots of coffee and pitchers of steaming milk, baskets of oranges and baskets of rolls, bowls of butter and bowls of jam. They were rewarded with smiles and thanks by Lord and Lady Penworth.

Lady Elinor and Lord Tunbury were oblivious to everything, including the food that was placed before them. Instead of being insulted, the servants were amused. Those who hadn't observed the scene in the library had heard about it. They rather relished the discomfiture of Landi, whose connection to the princely Savelli family was of the flimsiest. The young lady would doubtless be far better off with her English suitor, even if he failed to make *una bella figura*, an elegant appearance.

About the other young Englishman, the handsome one, they were not quite certain. This morning he did not seem as happy as the others. In fact, he seemed quite disturbed about something. Not the betrothal of his sister, though. He could be roused to smile at the couple, but soon he relapsed into a brown study.

Eventually there was nothing left to place on the table or remove from it. There were no cups to fill, no crumbs to brush away, and there had still been no interesting remarks, no revelations about the events of the evening, not even a mention of the cavaliere. Disappointing. The two servants looked at each other, shrugged, and returned to the kitchen.

"What on earth is the matter with you, Pip? You look as if you have indigestion." Lady Penworth's mothering style had never veered toward sweetness.

Rycote flushed. "I was thinking that perhaps I should return to Rome. We have been away for more than two weeks, and I can't help worrying about Lissandra." The sudden silence at the table made him flush more deeply. "Donna Lissandra. And her family, of course."

"Of course." Lady Penworth sipped her coffee.

"It's that French fellow, Girard. I don't like the way he keeps hanging around her." Rycote wriggled uncomfortably.

"She is a lovely and charming young lady," said Lord Penworth, looking at his son with some compassion. "It is hardly surprising that she should have suitors."

"Not like him!" Rycote pushed to his feet, strode over to the balustrade, and leaned on it to stare out over the garden. The others watched him. Finally he turned back. "It's not only that. It's her brother."

"I understood that he had fled with the other followers of Garibaldi some years ago." Lord Penworth was looking cautious now.

"But he's back."

Lord Penworth looked actually alarmed now, but his son failed to notice this. Rycote kept his voice low and glanced about only to make sure none of the servants was within earshot. "Girard was following her one day, thinking she'd lead him to Pietro. She knows he's watching her, so she'll be careful. But I don't like it."

Penworth picked up his coffee, lifted it to his mouth, then decided against drinking it and put the cup back down. He took a deep breath and gave his son a level look. "I can understand your concern. However, you will remember that we are guests in this country. I may not be a member of the government, but I do hold my seat in the House of Lords, and it would ill become me—or a member of my family who is traveling with me—to become involved in what might be considered treasonous rebellion."

"You would hardly expect me to leave an innocent lady exposed to danger," said Rycote indignantly.

"Of course not," said Lady Penworth, putting her

napkin aside and standing up. "I agree. It is time we returned to Rome. After all, we have a wedding to plan." She patted her son on the cheek. "Don't worry, dear. It is all a matter of perception, and I am sure we can all see to it that things are perceived as we would like."

"My dear, we cannot leave until Savelli returns." Penworth spoke mildly but firmly. "We have to tell him about Harry and Elinor's discovery yesterday. That is a matter of no little concern. You must see that."

Lady Penworth smiled at him. "Of course I do, and I agree completely. But the prince will be returning today, and it will not take you long to tell him all about the stolen goods. I am sure the contessa will be delighted to see us leave, now that she realizes that Elinor will not marry her son. The servants can set to work on the packing while you and Rycote finish arranging the notes and sketches for the prince, and we should be ready to depart tomorrow. You young people may keep out of the way." She waved a dismissive hand at them all as she marched into the house.

Penworth looked after her with a resigned smile. "It appears we will be returning to Rome tomorrow."

Tunbury had been attending to all this with only half an ear. He had been busy admiring the way a lock of Norrie's hair had escaped its chignon and curled around her ear. In shadow it was almost black, but when she turned her head and the sun hit it, all sorts of colors appeared in it. It was quite fascinating, and he was going to have the rest of his life to determine all of those colors. Every morning he would be able to sit with Norrie and look at her hair. And other parts of her.

"Tunbury, stop looking at my sister like a besotted idiot, and pay attention," snapped Rycote. "We're returning to Rome tomorrow."

"Fine," said Harry, still looking at Norrie. "We could go on a picnic today, if you like."

"Lovely," she said, looking back at Harry. "Is that all right, Papa?"

"Hmm?" With an abstracted air, Penworth continued looking at the doorway through which his wife had disappeared. "That sounds fine. Enjoy yourselves." He stood up and went after his wife.

Rycote was still frowning, as if unable to decide whether he was pleased or not with his mother's pronouncement. Pushing himself away from the table, he followed his father.

❧

Elinor held up the rose dimity, looked in the mirror, and tossed it on the pile of discards. "No, that one won't do, either."

Martha looked at her with a mixture of amusement and exasperation and held out the pale green muslin dress she had just finished pressing. "This one, Lady Elinor?"

Elinor looked at the maid and smiled ruefully. "I'm being ridiculous, aren't I?"

"Not at all, my lady. You just never felt the need to please a young man before. Now let me help you into this." She lifted the flounced skirt over Elinor's head, careful not to disarrange her hair, and tied it over the petticoats. Then she fastened the undersleeves into the bodice and allowed Elinor to close the tiny pearl buttons running down the front. She fluffed the lace ruffle at the neckline so it stood up properly, tweaked the flounces so that the green and white embroidery showed to best effect, and then stepped back and smiled approvingly. "There now. You look just like a breath of spring."

With a half-laugh, Elinor turned to look at herself in the mirror. "It's all backwards, isn't it, Martha? I feel as if I'm just starting the courtship, only we're already promised to each other. And it's not as if we haven't known each other since childhood." She turned from side to side to see how the flounces fell as she moved. Very nicely, she decided.

"Ah, but getting to know each other as man and woman isn't the same as knowing each other as boy and girl, is it? You'll have plenty to learn about him, and him about you, never you fear. Now, it's the leghorn bonnet you'll want with this. The ribbons match and the wide brim is protection from the sun. And which parasol?"

"The white Battenberg lace, and the white lace mitts." They were impractical for a picnic, but the lace made her feel delicate and fragile, and that, she thought, was how a girl being courted should feel.

Millie smiled her approval, and when Elinor reached the portico where Harry was waiting, she saw approval in his face as well. She admired the way he looked in return. His fawn trousers and brown frock coat fit him beautifully, showing his broad shoulders to advantage. His waistcoat was a mix of tan and brown, and his pale hat, with its soft, low crown and wide brim, looked quite dashing. How silly of him to think he looked ungentlemanly. He looked bold and brave and, and…. Her breath caught as she thought of the wonderfulness of him.

He handed her up onto the buggy's seat. It wasn't the most dashing of vehicles. The seat was little more than a board, and the space behind, now occupied by a picnic basket and blanket, looked as if it had last been hauling bales of hay. The whole was pulled by a horse that looked as if he would be happier pulling a plow. He probably had been pulling a plow yesterday, but Elinor didn't care. She was sitting beside Harry, and she was setting off into an entirely new part of her life, uncharted territory. Rather like those old maps that said, "Beyond this place be dragons." Only it wasn't dragons. Her map said, "Beyond this place be Harry." That was all she needed, or so she told herself.

They drove along in silence, an unusual circumstance to Elinor's mind. Not only was she sitting stiffly erect, while Harry was sitting precisely the same way, but she couldn't think of anything to say. She couldn't remember the last time she had nothing to say to Harry, or he had nothing to say to her. Or if they should happen to be silent, it was always a comfortable kind of silence. This silence was more like a nervous uncertainty. She stole a glance at Harry. He was looking unsure of himself. That was not like him. Not at all. Harry always looked at ease, even when he wasn't. And he was stealing glances at her, as if he hesitated to look at her straight on.

What was going on?

Had he decided she was too naïve, not worldly and glamorous enough? Was he having regrets? He couldn't be. Not now, not when he'd finally spoken. She didn't think she could bear it to have all her happiness snatched away.

❧

Harry's gut had begun churning right after breakfast. His sisters. He'd forgotten to tell Norrie about his sisters.

Who was he trying to fool? He hadn't just forgotten to tell her about his sisters. He'd forgotten all about them, period. Again.

What kind of a brute was he that he could forget he had sisters? What was wrong with him?

Rycote never forgot he had sisters. He might complain about them, but he always looked out for them. He never simply forgot their existence.

He, on the other hand, had barely been able to recognize his sisters when he had finally remembered to go see them.

Of course, they had changed a lot in the years he had been away, and he had hardly ever seen them in the years before.

What kind of an excuse was that? Whose fault was it that he had not seen his sisters in years? That he barely knew them?

And now he had gone off and forgotten them all over again. He was as bad as his parents.

No, he was worse than his parents. He knew better. He had the Tremaines and—deliberately or not—they had taught him how families were supposed to behave, how brothers were supposed to behave.

He had responsibilities to his sisters, and they couldn't be ignored. Not any longer. He had tucked his sisters off in a corner of his memory where he kept the rest of his family, where he kept the things he didn't want to think about. Now that was changed. When he had seen his sisters this time, he had made promises. He didn't make promises often, because when he did, he kept those promises.

The problem was that these promises were going to affect Norrie too. Unless she changed her mind. God, he didn't think he could bear it if she changed her mind. It was one thing to have no hope; it would be another to have paradise snatched away just when it was within his grasp.

She looked so innocent when she came down, so pure, all lacy and fragile, and he had to seat her in this sorry excuse for a carriage. He darted a glance at her. She was sitting there so peacefully. But he had to tell her, and the longer he put it off, the harder it was going to be.

He pulled the horse to a halt, a very minor change in its speed, tied off the reins, and turned to her. "Norrie…" The hint of fear in her eyes froze him. What was going on? Norrie was never frightened.

"You've changed your mind," she said.

"What?" He was too confused to say anything else for a moment. "What are you talking about?" he finally managed to say.

"You haven't?"

"Of course not. What an asinine thing to suggest."

"Then why have you been sitting there look-ing tragic?"

She sounded irritated. That was better than fright-ened, he thought. "I have to tell you something. It's about my sisters." Best to just blurt it out.

She blinked. Then she blinked again. "Your sisters." She stared at him in silence.

He nodded.

She shook her head as if to clear it of confusion. "Good heavens, you have sisters. I remember now. Two of them. Is that right?"

He nodded again. "Julia and Olivia."

"That's right. You told me their names once. I'd forgotten all about them." She turned on him. "But you never talk about them. You haven't said anything about them in, in years. I don't know anything about them."

He could feel the heat rising in his face. "Well, I don't really know them very well myself. I haven't seen them much. They were still babies when I went off to school."

"Babies," she repeated.

"And then I was almost never home on vacations."

"No, you weren't. You were with us."

"That's right."

"Where were they?"

He didn't think he could feel much more uncomfortable. "Not with our parents. They were at the Abbey with their nurse, and then with their governess."

"But not with their brother."

"Norrie, there wasn't anything I could have done for them." He was pleading. "Not then."

She thought about it, then nodded. "Not then. But now?"

He couldn't quite meet her eye and spoke quickly. "You see, Julia is seventeen. She ought to come out next season, only she thinks our mother will make it a disaster so I promised I would help her."

Norrie softened right in front of his eyes. "Well,

of course you must help her." She paused to think. "Absolutely. Your mother will have no notion of how to bring out a daughter. The places she goes are hardly suitable for a young girl, and she probably isn't invited to the places that young girls should go."

Of course Norrie would understand that right away. But did she see…? "The thing is, once we're married, you'll probably have to help too."

"Indeed." She beamed at him, looking quite happy at the prospect. "We'll have to take a house for the season that's big enough for her to stay with us. That will be much better for her than staying with your mother. She isn't likely to kick up a fuss, is she? Your mother, I mean." He started to say no, but Norrie wasn't actually listening to him. She was making plans. "My parents will let us use Penworth House for a ball, I'm sure. And I can take your sister shopping and see to it that she has the right wardrobe. It will be great fun. What is Julia like?"

This time she did wait for an answer, only he didn't really know what to say. "I haven't actually seen much of her recently, but she seemed a bit reserved when I went to visit."

Norrie had stopped planning and was looking at him. "She was just a baby when you first came to stay with us, wasn't she." He nodded. "And you've never been back much since then." He nodded again. "And the other sister? How old is she?"

"Olivia. She's twelve."

"She wasn't even born yet when we first met you."

He nodded. "That's right." He didn't admit that she'd been almost two when he first saw her. Once he'd come to know the Tremaines, he'd done his best to forget he had any other family.

"Oh, Harry, you've got two sisters and you don't even know them. That's so sad."

"You won't have to deal with them. I promise. They aren't your responsibility."

"Don't be ridiculous. You should have been taking care of them for years. All right, you couldn't have done much for them while you were in school. But you never even spent time with them—that was very bad of you. However, from now on they will be *our* responsibility, and I can promise you that I am better prepared to deal with two almost-grown girls than you are." She threw her arms around him. "What a lovely way to start out."

Sheer astonishment froze him for a minute. She wasn't going to turn away from him. She wasn't even going to turn away from his sisters. He pulled her across his lap and held her tightly, knocking her bonnet askew so he could bury his face in her hair. She fit so perfectly into his arms, as if this was where she belonged. This *was* where she belonged. He would hold her, protect her, treasure her always. Nothing would ever harm her, not while he was here.

A lengthy kiss and much murmuring of endearments were eventually interrupted by a snort from the plow horse. Harry looked up to see the horse looking longingly at a patch of grass and he sighed regretfully. "I suppose we should get on our way."

"Mmmm. I suppose. Where are we going?"

"A nice shady, secluded spot I found one day." He smiled at her.

She smiled back. "That sounds lovely."

As he gathered up the reins once more, she settled next to him, pressing close to his side. "Ouch!" She pulled back. "What on earth is in your pocket?"

He glanced down and grinned. "My revolver, remember?"

"Good to know you'll be able to keep us safe if we're attacked by any large stones."

Seventeen

HARRY SPREAD OUT A BLANKET ON A LEDGE THAT WAS cushioned with the soft grass of spring. Patches of trees provided privacy on either side, and below them a hillside planted with vines led down to the plain, where a patchwork of fields stretched before them, pale green where the grain was growing, brilliant yellow where some plant she didn't know was blooming.

She took Harry's hand—it was trembling slightly, she was pleased to notice—and allowed him to seat her. She closed her parasol and set it aside, then reached up to unpin her hat and set that aside as well. She closed her eyes and tilted her head back to enjoy the warmth of the sun. It was only then that she opened her eyes and looked at Harry.

He was kneeling beside her on the blanket, his hands clenched on his thighs, watching her. His eyes were dark.

She smiled at him and held out her hand. Would he understand?

He did.

Almost before she knew it, she was on her back and

he was pressing down on her. One hand was fisted in her hair, holding her head tilted for him as his mouth began its exploration. Soft kisses, his lips barely brushing her skin, fluttered over her face, making her yearn for more. Her hands reached up to clutch at his shoulders until finally his mouth covered hers and she moaned with joy. Yes, this was what she wanted, this was what she had been longing for. But there was more, much more. She clutched his shoulders to make certain he could not leave before she discovered what that *more* was.

⤞⥤

He could feel her beneath him, soft and yielding, as he tasted her, his tongue exploring the softness of her mouth, her tongue tentatively darting forth to tangle with his. Just as he caressed her, she was reaching up to caress his face, his shoulders, his chest. He could feel her pleasure in the little shivers that ran through her body. While one hand cradled her head, the other began to undo those tiny buttons on her bodice. He had not planned to do so, but once he began it seemed the only thing he could do.

Her hands suddenly ceased their caresses and she pulled back from his kiss. "What are you doing?"

"Undressing you." *Don't ask me to stop.*

She stared at him, motionless. Then she smiled, a purely female smile. An eternally female smile, full of welcome and promise. Eve must have smiled so at Adam, Helen of Troy at Paris, Guinevere at Lancelot. His heart leaped within him, and he was filled with the eternally joyful male reaction to that smile.

"Oh you wicked, wicked creature."

His mouth came down upon hers again and she welcomed him in a joyously passionate kiss while his fingers dealt with the remaining buttons. He pushed her bodice out of the way and her breasts, her beautiful rounded breasts, spilled out of her corset. He stared at them for a moment and reached a hand to cup one. Here were the breasts he had dreamed of, coveted, for so long. They were perfect. He groaned and then bent down to worship them with his mouth while her fingers tightened in his hair and she made little sounds of pleasure.

It took a moment for him to realize that those sounds had ended abruptly in a gasp that sounded strangely like fear and she was no longer arching beneath him. Before he could raise his head to ask what was the matter, he heard a harsh metallic click as the hammer of a gun was drawn back. He would have recognized the sound even without the sensation of a cold metal barrel pressed behind his ear. But the gun barrel was unmistakably there.

"I do regret interrupting you at such a time, but I fear I require your attention." Landi's voice, less amused than vicious, came from somewhere behind him. "Now you will stand up, slowly and carefully."

There was nothing else he could do at the moment. He pushed himself up to his knees, pulled the bodice of Norrie's dress together, and reached over for his coat to cover her. Her eyes were wide with shock and he tried to reassure her with a smile. It probably wasn't successful, but he stood up, keeping himself in front of her, and turned around. He could screen her at least.

Landi had moved back to stand about twenty feet

away. He was flanked by a grotesque pair of villains, one a scrawny creature whose leering grin showed half his teeth missing, the other a bearded barrel of a man. Both were dressed in filthy rags and carried ancient fowling pieces. In contrast, Landi stood posed gracefully, a sneer on his face. His loose shirt made him look like a pantomime Pirate King, but he held his modern rifle as if he knew what to do with it.

Harry heard Norrie get to her feet and moved slightly to keep her sheltered behind him. "What are you playing at, Landi?"

"Playing, *milord*?" The title sounded contemptuous. "No, it is no game, I fear. Or rather, you should fear. You have interfered in my business, and that is not permitted."

"If you for one moment think that these melodramatic threats will impress Lady Elinor…"

Landi laughed. "No, no. It is too late for that, is it not? That was simply a chance that demanded to be taken. I was speaking of my—what shall we call it?—my antiquities business."

"So you're the thief. I'm not entirely surprised. It's the sort of shabby business someone would expect of a parasite like you."

The laughter disappeared from Landi's face. "It is so easy for you to be superior, is it not, Englishman? You with your arrogant assumptions that your wishes are all that matter, that everyone will bow to you. Unlike you, I had no wealthy father to provide my fortune, and my cousin shows no inclination to share his, so I need to make my own. I will not allow you or anyone else to disrupt my plans."

"What makes you think I have done so?"

"Do you think I am stupid? Yesterday the gold, the statues, the urns were where I left them. Today they are gone. You were the only one wandering about yesterday, you and the lady. I am afraid I cannot let you enrich yourself at my expense. Where are they?"

Harry could feel Norrie moving restlessly behind him and held a hand back to urge her to stay there. He could protect her with his body—for the moment, anyway. "If I give you the information, will you depart and let us be? Will you accept our word that we will tell no one?"

Landi narrowed his eyes and smiled. "Why not? I was not planning to remain here any longer. I will be safely away before you can walk back to the castello."

Harry tried to look stupid enough to believe that. *He'll kill us both the minute we tell him what he wants. Norrie, remember the revolver. Give me the revolver.*

Landi continued to smile. "I doubt any of this will come as a great surprise to my cousin. He knows I have no more fondness for him than he has for me. He likes to order me about because he knows I resent it. How fortunate for me that he was away when you made your discovery."

"What makes you think he doesn't know by now?"

The smile vanished from Landi's face. "Explain yourself."

"Did you think that we would keep it a secret?"

"Why not? Then you could take it for yourselves. No, you think yourself too honest, too honorable for that." The words were pronounced as insults. "But keep silent you did. No one spoke of it last night, and everyone would have talked of nothing else if they knew. And you left the villa this morning before the prince had returned."

Harry shrugged. "We had no way of knowing who the thieves were, so naturally we did not shout out the news. But I told Lord Rycote and Lord Penworth, and they will have told the prince immediately upon his return."

Landi spat out a curse and looked off into the distance. He swung back and tightened his grip on his rifle. "Then you had best pray that he has not yet removed our goods."

"And if he has, what will you do? Kill us? Don't you think our dead bodies might raise some questions? You cannot expect our families to let our deaths go unavenged. You do not know the Tremaines if you think you can escape discovery."

Landi shook his head in pity. "Alas, I fear your deaths would be blamed on brigands. They infest these parts, you know." He waved at his companions. "And I myself do not plan to linger here." He smiled at Harry's start. "No, I have not betrayed myself to them. They speak no English, so you can expect no help from them. On the contrary, I believe they are hoping you will be stubborn and require...persuasion to give us the information we want. Do you really want to watch my friends here abuse Lady Elinor, watch her in agony when you know that a word from you could end her suffering?"

Bile rose to choke him. He knew it was stupid but his body coiled to spring. Before he could move, Norrie burst out and took her stand in front of him.

She flung the coat back at him, and he gave a grunt of pain as something struck him in the groin. It took him a moment to realize that it was the revolver. The blessed girl had remembered the revolver!

She stood there, arms akimbo, and—good God, her bodice was still hanging open! And those pigs were staring at her, drooling. Words were spilling out of her in a torrent of fury. "You bastard. You worthless slime. You filthy pig. You steal from your cousin, who supports you and your mother, and you threaten us? How dare you!"

Harry took a deep breath and wrapped his fingers around the revolver under the coat. As soon as he was sure he had it untangled and firmly in hand, he whispered to Norrie, "Dive left on three and run like hell."

The attention of the two brigands was focused entirely on her bosom. Landi sucked in a breath and looked at her with an appreciative smile. "Ah, *bella*, you should have married me. It would have spared us all this unpleasantness."

"*One.*"

Unseen behind Norrie, Harry removed the revolver from his coat.

"*Two.*"

She gave Landi a contemptuous look. "Marry a creature like you? I can imagine nothing more disgusting than the touch of a cowardly cur."

Harry cocked the revolver as she spoke.

"*Three!*"

Norrie dove left, and Harry swung the Colt up. His first shot hit Landi, and before the two brigands had recovered from the sudden turn of events, his second shot took down the barrel-shaped lout on the right. He swung to the left and pulled up just in time.

Instead of running as he told her to, Norrie had gone straight for the scrawny fellow and taken him down with a classic Rugby tackle. His ancient fowling piece flew off to the side, going off with an explosion that damaged some grass but nothing else. Norrie had him down and was kneeling on his chest, bashing his face with a rock. A quick glance showed that Landi had vanished from sight, so Harry went to her aid, not that it seemed to be needed.

He stuck the revolver into his waistband, flinching slightly at the heat of the barrel, and put his hands on her waist to lift her up. The brigand moaned, half dazed, and tried to rise. Harry knocked him back down with a kick. "It's all right, Norrie," Harry murmured. "It's over."

The rock was still clutched in her raised hand. She looked over her shoulder at Harry, then at the space where Landi had stood, and then back at the brigand cowering at her feet. Tears filled her eyes. "He leered at me," she said.

She started to shake, and he turned her to him and wrapped his arms around her, rocking her gently. "It's all right, my love. It's all right."

Eventually she stopped shaking and straightened up. "They were going to kill us, weren't they? Whether we told them or not."

Harry hesitated but nodded.

"He was looking forward to it. And besides, he leered at me."

"And so deserved anything you might give him." Harry kept his face solemn. "I was impressed by your tackle."

She shrugged and lowered the hand still holding the rock. "You and Pip taught me years ago." Her voice was not quite steady yet.

Harry stared at her in a mixture of awe and amusement. "Who would have thought football would be so useful?"

The brigand was starting to make noises.

Harry looked down at him, then kicked him over onto his stomach and put a foot on his back. "I think you may need to sacrifice a petticoat. I don't think any of those rags he is wearing are sturdy enough to truss him up."

"Gladly." She sounded calm until she looked down and realized that her bodice was still hanging open. She hastily put it to rights before she lifted her skirt, then a petticoat, then another.

Harry stared. "How many of those do you wear?"

"Only four today, since we were going on a picnic, but the nicest ones are on top and I don't want to sacrifice them. I don't think he deserves anything better than the bottom one."

"I'm sure you are right." Harry's mouth felt dry as he stared at the legs she uncovered as the bottom petticoat fell to the ground and she stepped out of it. His private parts were reacting in a thoroughly inappropriate manner. This was not the time for such thoughts, but he wasn't thinking. His body was behaving quite independently of his mind. God, she had incredible legs. He closed his eyes and thought about cold baths and congealed porridge. With a shake of his head, he took the petticoat she handed him and tore it into strips.

As he tied the captive's hands behind him, the fellow was foolish enough to begin a string of filthy curses aimed at foreign hellcats. Harry sighed, pulled out his revolver again, and held it under the fellow's chin. Silence followed immediately.

"The lady speaks excellent Italian." Harry spoke in Italian. "However, I do not believe she understands precisely what you said. That is just as well, is it not?"

The brigand jerked his head in agreement.

"Yes. And while we are at it, I think that when we deliver you to the authorities, you might wish to tell them that it was I who administered those bruises on your face."

The brigand started to object.

"No, I am not seeking the glory—there is no glory in defeating a cockroach. However, you do not really want to have to tell people that you were taken down and beaten by a little slip of a girl, do you?" A guttural snarl escaped as Harry prodded him with the revolver once more. "Do you? I can just imagine what the other prisoners will think of you."

Another curse was followed by a nod of acquiescence.

Harry smiled and finished tying the fellow up. Norrie had restored her clothing to respectability and was twisting her hair into a neat bun. Harry picked up the brigand's flintlock fowling piece and handed her the revolver. "Stay here with him. I want to see about the other fellows."

She hesitated a moment before taking the revolver but nodded and took it in her hand. It apparently weighed more than she had expected, because she came near to dropping it, but she steadied it and her shoulders straightened. She swung the muzzle around to point at the brigand and seemed pleased at the look of panic on his face.

She was still pointing the revolver at the brigand when Harry returned, but her fingers had grown stiff. He had to almost peel them from the pistol. After tucking it into his belt, he put his arm around her, and she sagged against him.

"It's all right now," he said. "The fat fellow is dead, and Landi is gone. I think I hit him—I saw a trail of blood, and he left his gun behind—but he seems to have vanished. It looks as if they had horses tied just beyond those trees, and he must have driven off the others. There are hoofprints, but no horses, so I couldn't go after him." She pulled away and gave him such a look of horror that he wanted to laugh. "No, I wouldn't leave you behind to go chasing after him, but he didn't know that, now did he?" She subsided, and he returned to the problem. "We can put this one in the back of the buggy, but we'll have to leave the dead one. Even if they would both fit, I can't stomach putting them on there together."

Norrie looked sick. "No. That would be…" She shivered. "I'm sorry. I'm being silly."

"Oh, yes, what a foolish girl you are. Instead of shrieking and swooning, you keep your head and pass me the revolver right under Landi's nose. Then you tackle a bandit and beat him up when you are told to run for safety. What a useless little ninny, to be sure."

She managed a smile. "We did do pretty well together, didn't we?"

Eighteen

THE TRIP HOME WAS MANAGED WITH NO MORE dispatch than the morning trip. Neither gunshots nor bloodshed had disturbed the plow horse, nor had he discovered any reserves of energy during his wait. He was content to plod onward, one thudding foot at a time, and no amount of urging could increase his pace. At least that meant that their passage raised little dust.

Although the sun was still high, Norrie shivered from time to time. Tunbury had wrapped his coat around her and kept her close by his side, but his stomach churned with anger—at Landi and his villains, obviously; at Savelli, for having sheltered this viper; even at the Etruscans, for having left behind treasures to steal—but most of all at himself.

How could he have been so stupidly careless? No matter what Norrie might say, he should have protected her, and instead he had led her into danger. He should have realized that the thieves would not take the loss of their goods lightly. Without her quick thinking, they would both be dead now.

By the time they arrived at the villa, his scowl

was sufficiently ferocious to make the servant who appeared at the door blanch and take a step back. Tunbury snapped a few commands that brought the servant to the wagon to peer over the side.

The fellow gasped at the sight of the bruised and battered captive. "*Bandito. Sì.*"

While a second servant ran off to find the prince, Tunbury swung Elinor off the seat and carried her in, holding her too tightly to allow for protests, were she so inclined. He hesitated briefly at the door of the sitting room but swung away and continued up the stairs to Elinor's room. "Fetch her mother," he commanded Martha, "and prepare a bath for her."

"I can stand, you know," Elinor said, her face pressed into his shirt.

He placed her carefully on her feet next to the bed, lest she fall. She did sway slightly, but remained erect and even smiled at him. Her bodice was buttoned now, but her dress was streaked with blood. He put his hands on her shoulders and touched his forehead to hers in mute apology.

"I will wait until your mother gets here. Then I must tell the prince and your father what happened."

"You are going to try to find him, aren't you?"

"Yes."

She shook her head and sighed. "But you will come to me when you return."

"Yes."

He kissed her fiercely, possessively.

There was no time for further talk. Lady Penworth flew in, a Fury prepared to take on the world in defense of her child. The look she threw at Tunbury knocked him back three paces while she wrapped her arms around her daughter.

"I'll explain. Go now, but be careful," Elinor told him.

After a quick look at the servants pouring into the room with pitchers of hot water, a pot of tea, and a bottle of brandy, he fled downstairs.

Things were no better there. Lord Penworth seized hold of him at the bottom of the stairs. "Where is Elinor? How badly is she injured?"

"She isn't hurt." Tunbury tried for a calming tone despite the sick fury writhing within him.

His effort was not particularly successful. Penworth was, if anything, even more distraught than his wife. "They said there was blood." Iron fingers sank into Tunbury's shoulder, as if to claw answers from him.

"Not her blood. We were attacked, but she was not injured." At least not physically, Tunbury thought, but did not say.

Just then, Savelli appeared, striding into the hall and looking thunderous. "What is this I hear about bandits—my cousin—attacking my guests?"

"Could we go someplace private?" Tunbury stood stiffly, taking advantage of his height and looking down at the prince.

Savelli checked momentarily, then nodded and led the way into a study. Its civilized trappings, with leather-covered volumes residing in glass-fronted cabinets and plush curtains dimming the light, seemed an incongruous setting for a melodramatic tale.

It did not take long to recount the day's events, but even an expurgated account was enough to turn

Penworth white and send him charging from the room
to see for himself that his daughter was uninjured.

Savelli, on the other hand, seemed turned to stone.
Gone was the enthusiastic antiquarian, the languid
aristocrat, the courteous host. All that remained was
the stern autocrat who ruled this little kingdom. For
all his fondness for the pleasure-loving Etruscans, the
prince was a stern, proud Roman to the bone. He
reached out a hand to ring for a servant and, when one
appeared, fired off a dozen questions and responded
to the answers with a series of orders so rapid that
Tunbury had difficulty following. Then he snapped
out at Tunbury, "Come with me."

It did not occur to Tunbury to refuse. He followed
the prince into the stables.

Savelli tossed a glance at an empty stall and barked
a short, bitter laugh without breaking stride. "I see
he has stolen my best horse as well, and will doubtless run him into the ground, fool that he is." He
came to a halt at the entrance to the tack room.
On the floor, still bound with the strips of Norrie's
petticoat, was the bandit, watched over by a pair of
sturdy grooms. Savelli flicked his hand and one of
them kicked the captive over. The bruises Norrie had
given him seemed to have multiplied under the care
of the grooms. The prince gave another short bark
of laughter. "I see you dealt appropriately with this
piece of carrion."

The piece of carrion opened his mouth as if to snarl,
but a look from Tunbury was enough to silence him.

Savelli was nodding. "Yes, I recognize him. He was
discharged for insolence some time ago." He looked

at the grooms. "Get what information you can out of him first."

Tunbury did not ask what would be second. He did not care. The mere thought that this creature very nearly had Norrie in his power…

Savelli turned back and stalked out into the court-yard where half a dozen mounted men and a pair of saddled horses waited. "My servants tell me that Armando already returned to the house. His mother is in considerable distress. It appears he helped himself to whatever jewelry and money she had in her room. He has about half an hour's lead on us, and he may have friends willing to help him. I do not know if we will be able to catch him, but I intend to try. Do you wish to come?"

Oh yes. He most definitely did.

❧

Full night had fallen by the time they returned. Lantern light threw bizarre shadows about the stable yard as the weary riders slipped from their horses and silently passed the care of their mounts to the grooms. Failure and disappointment cloaked them, and they parted wordlessly. Prince Savelli, his posture still rigid but his eyes bleak, strode off through the arch leading to the entrance hall. Tunbury began to follow, then checked his steps and turned to the garden.

He went quickly and quietly up the stairs to the terrace. Clouds dimmed the moonlight, but he had no difficulty finding Norrie's room. The curtains were not quite closed, and he could see that a light still burned so he rapped softly on the glass.

Almost immediately the curtain was pulled aside and the French doors were flung open. Norrie pulled him in and threw herself against him. He wrapped his arms around her and rested his cheek against her head. The sweet soapy scent of her hair cleaned the stink of dust and horses from his nostrils and the tension began to ease.

"We didn't catch him. I'm sorry."

"That doesn't matter." Her voice was muffled by his coat. "As long as you aren't hurt. I was so worried."

"Ah, there was no need for you to worry." She felt so good in his arms, so soft, so perfect. He rubbed his cheek back and forth against her clean, silky hair. "At least a dozen of us were hunting him. How much safer could I be?"

"Of course I worried." She twisted her hands in his jacket and tried to shake him. "Who knows what might happen? Armando is a rat, and a cornered rat is dangerous. You are not to go putting yourself in danger. I forbid it. Now that you finally got around to declaring yourself, I don't intend to lose you."

He smiled and dropped a gentle kiss on her hair. "You won't ever lose me. I'm here to stay, and I promise to do a much better job of protecting you in the future. I don't intend to lose you, either."

For long minutes they stood there in silence, just holding each other. Then Norrie said, "Adventures aren't quite the way I imagined they would be. I thought I wanted to have adventures the way you did—I was quite envious of you. But I wouldn't really like too many more like that one."

"No more would I. Ah, Norrie, every time I think about what could have happened…"

"I was afraid, you know. Terrified, even."

"Of course you were. So was I."

"You were?"

"Can you doubt it? Only a fool isn't afraid when a lunatic is waving a gun at him."

She buried her face in his shirt again. "It wasn't just that I was afraid. I didn't like that. But I hated those men. I really hated them. I never felt that way before. It bothered me."

He pulled her tighter to him. "And I pray you will never need to feel that way again. I promise you, Norrie, I will do my best to make sure you never need to feel that way again."

She let him hold her until finally she pulled back her head and looked up at him. A smile was beginning to tug at her mouth. "But after all, what did happen was that we won. We make a good team, don't we?"

He had to return her smile. She was back to being fierce. "Yes, we do."

"And you won't mind if in the future our adventures are not quite so adventurous?"

"I have very different adventures in mind for us." His hand was making circles on her back, and he suddenly realized that she was wearing nothing but a nightdress and wrapper—no corset, no petticoats, almost nothing at all. His body had realized this well before his mind had noticed, and if she hadn't noticed already, she soon would realize what it was that was pressing against her.

He ought to leave. He really ought to leave. He shouldn't be here in the first place. He knew that, but instead of letting her go, his arms were tightening and pulling her closer. Her head tilted so that her lips were just waiting for him, parted in invitation. He couldn't refuse.

He explored her mouth slowly, tangling his tongue with hers, reaching deep into the soft cavern. Slowly, then not so slowly as desire overcame him. Yes, this was what he wanted, and her arms tightened, pulling him closer. This was what she wanted too. His hands cupped her buttocks—somehow her nightdress had been pulled up—and pulled her hard against him. He heard a groan of longing and realized that it came from him.

He shouldn't—they shouldn't. He lifted his head and tried to think. "Norrie, I'm sorry. I shouldn't be here." He could barely get the words out.

She pulled his head back down. "Don't you dare leave. Don't you dare."

He couldn't quite believe it. Could she really have said that? Was she inviting him to her bed? Did she even understand what she had said? But she was pulling him back, pulling him toward her bed, pulling him toward everything he wanted. Oh, God! She was!

He had to ask. "You're sure, Norrie? You're sure?"

She was pushing his coat off his shoulders and pulling out his shirt. "Of course I'm sure."

He had to let go of her to get his arms out of the tangle of cloth, but his mouth followed her, nibbling her jaw, dropping kisses along her brow. His arms finally fought free of his clothes, and he caught her up again as they stumbled onto the bed. She was laughing, joyous laughter.

His heel snagged on the coverlet. "Just a minute."

His voice was hoarse as he lifted himself up and sat to tug off his boots. Had it ever taken him this long to get his boots off? He stood up to undo his trousers and realized that Norrie had stood too. She had discarded her wrapper, and as he watched, she lifted her night-dress and pulled it over her head.

And then she was naked.

All he could do was stare in awe. Not even in his dreams… "Norrie," he whispered, "Norrie, you're so, so perfect."

She lifted a hand, ever so slowly, and reached toward him. Her fingers touched his bare chest, ever so lightly, and trailed over his skin. "You're beautiful. You really are Hercules," she whispered.

He couldn't move. Her touch had him frozen. The moment stretched on and on. Then she raised her eyes to meet his and caught her lower lip in her teeth. Her sudden uncertainty was all he needed. "Not a demigod," he said thickly. "Only a man."

In an instant his remaining clothes had fallen to the floor and they were on the bed, skin to skin.

His hands skimmed over her, touching everywhere, deciding where to settle first. Every place he touched brought a response from her—a little noise, a move-ment. He wanted to go slowly, he needed to go slowly for her. His hands trembled with the effort to hold back.

His touch seemed to burn. Her whole body seemed to be on fire. Suddenly every bit of her was so sensi-tive. She hadn't known she could feel so much. And then his hand was between her legs and touching her there. She gasped, and then there was more and more and more—and she was flying, exploding.

When she opened her eyes, he was above her, smiling. He kissed her and she could feel him down there, not his hand but him, pressing into her, slowly filling her. Yes, this was what she wanted, yes. He was moving inside her, faster now, faster, and she was flying again.

With a strangled cry he shuddered and collapsed on her. The weight of him should have felt heavy, but it didn't. It just felt right. She lifted her arms to hold him there and gently rubbed little circles on his back while his breathing gradually slowed to normal.

He rolled over eventually and pulled her with him, held against his side. He was smiling, but he looked half stunned. She wasn't quite sure what to make of it. "Are you all right?" she asked.

"All right?" He gave a choked little laugh. "God, Norrie, that was incredible. And I'm supposed to be asking you. Did I hurt you?"

"Goodness, no. Is it supposed to hurt? I thought it was wonderful."

He cradled her cheek in his hand and gently caressed her. "Wonderful. Just wonderful."

Nineteen

THE TRIP BACK TO ROME HAD BEEN QUIET. LADY
Elinor and Lord Tunbury were too busy gazing
at each other to pay much attention to the others,
and Lord and Lady Penworth spent much of the
time dozing, except when Lord Rycote's fidgeting
prompted exasperated mutterings from them. The
moment the coach pulled into the courtyard of
the palazzo, Rycote leaped out and vanished through
the door leading to the Crescenzis' chambers.

The elderly retainer—Rycote had never figured
out just what his title was—backed out of the way,
and Donna Lissandra erupted from the sitting room.
She halted abruptly when she saw Rycote. Her fierce
expression dissolved and she ran to him, stopping just
short of throwing herself into his arms.

"It is you," she said. "Ah, thank heaven it is you."

More than a little gratified by this reception,
Rycote put an arm around her shoulders. "Yes, I am
here. Now tell me what is wrong. Has that swine
Girard been bothering you?"

"It is not just Girard, swine that he is. Maria is the

one who made the trouble. And such trouble! She told him that Pietro was hiding in Rome. My father was furious with her and sent her off to the country, but Girard has been haunting us. Every time my mother and I step outside the house, even to go to church, he is there, following."

She started to lean against him, gratifying him still further, but then leaped back. "Madonna! Your whole family has returned, no?" At his nod, she turned and ran for the stairs to the *piano nobile*.

Confused, he followed. "Lissandra, wait. Tell me what is wrong."

She flew up the stairs, ignoring him completely, and burst into the hall, where the English party was standing in some confusion. With her hands at her breast she began, "My lady, my lord, please, I..." Her voice faded away, and she descended into a faint, slowly enough to enable Rycote to catch her.

He lifted her up and looked around wildly.

Lady Penworth looked amused. "Just put her here on the sofa, dear," she said.

He did so, but promptly knelt beside her, chafing her hands. His mother clasped his shoulder to pull him away.

"Calm yourself, Pip. Now go and find a glass and some brandy." When he got up to obey, she waved the others back as well. "Let us give the poor girl room to breathe." Lady Penworth then knelt beside Lissandra herself, taking her hand and speaking softly enough so the others could not hear. "It's all right, my dear. That was a beautiful faint. Just lie there and give my hand a squeeze when you have decided what to say."

Lissandra's eyes flew open and she gasped.

Lady Penworth shook her head and smiled. "I'm only trying to help."

The girl burst into tears. "I am so sorry. I had no intention of making trouble for Lord Rycote. Or for any of you. I just did not know what to do."

Pip hurried in from the library, carrying the brandy decanter and a glass. At the same time, the door on the opposite side of the hall flew open and Pietro Crescenzi entered with a dramatic gesture. Pip frowned at him. "What are you doing here, Pietro?"

"My sister is innocent, and my parents know nothing of this," he declared.

"That is no doubt perfectly true," said Lord Penworth with a wry smile. "I am coming to learn that parents frequently know nothing of what their children are doing."

"I think, dear, that this must be Lissandra's brother. The revolutionary one." Lady Penworth came to stand beside her husband and tilted her head to look at the newcomer. "There does seem to be a resemblance."

"Hmm? Yes, I suppose so." Penworth frowned at the young man. "But aren't you supposed to wear a red shirt or some such?"

"He's been in Rome in hiding, Father." Pip glowered at Pietro. "But I thought he had promised to behave like a gentleman and not involve his sister in his activities."

"Ah, no, it is not his doing." Lissandra appeared to have quite recovered, and clasped Lady Penworth's hand between hers. "It is I who insisted that he hide here. My father would be distraught if he knew. Please do not tell my parents. I will find another place for him immediately."

Penworth was still frowning at Pietro, who was swaying slightly. "I do not wish to be rude, young man, but is that blood on your shirt? And if so, is it yours?"

"It almost certainly is, I think, judging from his pallor," said Lady Penworth. "Perhaps we should all sit down, and somewhere less open. Lissandra, help your brother into the library."

They went in procession, Lord and Lady Penworth leading the way, Lissandra helping her brother, and Pip helping her. Harry and Elinor, who had been paying virtually no attention to the drama being enacted, trailed behind, walking just close enough for their arms to brush.

"Is there something between your brother and the Crescenzis' daughter?" Harry asked softly.

"Oh yes, hadn't you realized?"

He smiled. "All my attention has been on you. I have very little left for him."

Elinor grinned. "I think she's good for him. He was getting much too stuffy."

"However he managed that in your family, I can't imagine." Harry grinned back, so Elinor jabbed an elbow into him.

Once everyone was settled in the library, where the dark paneling had a soothing effect, Lissandra attempted to fuss over her brother. He, however, was determined to speak.

"My lord, my lady, I beg your forgiveness. It was an emergency." He shook off his sister. "I should never have imposed upon you this way."

"It was that spiteful old witch Maria," burst out Lissandra. She turned to Pip, who took her hand. "After you were so good as to warn me, I was very careful. Never once did I allow Girard to follow me. But I never thought to watch for Maria. I knew she was angry, but it was inconceivable to me to think she would ever betray our family."

"What did she do?" Elinor asked, fascinated.

"Followed Lissandra and then led the French to the house where I was staying," said Pietro bitterly. "My comrades and I fought them off, but Giovanni was killed. It was his house, and I do not know what will become of his family."

"Pity you didn't think about that earlier," Pip snapped. "It's all very well and good to go about risking your own life if that's what you choose to do, but you should not endanger innocents like his family and your own."

Lissandra frowned at him and tried to pull her hand loose. He wouldn't let go, so she left it while she turned to the others. "Our father was very angry. He dismissed Maria from his service and sent her back to the village she came from—ah, you should have heard him. 'Viper' was the kindest term he used. But he was even more angry with Pietro. He said he was a disgrace to the family and he disowned him." Tears of pity filled her eyes as she looked at her brother.

Pietro looked tragic himself. "Why can he not see that this is the future? Only once Italy is free and united will she be strong. Can he not see that the real disgrace is allowing France and Austria to tyrannize us? Too long have we been denied our liberty."

While he continued for some time in this vein, Lady Penworth whispered to her husband, "I believe they must have learned their English by reading Byron."

He smiled in agreement. "That fellow has a lot to answer for."

Finally, a cough from Lord Penworth drew the young people's attention. "Yes, well, I think we had best leave the politics for a different time. I was hoping, Miss Crescenzi, that you might explain what your brother is doing here in our apartments."

"And, while you are at it, explain what has happened to the servants," added Lady Penworth. "I must confess that I had been looking forward to a cup of tea and a hot bath when we arrived." Her arched brows indicated less than total sympathy with the Crescenzi children.

Completely ignoring his earlier criticism of Pietro, Pip leaped to Lissandra's defense, putting himself between her and his parents while still holding her hand. "I am certain Donna Lissandra would not have imposed on our hospitality except in the direst of circumstances."

"No doubt. However, since you have not been here and she has, I suspect she can provide an explanation more easily than you can." Lady Penworth was having difficulty suppressing a smile at her son's unusually dramatic behavior.

"A hundred thousand apologies, most gracious lady." Lissandra clasped her free hand to her breast. "But my brother was wounded and could not travel. I could not think of any other place where Girard would not search for him. But here, in the chambers of a noble English family—Girard would not dare force an entrance."

"Not bad thinking," Harry said with a judicious nod.

"I will remove him at once," she said. "We can surely find another place."

"Nonsense, Donna Lissandra," said Pip. "Our family will be glad to shelter him until his safe escape can be arranged."

Lady Penworth raised her brows and was about to speak, but her husband put a hand on her arm and she contented herself with a second inquiry as to the whereabouts of the servants. It appeared that they had all been given leave to visit their families for a few days, lest news of Pietro's presence leak out.

"Pity," said Lady Penworth. "Because I really would like a hot bath."

At that, Lissandra burst into tears.

Pip pulled her into his arms and glared at his mother, who simply raised her brows again.

Lord Penworth muttered, "Stop teasing them," to his wife.

Pietro leaped to his feet and declaimed his intention to depart that instant, Lissandra wailed, and Pip assured her that everything would be taken care of, all at increasing volume.

"It's as good as a play," said Elinor to Harry.

"Yes," he agreed, "but I think we'd better take a hand and straighten things out before your mother enjoys this too much." He stepped into the middle of the chaos, grabbed Pietro by the shoulder to swing him around, and clapped his hands loudly an inch from Pietro's nose. That halted Pietro in mid-oration.

Elinor, meanwhile, picked up a vase of somewhat wilted flowers, pushed it under Lissandra's nose, and then raised it as if to dump it on her head. Lissandra's wailing ended on a gasp.

Elinor and Harry exchanged congratulatory smiles.

"Oh, well done, children. I am pleased to see you working so well together." Lady Penworth beamed at them.

Lord Penworth gave a harrumph worthy of a much older man. "Suppose you tell us just precisely what is going on here. Signor Crescenzi, I gather you are persona non grata in Rome. Might I ask precisely who is objecting to your presence?"

"My lord, I was requested to return here by…"

"No, no, no." Lord Penworth shook his head decisively. "I absolutely do not want to know what you are doing here. As far as I am concerned, you came to visit your family, and that is all. What I do wish to know is, who is hunting you?"

"Ah," said Pietro, smiling as the light dawned. "As an English lord, you would have, of course, no interest in our Italian politics and could not be seen to do anything that might suggest that your government took any interest in the matter."

"Good to see that he isn't a complete fool," Harry muttered to Elinor.

Penworth nodded, so Pietro continued. "That Girard is the one who seeks me. It is not that I am of any great importance, you see, but he has tried to force his attentions on my sister, who naturally scorns the pig. I fear he wishes to have me in his hands, thinking that then he can bring pressure on her."

"The devil you say!" Pip looked horrified.

Even Lady Penworth looked taken aback. "Why, the utter cad," she said.

"That settles it," Pip said. "Father, we cannot stand by and permit such an outrage."

"No, of course not," said Lord Penworth quietly. "The first thing we must determine is how badly injured this young man is."

Pietro waved dismissively. "Truly it is not serious."

"Ah, my lord," broke in Lissandra, "the blood— you would not believe the blood."

"*Basta*, Lissandra." Her brother hushed her. "Enough. It was nothing more than a graze."

Penworth nodded. "I trust you will not consider me overly intrusive if I ask to examine the wound? I do have some experience with injuries."

With his wife hovering over his shoulder, the marquess expertly removed the bandage to examine the wound in Pietro's side. It was indeed little more than a graze, though deep enough to have bled profusely. Penworth nodded in satisfaction and Pietro maintained a stoic air.

"And when did this occur?" Lady Penworth sounded mildly curious.

"Yesterday it was." Lissandra waved her arms dramatically. "When Eduardo brought him here… Pietro had gone to Del Falcone, but that is the first place Girard would look so Eduardo brought him here. I very nearly swooned at the sight—so pale he was. And then my father began shouting and threatened to disown him, so I whispered to Eduardo to take him up here to your apartments.

I know it was wrong of me but I could not think what else to do."

Pip took her outstretched hand and patted it reassuringly. "Not wrong at all. That was very clever of you indeed."

Lady Penworth glanced at her son in amusement before returning her attention to Pietro's injury. "Well, there seems to be no sign of infection, and the wound appears to have been properly cleaned. There has been no fever?" When Pietro shook his head, she continued, "In a week or two, you should be as good as new."

"Yes," Penworth agreed. "I do not see any need for a physician at present, so there should be no problem with your remaining here until you can leave Rome to rejoin your friends."

The Crescenzi siblings immediately burst into prolonged and flowery protestations of gratitude, which Lady Penworth brought to a close with a gesture demanding silence. "I do hope, however, that you have some notion as to how we can manage for servants. I am still, as I mentioned earlier, longing for a hot bath and a meal."

Lissandra, who had been hanging on Pip's arm and looking at him with something resembling adoration, was called back to the present and assured everyone that she could easily collect servants whose loyalty and discretion were beyond question. "And," she added triumphantly, "Abondanza can even cook."

Happily leaning against Harry, Elinor turned to stifle a laugh in his jacket. "Just as well," she murmured, "because I can't cook at all, and neither can Mother."

"A fine wife you'll be," Harry replied. "I'll have you know that I can roast a piece of meat over a fire, and I have even been known to fry up some bacon and eggs."

"Can you really?" She looked up at him and found herself lost in his eyes.

His arm tightened around her and he moved her slowly out of the library and into the hall. "A fine wife," he repeated, his voice hoarse, and his mouth came down, brushing gently over hers at first before settling possessively, while his arms tightened around her as if they could melt into one.

"Not now, children." Lady Penworth rapped him on the shoulder as she walked past, leading the others. "We need to get settled in."

They parted, slowly returning to earth. "We have to get married soon," said Harry.

Twenty

IT HAD BEEN A LONG NIGHT. IT HAD ALWAYS BEEN hard, knowing Norrie was lying in her bed only a few doors down the hall. But now, having shared that bed once, it was sheer torture. He tried closing his eyes, and the memory of her lying there naked, reaching up to him, had him thrashing about. Staring into the darkness was no better. His body remembered the feel of her, every wonderful, welcoming inch of her.

He forced himself to stay in bed until the sun was at least fully up, but that was as long as he could manage. Not wanting to bother the servants at this ungodly hour, he managed to shave himself in the cold water left from the night before and dressed carefully, less from vanity than from a desire to use up as much time as possible. He wanted to see Norrie, but he could hardly expect her to be up with the sun.

But no sooner had he stepped into the hall than he heard her door. And there she was, looking as if she had slept no better than he. He pulled her into the window alcove where they were hidden by the draperies, and she melted into his arms.

He could not restrain a growl of hunger, and she answered with a whimper of desire. The moment his mouth touched hers, her lips parted to welcome him. Their tongues tangled together in a dance of desire. Was there any joy equal to the joy of kissing Norrie?

Well, perhaps one. He was working his way through the yards of skirts when the rattle of crockery recalled him to the present time and place. That would be Millie bringing a cup of tea to Lady Penworth. He stood, his forehead pressed to Norrie's, as he waited for his breathing to calm.

"I couldn't sleep for wanting you," he said, once he could manage to speak.

"I couldn't sleep, either." Her breathing was as ragged as his.

"Don't change your mind. I couldn't survive if you changed your mind."

She looked at him as if he were mad. "Why do you keep talking such nonsense?"

"Because I can't believe it's true, that this isn't just a dream."

Now she grinned at him. "Then you had better hope it doesn't turn into a nightmare. It's not that I mind being adored up here on a pedestal, but I don't think I can take it for too long. I am human, you know."

"Oh yes, I know. You're headstrong and reckless and bossy and fractious when you haven't been fed and far too sure you're right all the time…"

With a look of mock outrage, she pulled back and thumped his shoulder. "And you go off into a cloud of gloom while you feel sorry for yourself and berate yourself and shoulder responsibility for things that are in no way your fault."

"But you love me anyway."

⁓

Eventually they made their way to the quiet breakfast room in the rear of the palazzo, opening onto a small courtyard. The shutters were flung wide, letting in the songs of the birds as well as the soft May morning. At the table Elinor poured a cup of coffee and handed it to Harry. Their fingers brushed as the cup was passed, and a shiver ran through her, a thoroughly delightful shiver. The cup remained there, held in the air between them as they stared, smiling, at each other.

"Harry, either take the cup or give it back to her before you drop it." Lady Penworth sounded a bit acerbic, though there was a smile lurking at the corners of her mouth. "Elinor, you need to get your head out of the clouds. We need to begin organizing things for our return. Fortunately, we can return through Paris and will be able to order most of your trousseau there. Now, we should be in Paris by the beginning of June at the latest. I think we should go to that Mr. Worth we encountered at Gagelin's. His designs struck me as quite delicious." She smiled at her daughter. "At the very least, we should have him do your wedding gown. An order placed in June should allow enough time for it all to be completed in time for a September wedding."

"September!" Elinor's head snapped up and she looked at Harry. The consternation on her face mirrored his feelings.

Lady Penworth was startled. "Is that too soon? I thought…"

"September is four months away. Four whole months!" Elinor protested.

"Four months?" Harry was having trouble keeping his voice down. Surely Lady Penworth was joking. "You want us to wait four months?"

Lady Penworth sat back and looked at them. Harry knew that look. It was her *grande dame* look. It was not put into use very often, but when it was, few could stand up to it. He had seen prime ministers quail before it.

"A year is not an exceptional wait," Lady Penworth pointed out. "Four months is a very brief engagement." Ignoring their sounds of protest, she continued, "Have you written to your family yet, Harry?"

He felt the blood drain from his face. "I do not need the earl's permission to marry," he said stiffly. Under the table he reached for Elinor's hand and held it tightly. She squeezed back in support.

"Of course not," said Lady Penworth. "However, do you not think your parents are entitled to hear of your plans, simply as a matter of courtesy? They may even wish to be involved in the planning."

"My parents—the earl and countess—have nothing to do with my life and will have nothing to do with my marriage." He could have been a statue, he held himself so still.

Lady Penworth contemplated him in silence. Eventually she said, "Does your family even know where you are at present?"

He shrugged. "I did not inform my parents, but

there is no secret about it. My sisters know, and my bankers would know where to find me."

"Harry, I know that there have been difficulties in your relationship with your family, and you obviously think that relationship is none of my affair. However, you are bringing my daughter into your family…"

"No," he said flatly. "I will keep her far away from them. I will keep her safe, and the earl and countess will not be allowed anywhere near her."

Elinor was upset. She was darting her eyes from him to her mother and back again. "Mama, I think we should speak…" she began but her mother held up a hand for silence.

In the tone of voice that had always had her children quaking, Lady Penworth spoke. "Lord Tunbury, you are displaying a childish ignorance of the world. In the future, you may maintain as great a distance as you like between your parents and my daughter. I have no objection to that. However, I will not permit you to marry her in some hugger-mugger fashion, and I will not have your family excluded from the ceremonies surrounding that marriage. No one will think it is you who excluded them. People will assume that your family disapproves of the connection, that they have some reason to disapprove of my daughter."

"Mother!" Elinor protested.

"No one could possibly think such a thing," said Harry hotly. "No one who knows Norrie or your family could imagine any objection to her."

"Do not be foolish. Lord Penworth has political enemies who would be more than willing to try to embarrass him by smearing his daughter." She pinned him with a glare. "And please do not tell me that you care nothing for what society thinks, that no one you consider a friend would take such rumors seriously."

He snapped his mouth closed. He had been about to say precisely that.

Lady Penworth continued, "It is one thing to spend little time in society because you are bored by it and indifferent to its amusements. It is quite something else to be excluded from society, justly or unjustly. And I might point out, Lord Tunbury, that I have never found my daughter indifferent to the allure of society's balls and parties."

"Mother, stop!" Elinor bit her lip and peered at Harry. He pushed back from the table.

"I quite see your point, Lady Penworth," he said stiffly. "If you will excuse me." He stood up, bowed slightly, and strode from the room.

He could hear Norrie as he left. "Mother, you should not have done that. You don't understand. You have no idea at all."

When she caught up with him, he was in the library, his arm braced against the window frame as he stared unseeing into the street. He felt her near him before he turned and saw her. Pulling her into his arms, he buried his face in her hair. She started to speak, but he shushed her and held her, rocking gently, drawing strength and comfort from her. This was paradise, having her in his arms. If only they could remain like this for all eternity. If only he could keep the snakes out of paradise.

"She's right, of course. Your mother. We will have

to wait and do the expected thing, have the expected kind of wedding."

"She can't be right. I won't have it. She can't possibly expect us to wait that long."

"Ah, Norrie," he murmured, not lifting his head from hers. "If I were a better man, I would leave. You would be far better off without me. You could find someone worthy of you."

"Don't you dare even think such a thing." She tightened her arms around him and lifted her head just enough to glare at him. "You are going to marry me, and if you think I am going to free you from your promise, you had better think again."

The beginnings of a smile tugged at his mouth, and he felt some of the tension easing. But not all of it. "I left once, but that was when you still thought of me as just another brother. That was painful enough. Now? It would tear my heart out to lose you."

⚬✄⚬

Pietro grew stronger, watched over by his sister, who was in turn watched over by Pip. Elinor and Harry alternated between floating along blissfully, snatching private moments in alcoves and empty rooms, and simmering with frustration. Lady Penworth watched over her family with a mixture of amusement and concern. Lord Penworth, wishing to be prepared for the problems he foresaw, wrote to Freeborn, asking him to call.

The consul arrived looking cheerful, white side whiskers newly adorning his thin cheeks. In addition to his own warm words of welcome, he insisted upon delivering Mrs. Freeborn's greetings to Lady

Penworth and Lady Elinor and her invitation to tea
the following afternoon. "I wouldn't be at all surprised
if she wishes to hear every last detail of your visit to
the Savelli castello," he added with a chuckle. "She's
never been there, but she loves to read about castles
with dungeons and towers."

Before a discussion of gothic novels could begin,
Penworth drew the consul toward the library. "First
I must speak to you privately. I am in need of your
advice on a highly confidential matter."

When they emerged to join Rycote and Lady
Penworth, Penworth looked less worried and Freeborn
looked, if anything, even more cheerful. "Bless my
soul," said the consul, "this takes me back. It's like the
excitement of '49 all over again. I handed out so many
diplomatic passports as the French were pouring in and
the Republicans were pouring out that I could barely
sign my name fast enough.

"Lord Palmerston was foreign secretary then and
sent me a blistering letter of reproach, telling me to
stop, though it arrived too late to make any difference." He winked. "Of course, the fellow who delivered the letter told me he wanted to shake my hand.
Never was sure if that was because I'd handed out the
passports or because I drove Palmerston crazy."

"I don't want to cause you any difficulties," said
Penworth. "Surely we can find a way to get young
Crescenzi out of Rome without involving you."

The consul dismissed that idea with a shake of his
head and a wave of his hand. "I couldn't possibly let
you leave me out of this. Especially since Palmerston is
now prime minister. How could I possibly pass up the

chance to upset him again? I'm afraid, though, that he won't find anything to object to in a single passport." He looked momentarily regretful, but then good cheer returned and he rubbed his hands gleefully. "It makes me feel quite young again."

Rycote, however, was frowning and feeling far less euphoric. "It seems to me that the problem may be just getting him out of this building. Every time I step outside I notice men loitering about in doorways, keeping an eye on everyone who approaches."

"Everyone who approaches, eh? That's good, that's very good," said Freeborn. "If they are looking in the wrong direction, that means they don't know he's already here."

"That doesn't mean they won't notice if he walks out the door," Rycote snapped. All that good cheer was getting on his nerves.

Freeborn patted him on the shoulder paternally. "No need to worry. We could always roll him up in a carpet like Cleopatra and carry him out." When Rycote glared, Freeborn laughed and continued, "No, there really is no difficulty. I'll call for you in my carriage. One of the seats covers an empty space. Once he's well enough to bend easily, he can hide in there and we can take him all the way to one of the border exits."

"Why, Mr. Freeborn," said Lady Penworth, smiling in delight, "I believe you are really a swashbuckler at heart."

Freeborn blushed slightly and ducked his head. "Lady Penworth, I do believe you may be right."

❧

Pip heaved an almost silent sigh as Pietro entered the breakfast room. He didn't actually dislike Lissandra's brother, but he disliked dramatics at breakfast time, and Pietro was permanently swathed in dramatics.

Moving easily after a few days' rest, the young Italian was frowning over a message Eduardo had delivered in a basket of pastries.

"What is the matter?" Lissandra looked up from the brioche she was buttering.

"I do not know how I can help him." Pietro stood there uncertainly. "A friend—well, not really a friend but a comrade, I suppose—says he has been betrayed and must leave Italy."

"Who is it?" Lissandra turned to Pip with a smile. "I know many of my brother's comrades."

"This is no one you would know. He is someone I encountered briefly just after we established the Republic in Rome." Pietro shrugged. "I had not thought him deeply committed to us, since he managed to drop out of sight long before the end. Armando Landi."

Harry spewed out a mouthful of coffee and nearly knocked the table over as he sprang to his feet. Elinor looked at Pietro in horror. More practically, Pip managed to catch the coffee tray before it flew into space.

Harry advanced on Pietro, seized the young man by his lapels, and snarled, "Where is he? Where can I find him?" Elinor, at Harry's side, looked no less furious.

Pietro could scarcely manage to keep his feet as he staggered back, held up by Harry's grip, but he shook his head. "I do not know," he finally managed to gasp. "Why? What do you know of Landi?"

Lissandra was hurrying over to protect her brother from this sudden onslaught, and Elinor was helping Harry try to shake information out of Pietro. Pip had to push all of them apart. "Calm down or we'll never get anywhere," he told Harry before turning to Pietro. "This has nothing to do with your politics. If you and your Garibaldini friends are foolish enough to be taken in by him, I don't see much chance of your surviving, no less creating a unified Italy. Landi is a thief and a brigand, and he tried to kill my sister and Harry."

That statement triggered a dramatic flood of verbiage from both Pietro and Lissandra. It took some moments before they were calm enough to hear explanations, by which time Lord and Lady Penworth had arrived for breakfast. This, in turn, required a second round of explanations, frequently interrupted by outbursts from Pietro, calling down imprecations on traitors and proposing outlandish but grisly punishments. Harry kept growling that he just wanted to know where he could get his hands on Landi, and Elinor insisted that she would not allow him to go by himself.

"This is ridiculous," said Pip, but no one was listening to him. He went out, and when he returned carrying a pitcher of water, Harry and Pietro were still holding center stage, with Lissandra and Elinor as chorus. Pip tossed the water at the two principals, producing a shocked silence.

"Well done, Pip," said Lord Penworth before any of them could recover. He held up a hand and received at least momentary attention. "I realize none of us has any fond feelings for Signor Landi, and I know, Pietro, that you feel deeply his betrayal of both yourself and your cause. However, I would like to inject a note of practicality."

Pietro flung out his arms. "Do not fear, my lord. You and your family will be safe from this villain. My comrades and I will wipe him from the face of the earth. It will be as if he had never existed."

Lord Penworth closed his eyes briefly and let out a long breath. "I am sure that is very gallant of you, Pietro…"

"No, no, my lord. You have done so much for me already, and for my family, that I seize this chance to be of service to you."

"The hell with that" said Harry, grabbing hold of Pietro's shirt. "He threatened Norrie. He's mine."

Lord Penworth cleared his throat persistently until the tumult once more subsided enough for them all to listen to him. "Crescenzi, I understand your anger at the betrayal. Landi's attempt to use you and your colleagues in an effort to escape punishment for his crimes is utterly contemptible. But bear in mind that you are not the only ones who have been betrayed. His Excellency, Prince Savelli, has been most bitterly betrayed as well."

Penworth was the veteran of numerous Parliamentary debates and his voice began to soar in rhetorical outrage. "For a man to betray his own family, to steal from his own cousin, a cousin to whom he is indebted for so much kindness…"

Pietro could not contain himself. "It is beyond comprehension that a man could be so lost to honor."

Harry swung around at Crescenzi in exasperation,

but Penworth held him back with a tight grip on his shoulder.

"Landi has betrayed not only your comrades and his own family but the very heritage of his country." The others looked at Penworth in some confusion, but the marquess continued, in full flight, complete with oratorical gestures. "These antiquities he has stolen belong not only to Savelli, on whose land they were found, but to all of Italy. Nay, to all of mankind.

"They are of value not simply for their artistry, or for the precious gems and metals they may contain. They tell us of an entire civilization that once flourished here. When antiquities like these are stolen, sold to greedy and ignorant collectors, they are stolen from all mankind, and Italy especially is robbed of her heritage. Private vengeance palls in the face of such perfidy."

Harry looked ready to erupt in fury, but Penworth only tightened his grip.

Pietro looked both impressed by a rhetoric that surpassed his own and confused by its message. "I do not entirely understand, my lord. Are you saying we should let the man escape?"

"No, no," said Penworth, sounding practical once again. "But I think we must not act too precipitously. It would be wise to consult with Prince Savelli before determining a course of action. You and your colleagues will be able to keep a watch on Landi, will you not?"

"Ah, yes, that is wise." Pietro nodded sagaciously. "We will arrange a hiding place for him and tell him to be patient while we arrange his escape. Then he will keep still while we plan his destruction."

"Excellent." Penworth nodded approvingly as Pietro went off, followed by his sister.

Pip muttered a soft curse. "That fool is probably planning to use his sister to carry messages again. I can't allow this." He hurried after them.

Lady Penworth raised her brows. "*Pip* can't allow this?" She turned to seek an explanation from her daughter, but Elinor and Harry were demanding an explanation from Lord Penworth.

"You can't just turn him over to his cousin." Harry paced furiously, swinging out a fist to punch at the furniture. "The way he spoke to Norrie…what he was going to do to her…" He shook his head, incoherent.

"I understand how you feel, Harry, but think for a moment." Lord Penworth put his hands on the younger man's shoulders once more and gave a small shake. His was once more the voice of common sense. "Stop and think. If we were in England, we could call in the authorities and know that Landi would be tried and hanged for his crimes. But we are in the Papal States. I know nothing of the laws here, of the way the courts operate. Do you?" Harry could say nothing, so Penworth continued, "For all we know, we could be tangled up in legal proceedings for months."

"Months!" Elinor looked horrified.

"Months," repeated her father, his gaze fixed on Harry. "And who knows what sort of inquisition Elinor could be subjected to. Do you want to risk that?"

Harry could only shake his head.

"To say nothing of the difficulty we would have in attempting to explain young Crescenzi's presence here."

Harry sighed in surrender.

"Therefore, we will have to trust Savelli's judgment," Penworth continued inexorably. "And I do not think he is inclined to leniency."

Lady Penworth interrupted impatiently. "Well, if that is taken care of, Elinor, will you please tell me what has been happening between Pip and Miss Crescenzi? Am I correct that things have proceeded?"

"Yes, Mama," said Elinor with a slight smile. "I think one could say that things have definitely proceeded."

"Dear me. I have obviously been spending too much time thinking about your situation and neglected your brother." Lady Penworth tilted her head and considered. Then she smiled. "I should have known he would choose as well as you did. The brother is a bit foolish, but on the whole I think she will be very good for him. She sees him as a hero, and he needs that. He is too apt to doubt himself."

Elinor let out an incredulous snort. "Pip? Doubt himself? My brother, who always knows how everyone should behave?"

Lady Penworth shook her head. "Did you never realize? He fears that he lacks Harry's courage and his father's instinctive honor. That is why he sets such high standards of behavior for himself. But unlike his sisters, Miss Crescenzi actually needs his protection. By providing it, and providing it so ably, he has gained the self-assurance he lacked."

With that, she swept out, leaving Elinor with her mouth hanging open.

"Your mother's perception is frightening," said Harry.

Twenty-one

FOLLOWING THE ADVICE OF MR. FREEBORN, LORD Penworth dressed with great formality and paid a call upon the Marchese Crescenzi. The marchese, dressed with equal formality, received him seated in his chair of throne-like appearance and little comfort. Since neither one could speak more than a few words in the language of the other, Mr. Freeborn was also present as an acceptably disinterested translator.

The opening minutes of the audience—minutes that seemed interminable hours—were devoted to an exchange of florid civilities and compliments. Lord Penworth had attended royal visits and diplomatic presentations that seemed casual in comparison, but Mr. Freeborn had assured him that the marchese would be insulted by any lack of ceremony. Penworth found the room itself almost more oppressive. The marchese must have suffered from the cold because the room was intolerably hot. Penworth could feel the sweat trickling down his neck and felt a moment of sympathy for the two footmen standing by the door. Not only were they garbed in velvet liveries, but they had to wear powdered wigs as well and must have been required to stand in this stifling atmosphere for hours.

The room itself suffered from a surfeit of things. So many chairs and small tables were crowded into the room that it had been difficult to navigate a route from the door to the marchese. Penworth held himself stiffly in the chair to which he had been waved, a carved and gilded concoction that had creaked alarmingly when he sat. Aside from worries about the likelihood of the chair collapsing were he to move, there was the danger that a careless elbow would knock over the velvet-covered tables topped with bibelots that flanked him. The dim light in the room helped to disguise what was obvious once one neared the objects in the room: All were worn and shabby.

It was with relief that he received the unspoken indication from Freeborn that they could now move on. The actual business of proposing a marriage between Donna Lissandra of the noble house of Crescenzi and Viscount Rycote, eldest son and heir of the Marquess of Penworth, was accomplished easily enough once it was made clear that all that was expected by way of a dowry was the lady's own distinguished lineage. Even if Penworth had not deduced the straitened circumstances of the Crescenzi family from the fact that they were renting out part of their palazzo, Freeborn had warned him that young Pietro's political activities had resulted in the loss of much of the family's wealth.

The marchese also received assurances that Donna Lissandra would of course be free to practice her religion, and Viscount Rycote was even prepared

to have the marriage ceremony performed by a
Roman Catholic priest. The location of the ceremony
required a bit of negotiation, however. Although there
was much to be said in favor of having the bride married from her own home, and Lady Penworth herself
thought that the church of Sant'Agnese in the Piazza
Navona was a decidedly attractive venue for a wedding, there was the problem that the English tended to
be exceedingly insular. Rycote was heir to a position
of considerable importance and his wife would be
expected to take her place in English society. This
might all be made easier if her first appearance were at
a wedding of splendor in London.

After due consideration, the marchese conceded
that a London wedding would make sense. Left
unmentioned was the fact that this arrangement
relieved the Crescenzis of the considerable cost of
a wedding celebrated in a manner fitting to their
daughter's station.

Also left unmentioned was the obvious fact of the
marchese's ill health. By the time their negotiations
had been concluded, the marchese's face was pallid
and pinched with pain, and he seemed to be holding himself erect by a determined act of will that
won Penworth's admiration. When the English lord
declared himself honored to ally his family with that
of the Italian lord, he meant every word of it. When
the Italian lord returned the compliment, it was with
equal sincerity.

Donna Lissandra was then called in, accompanied
by her mother and Rycote. Marchese Crescenzi
announced to his daughter with great formality that

he had arranged a marriage for her. She was admirably demure as she kissed his hand in gratitude and promised to be a dutiful wife to the husband her wise father had chosen for her.

Rycote then carefully enunciated, in Italian, a speech that Lissandra had drilled into him, in which he expressed gratitude to his father for having chosen such an exemplary bride for him and then vowed to the marchese to honor and protect his daughter always.

A brief toast sealed the betrothal, and then everyone withdrew to the next room, where an elaborate ceremonial meal awaited, while the marchese retired to his bedchamber.

❧

Tunbury, wrapped in a dark cloak that made him feel ludicrously melodramatic, stood with Savelli's men hidden in a barn just outside the walls of the city. Clouds covered the moon, so that even though the barn doors were open, only the faintest light came in. Somewhere a church bell tolled midnight, another melodramatic touch. Inside the barn a canvas-covered wagon loomed like some huge beast. Young Crescenzi paced before it, awaiting the arrival of Landi. The discipline of Savelli's men could not be faulted. Aside from Crescenzi's footsteps, nothing broke the silence. Tunbury breathed in the dusty scent of hay and felt an almost overwhelming need to sneeze.

Finally, new footsteps could be heard outside. Muttered phrases in varying tones suggested that several men approached. Tunbury could feel the men about him stiffen, and his muscles tightened in anticipation as well. Although he had promised not to interfere—his presence was contingent on that promise—he could not stop his hands from clenching into fists. Three shadowy figures appeared in the doorway

"You will wait in here." A harsh voice spoke in Italian.

"You still have not told me who is to meet me, how I am to get away." That was Landi, his voice a petulant whine.

"You are in no position to make demands." A third voice, commanding in tone. "Go inside and wait."

Landi stepped slowly into the cavernous gloom, and the other two disappeared back into the night. He halted and peered from side to side.

"Is that you, Landi? Come in quickly." Crescenzi stepped out of the shadow of the wagon.

"Crescenzi? Ah, Pietro, my friend, it is good to see you." Landi stretched out a hand eagerly.

Two of Savelli's men stepped out to seize him by the arms. Two others blocked the door behind him.

There was a brief scuffle, very brief, punctuated by a few curses. Then Landi was dragged to his feet. He glared about him, and his eyes fastened on Pietro. "Damn you! How could you betray a comrade?"

"A comrade? You swine. You are a thief who tries to use us to escape punishment for your crimes. I spit on you!" Pietro suited the action to the words.

Landi began to struggle again, but stilled when a light was struck and a figure carrying a lantern approached. It was Savelli. The light from the lantern made his elongated shadow snake across the floor. As the flame flickered, his stern features appeared demonic.

The prince came closer, his eyes on Landi, who grew pale and ceased his struggles. "You dare to speak of betrayal? You who betrayed both your comrades and your own family?" Savelli's voice was cold, his face implacable.

"I…" Landi's eyes darted from side to side.

"Do not even try to find excuses. We all know of your treachery. I took you in for your mother's sake, because her parents had made a foolish marriage for her. For you, I feel less than nothing."

"But for the sake of the family, of your name," Landi urged. "A trial will bring shame and scandal on your name."

Savelli smiled, as if actually amused. "Whatever makes you think I would permit a public trial? Do you doubt that I can handle by myself one who is a disgrace to the family?" He turned to Tunbury, who had approached during this colloquy. "I assure you, Lord Tunbury, this vermin will be treated as he deserves, and the insult to you and your lady will not go unavenged. Nor, Signor Crescenzi, will the betrayal of you and your friends be ignored. Discretion does not imply leniency. Traitors can never expect mercy."

"I do not doubt your justice, Your Excellency." Tunbury bowed formally, as did Pietro.

Landi looked at them, his eyes wild. "You are together in setting this trap for me? You will pay, I swear it."

Tunbury could not keep the loathing from his face. This creature, twisting like an animal in the hands of his captors, teeth bared like the rat he was, had lost all dignity. He had thought he wanted to deal out

Landi's punishment himself, that he wanted to smash the man for the threats and insults he had offered Norrie. Now, seeing him sweating with fear, he was grateful that Savelli would have his men take care of the swine. He would not have to soil his hands on the disgusting wretch.

The prince waved a hand in signal to his men, who disappeared into the darkness with Landi. "You will give my thanks to Lord Penworth," he said to Tunbury, as suavely as if at court. "I only regret that our association was shadowed by the actions of that creature. Perhaps one day we shall all meet again."

"I know the marquess shares that hope, as do I. He asked me to express his gratitude to you for taking care of this problem." Tunbury hoped his own poise approached Savelli's standard.

"Problem, yes," Savelli said softly. "I like that way of putting it." He turned his head slightly and gave Crescenzi a long look. "Perhaps young men who present a problem for their families would do well to remove themselves from Rome."

Pietro stiffened but then gave a wry smile. "That is no doubt excellent advice, Your Excellency."

Tunbury had had enough of civility and was relieved when Savelli turned to leave. All he wanted was to get back to Norrie.

❧

She was watching out the window when he returned to the palazzo. He looked up and smiled when he saw her, and she felt the tension fall away from her like a physical burden. It was all she could do to wait for him to come up the stairs. The moment he came through the door, she was in his arms, safe in his arms.

"It's all right," he murmured, his cheek resting on her hair. "He is no longer a threat."

Twenty-two

Mr. Freeborn waited in the parlor of the Tremaines' apartment, his hat and gloves placed neatly on the table beside him, a black-edged envelope held carefully in his hand. Without its cheerful smile, his lean face seemed more cadaverous than usual. He took a deep breath as Tunbury came into the room.

"You wanted to see me, Mr. Freeborn?" The question was more curious than worried.

"I'm afraid…" Freeborn stopped and started again. "Your family's attorneys were not certain of your direction, so this was sent to the consulate." He held out the envelope. "I am sorry to be the bearer of sad tidings."

Tunbury stared at it in surprise. A black-bordered envelope from the family attorneys could only mean a death, but whose? His parents were not old, and his sisters were only children. Had there been some accident? Were there some aunts or uncles important enough to warrant a letter chasing him across Europe? The surprise gave way to dread. Not his sisters. Please, not his sisters. Not when he was just beginning to know them. He reached out and took the envelope. "If you will excuse me?"

"Of course." A sympathetic nod from Freeborn.

The sympathy was making him nervous. Taking the letter over to the window, Tunbury tore it open to read. Then he read it again and looked up, stunned. "The earl? My...my father?"

"I am sorry, my lord. May I offer my deepest sympathy?"

Tunbury just shook his head in disbelief.

Freeborn gave the young man a considering look. "Perhaps you would like me to take the news to Lord and Lady Penworth?"

Tunbury nodded and sat down heavily, holding the letter carefully away from him as if he could distance himself from its contents. "I need a few minutes."

The consul nodded his understanding and left the room.

Tunbury stared off into the distance, seeing Bradenham Abbey as it had been when he was a child. Ironic, really, that the family seat of the Earl of Doncaster should have such an ecclesiastic name. But then, his parents had almost never been at the Abbey. An occasional house party, with crowds of noisy strangers filling the house all night while he, and later his little sisters, had strict orders to remain in the nursery wing. Hardly surprising that when he ran into his father one day when he was trying to sneak out to the stables, the earl didn't recognize him. His own father.

Or perhaps not his father.

He would never know.

He hadn't thought of that moment in years. He thought it had faded into the mists of time, or wherever unwanted memories went, but here it was, wrenching his gut again.

He shook his head. It wasn't as if he had had an unpleasant childhood. His mother gave birth to him and he was then handed over to servants—nurses and nannies and tutors. When he went to school, he learned that his experience had been no different from that of most of the other boys. It was the Tremaines who were the odd ones.

He had not quite been able to believe it the first time he went home with Pip for the long vacation. Lady Penworth was glad to see them, greeted them with hugs, and asked him what foods he particularly liked. Lord Penworth took them fishing. He spoke to them. He even listened to what they had to say, asked questions, and listened to the answers. And Pip took it all for granted, as if this was the way parents normally behaved.

Harry had been stunned.

He had spent every vacation after that with the Tremaines, never spending more than a few days in the loneliness of the Abbey. Until his twenty-first birthday. He had to go back then. An enormous celebration was planned for the coming of age of the heir of the Earl of Doncaster. There was a dinner followed by a ball with hundreds of people he did not know, and fireworks and toasts and speeches of congratulation from friends of his parents who did not know him. None of his own friends had been invited.

When everyone had left, he found himself alone with his father, with the earl. He still could not stop thinking of him as his father. That was when he had learned of his uncertain parentage. The earl was drunk, of course. He had been drunk himself, he supposed. All those champagne toasts. It had taken a while for the meaning of his father's words to sink in.

He had stared at the earl for what seemed like an eternity. The older man had looked at him uncertainly at first, but then his eyes had fallen and he had picked up his glass of brandy and drained it. *You disgust me*, Harry had told the earl then, *you and my mother both*. And afterward he had stormed out, demanded that a sleepy stableboy saddle him a horse, and ridden off to London.

That was five years ago. He had never gone back to see his father.

He had never spoken to the earl again.

The memories brought nothing but discomfort and regret. And a powerful sense of guilt, which had him pacing the room. Then Norrie was there, right in front of him. She wrapped her arms around him and leaned against him, resting her head on his shoulder. His arms went around her and he held her, taking comfort from her. He rested his cheek on her hair and breathed in the slight herbal fragrance. As always, her nearness was balm to his soul.

"The letter was from Dalrymple, the family lawyer. He said the earl had not been ill at all. But one morning his valet went to waken him and he was dead. A sudden apoplexy, they think."

"The letter was from the lawyer? Not from your mother?"

Harry would have laughed at that if he had been capable of laughter. Norrie couldn't quite manage to keep the censure out of her voice. "No," he said, "not from my mother. Not even a message from her."

"Oh, Harry." She tightened her arms around him.

"Ah, Norrie, I don't know what to say. I don't even know what I feel. Regret, certainly. I haven't seen him since that night he told me. We parted in anger. At least, I was angry. I told him I despised him. I don't know what he felt." Harry looked back at the memory uncertainly. "But I never spoke to him again. Whether he was my father or not, those should not have been my last words to him."

Elinor reached up to make him look at her. "No. You are not to feel guilty. You had no way of knowing you would not see him again. You cannot blame yourself. He cannot have been surprised that you were upset at what he told you. Anyone would be."

"But after I ran off, I never went back to see him. I never spoke to him again. I never even wrote. And I should have."

"Did he try to see you? Did he write to you?" When he shook his head, she went on. "Then the fault is not yours, not yours alone. After all, you were in London for a year before you went on your travels. He could have tried to see you at any time. He should have tried to heal the breach."

Harry managed a crooked but bitter smile. "That assumes he realized there was one. It could be that he was too drunk to realize I was upset. He may even have been too drunk to remember that he told me. He may have thought nothing of my disappearance. After all, he was accustomed to not seeing me for years on end."

"Stop that!" Elinor seized his shoulders and gave

him a small shake. "You will not think that way. It is as likely that he thought he had to tell you lest you one day heard rumors, and he could well have been drinking to give him the courage to speak. He had to know you would be upset, and that you could not but think badly of him. What man wants his son's disapproval? Perhaps he kept away from you hoping that time would ease the hurt."

This time Harry's smile was genuine. "Norrie, my love, will you try to find virtue in everyone?"

"No, but I do not want you punishing yourself for things that were not your fault." She stepped away from him and bit her lip. "Actually, I find I am worrying a bit about your mother. I have met her only a few times, but now that I know all this about her, I find it difficult to have much sympathy for her."

Harry snorted. "I would express my own feelings a bit more harshly."

"Shall we have to live with her?"

"Lord, no! Whatever put such a thought in your head?"

She smiled ruefully. "I wasn't looking forward to it. Actually, I would probably never have thought about it, but Pip and Lissandra were talking about Lissandra's mother, and Pip was saying perhaps her mother should come to live with them after her father dies."

Harry looked a bit taken aback by that. "Isn't he being a bit pessimistic?"

"Well, Pip likes to plan ahead, and I expect Lissandra was a bit worried. After all, the marchese does seem to be quite ill."

That produced a chuckle, and Harry pulled her into

his arms again. "Fifty years or so from now, should we lose your father, your mother will be more than welcome to share our home. But I can promise you, we will never make our home with my mother." He nuzzled her hair once more. There it was again, that slight herbal scent. "Your hair. What do you do to make it smell so fresh?"

"Rosemary and—ah!" He had stopped nuzzling her hair and had moved down to her neck. "A rinse of rosemary and thyme," she gasped.

"Delicious," he murmured and settled on her lips.

❧

Elinor fluffed out her skirt as she sat down at the breakfast table. She had chosen this dress carefully. There might or might not be rules about what sort of mourning was expected of a girl whose fiancé's father had just died. Possibly none, but just in case she was wearing a lavender dress sprigged with tiny white roses. It was subdued enough, but it was also very becoming. And the bodice closed in front with a long row of buttons. She darted a glance at Harry to see if he had noticed.

He had. The look he was giving her was so heated that she started to blush. She tried to give him a look of reproof, but she couldn't help smiling, and that made him smile. How she loved his smile. It positively melted her insides.

"You'll need to get back right away, of course." Lord Penworth looked at Harry with kindly sympathy. "Things are likely to be in disorder with Doncaster dying so unexpectedly."

The silence at the table made Harry realize that

Penworth had been speaking to him. The words sank in. His smile vanished and he took a sip of coffee and swallowed before he spoke. "My mother has, doubtless, all under control. She will have ordered all the appropriate clothing and draped the house as well."

Penworth frowned. "You are Doncaster now, and that means the responsibilities all fall on you. There are many people depending on you, not just your family. To say nothing of the fact that you must take your seat in the Lords."

Harry flushed at the reproof. "You are right, of course. I had managed to forget. Yes, I will have to go back soon."

"I'm sure you will be able to settle everything easily enough, but if you run into any problems, you can call on Galveston, the estate agent at the castle. You know him. And in London you can always use Middleton if you find Dalrymple unsatisfactory."

"Very well, sir."

"Yes, of course you will manage." Penworth smiled. "And we will all be back in a month or so."

Harry blinked at that.

Elinor did more than blink. She sat up in outrage. "What do you mean, a month or so? Aren't we all going with him?"

Lady Penworth reached over to pat her daughter's hand. "I know you are sorry to have the wedding delayed, but it won't be so bad. Only six months or so. You can be married in January. Harry will be out of mourning then."

"No." Harry leaped to his feet and Elinor was right

beside him. "No," he repeated, "I am not going back without Norrie. We can be married here."

"And all your worries about what people will say will be taken care of," said Elinor. "Obviously we can't have a big society wedding with Harry in mourning, so we will have a small wedding right here in Rome. And by the time we're out of mourning— six months you said?"

Lady Penworth nodded. "Yes, but…"

"In six months everyone will have something else to talk about," said Elinor, looking defiantly at her mother.

Attempting to defuse the situation, Lord Penworth broke in gently. "I don't know that you can get married here. It is a Catholic country, and I doubt you can just walk in and ask a priest to marry you. They must have all sorts of rules, just as we do at home. Banns and such."

"We'll ask Mr. Freeborn. He will know," said Elinor. "And if we can't get married here, and you want to stay, I'll go back with Harry and we can be married as soon as we reach England."

"Elinor Tremaine!" Lady Penworth drew herself up, fully prepared for battle.

"No, Norrie. I can't let you do that." Harry had her hand tightly clasped in his. He had to do this properly. What he wanted was to toss her over his shoulder and carry her off to a cave, but he was not going to do anything that might shame or embarrass her. He would do whatever her parents required, no matter if it killed him. "If we can't be married here, I will wait and travel back with you and your family." He smiled.

"And we will be married the minute we set foot in England." He lifted her hand and kissed it.

"And your estate?" asked Penworth sharply.

Harry scowled. "It survived the earl's neglect for years. It can survive mine for a few more weeks."

Penworth harrumphed, then looked at his wife.

She shrugged and said, "I am not happy, but…" She shrugged again. "It actually is a plausible solution."

"In that case," he said to Harry, "you had best call on Freeborn today."

&c

"Can you marry in Rome?" Mr. Freeborn smiled benignly at the new Earl of Doncaster. "Well, you can't have an Anglican religious service. This is the Papal States after all. But you can have a civil ceremony. That's easy enough."

Harry sat down with a whoosh of relief. He was wearing a black coat and dark gray trousers—he had remembered that, at least—but he had dressed hastily and the coat felt uncomfortably tight. He thought he might have snatched up one of Pip's coats instead of his own. He tried not to wriggle too much. He didn't want to rip it. "All right," he said. "A civil ceremony. That will do. Where do I go to arrange that?"

"Why, right here." Freeborn's smile grew broader, as he leaned back in his desk chair and gestured around his office. "As the British consul, I am authorized to perform marriages for British subjects."

"That's it? That's all there is to it?"

"There are various forms we'll need to fill out, and I expect Lady Elinor will want to dress up a bit, and you too. Then there are flowers and such like. The ceremony has to be here at the consulate, so the ladies may want to decorate the little room next door to this one. It can be made to look less like an office."

Harry looked around quickly. A broad desk, slightly battered-looking, shelves holding boxes of papers, walls an indeterminate shade of green or perhaps gray, heavy curtains at the windows. Yes, it looked like an office. Did that matter?

"But at the end of the day, you will be every bit as married as if the Archbishop of Canterbury himself had performed the ceremony," Freeborn concluded.

That was what mattered. Harry leaped to his feet and began pumping the consul's hand. "Thank you, sir, thank you. Tomorrow? Can we do it tomorrow? And then we must leave for England quickly. The next day? Can that be done? Thank you."

Freeborn shook his head in amusement.

❧

Things did not proceed quite as rapidly as Harry had hoped. His suggestion that the wedding be held the next day was met with a flat refusal from Lady Penworth. Even Lord Penworth had frowned on the idea.

"Absolutely not," said Lady Penworth, standing straight and stiff as a grenadier. "Bad enough my daughter is going to be married in a foreign country, far from family and friends. It is not going to be a hole-in-the-corner ceremony as if she were a housemaid sneaking off."

Elinor tried to protest, arguing that they could have

a religious ceremony once they were back in England, at the chapel at Penworth Castle or in the village church near Bradenham Abbey or even in Westminster Abbey, if that was what her mother wanted.

Lady Penworth sniffed. Of course they would have a religious ceremony once they returned to England. That was irrelevant. "I will confer with Mrs. Freeborn and Marchesa Crescenzi," she said. "Together we will decide how things will best be done. And Doncaster…"

Harry jerked around to face the door, half expecting to see his father there.

Lady Penworth sighed. "You will have to get used to the name, Harry. You cannot jump a foot in the air every time someone addresses you." Then she smiled at him fondly. "I know this is difficult for you, but I promise you, I am not trying to make it more difficult. Formality and ceremony will make it easier in the long run." Then she looked at the others. "Try to remember to call him Doncaster. The sooner he gets accustomed to it, the easier it will be for him to step into the role when he reaches London."

She swept out of the room, leaving the others staring silently after her.

"She's right about the name, you know," said Lord Penworth. "It took me the devil of a time to get used to being called Penworth. I had never expected to come into the title, and it was a bit embarrassing to be looking around every time someone spoke to me."

Harry smiled a bit weakly. He had always known at some level that he was the heir to the title. But that knowledge hadn't seemed to be part of his life.

It was nothing to do with him, with who he was or what he did. He looked at Pip, sitting beside his father and smiling sympathetically, and the realization crashed down on him that his whole life had just been changed and he had no idea what he was supposed to do.

Pip was prepared to take over someday as Marquess of Penworth because his father had prepared him for the role. All those vacations Harry had spent with Pip at Penworth, when the marquess had taken them riding over the estate, introducing them to the tenants, explaining why this crop was being grown in this field, why that field was lying fallow—all that had been training for Pip. And for him too in a way, he saw. At least he had some notion of the kinds of things he was supposed to notice.

But he had not spent any length of time at Bradenham Abbey since he was ten years old. He had known a few of the tenants then, played with some of their children when he could escape from nannies and tutors. But that was so long ago. He didn't know if they were still there, or even if they were still alive. Now he was going to have to take on responsibility for them, and he knew nothing about them. If someone sat him down in the middle of the estate, he would almost certainly be lost.

Some hint of the panic must have shown in his face, though he tried to hide it. Elinor slipped her hand into his and squeezed it. "We will manage," she whispered. "You will be a good and fair and caring earl because that is the kind of man you are."

Was he that kind of man? He was not at all sure.

Still, if Norrie could believe that, he would have to try to live up to it. With her by his side, perhaps he had a chance. He squeezed her hand back. As long as he had her by his side…

Twenty-three

IT TOOK A FULL WEEK. ELINOR HAD VERY LITTLE SAY IN the preparations. Even the choice of her dress was largely out of her hands. There had been no time for a new dress to be made, and her only dress even close to white was a quite simple one of cream muslin. The skirt was flounced, the sleeves long and full. In Millie's hands it had been transformed. The neckline had been lowered and covered with a wide lace bertha. The sleeves had been shortened into small puffs trimmed with satin bows. The flounces of the skirt were festooned with more lace and ribbons.

In three days it had become the wedding dress a girl dreams of. She had hugged Millie and then her mother and had been hugged back, and then all of them were hugging and laughing with tears running down their faces.

"You are a marvel, Millie," Elinor said, hugging the little woman once again.

"Well, I could hardly let my lady's daughter be married in a dress not fit for company. I have my pride, you know." Millie sniffed, but blushed and ventured a small smile. "It did come out nice, didn't it?"

"Indeed it did, and I do not know what we would have done without you," said Lady Penworth. "I don't know what I would have done all these years without you, my dear Millie."

Another orgy of hugs and tears and laughter followed before all traces of tears were washed away and Elinor tried on her wedding finery. Her hair was drawn softly back from its center parting and then crowned her head in a coronet of braids. As the final touch, her mother placed a veil of antique lace on her head. Elinor stared at it in the mirror and touched it with awed fingers. "Where did that come from?"

Lady Penworth smiled a tiny smug smile. "I found it in a shop here in Rome not long after we arrived and thought it would make a perfect wedding veil. Of course, I hadn't expected it to be needed quite this soon. No, no," she protested as Elinor flung her arms about her mother. "No more tears. We just finished washing the last ones away." But she hugged her daughter and wept a bit herself.

❧

Harry was given nothing to say about the wedding preparations, though he was allowed to arrange a suite in the Hotel Europa for the wedding night. Mercifully, no one expected him to spend it next door to the room of the bride's parents. Unfortunately, he was left with nothing to do and plenty of time to brood.

He refused to spend that time brooding about his family and the probable mess surrounding the estate back in England. Concentrating on the situation here in Rome meant that he was thinking about Pietro.

That young man was a blasted nuisance with his politics and his histrionics, and he was causing difficulties for the Tremaines. Perhaps he could remove that particular problem.

He managed to snatch Norrie away from talk of dresses and menus and pull her into one of the tiny rooms tucked into odd corners in the palazzo. He needed to talk to her, but before he could say anything, she had tangled her hands in his hair and pulled him down for a kiss.

Ah, how he loved her kisses, so eager, so welcoming. An invitation he could not refuse. There was a chair, one of the ridiculously carved and hideously uncomfortable chairs in which the palazzo abounded, but still a chair. He fell into it and she followed, tumbling into his lap.

He trailed kisses across her cheek and teased her with his tongue in the sensitive spot behind her ear. That made her wriggle against him in the most delightful way. Her bottom rubbed against his groin and he reacted in the inevitable fashion. She gave a little gasp when she realized what was happening, smiled one of those wicked little smiles of hers, and twisted around to rub her breasts against him, those lovely, luscious breasts.

He was only human, and a man, after all. What could anyone expect of him? He began pulling up those miles and miles of petticoats and skirts until he finally touched the silk of her stocking. After a momentary pause to enjoy the delicate feel of her, his fingers trailing up over her knee, he leaned back, pulling her on top of him.

The chair gave a horrendous creak, and the arm suddenly sagged beneath him. He froze in place and she sat up with a start. They stared at each other, and she cautiously lifted herself from his lap.

"Do you suppose we broke it?" she asked nervously.

He growled and gingerly removed himself from the ridiculous excuse for a chair. "I am in a fair way to smash every stick of furniture in this antiquated edifice from sheer frustration!"

She made a sound halfway between a snort and a giggle. A moment later they were leaning against each other in hopeless laughter.

"The day after tomorrow," he said when he could finally speak.

"Mmm." It wasn't much of a statement, but it sounded hopeful, so he kissed her again.

Regretfully he pulled away. "I pulled you in here for a reason."

"I know." There was that wicked smile again.

"No, I mean for a different reason. I have an idea about Pietro."

"That boy." She grimaced. "He really is tiresomely foolish."

"And I want to make sure he doesn't become dangerously foolish. So long as he is here, he puts your family at risk."

Norrie frowned. "There can't be any real danger for my family, can there?"

"Well, no one is going to throw the Marquess of Penworth into prison, but it could be awkward and embarrassing for him to be found with a fugitive revolutionary in his house. The problem is getting

Pietro out of here, and preferably far away. So I had an idea."

She looked at him with curiosity, but didn't say anything.

He grinned. "We could take him with us."

"What?" Her eyes widened and she did not sound pleased. "Oh, no you don't. I am not going to share my honeymoon with that...that posturing popinjay!"

"I should hope not. But an earl and countess will be expected to travel with servants. You will have Martha with you, of course, but I don't actually have a valet. I've never felt the need for someone to help me pull on my trousers. So Pietro could come along with us as my servant."

Her eyes widened again, but this time they were filled with laughter. "Oh, Harry, that would be perfect, absolutely perfect. You are clever!"

She spent the next half hour or so demonstrating her admiration for her fiancé.

Her father and brother were less enthusiastic about the proposal.

"I don't like it," said Lord Penworth. "Bad enough we've gotten caught up in this idiotic mess. Nothing I like less that the prospect of getting involved in Italy's political swamp. If it weren't for your brother's involvement with Donna Lissandra... Couldn't we just roll him up in a carpet and ship him out of the country?"

But grumble as he might, he could not help seeing that the plan had certain advantages, not least of which was that in a few days Pietro would be gone.

Rycote didn't like it, either. "He's much too

careless about other people's safety," he grumbled to Doncaster. "Look how he puts his sister in danger. What makes you think he'll be any more careful with Elinor's safety?"

"She'll have me to look after her, just as Lissandra has you," Harry said.

Rycote went over to the window to glare at the watchers, who didn't even bother to hide themselves these days. "It's his fault I can't step out the door without stumbling over them. Maybe once he's gone I can tell them they're wasting their time. The bird has flown." That thought seemed to cheer him a bit.

The one who seized on the idea with enthusiasm was Pietro. Fortunately or unfortunately, it was the theatrical aspect of the plan that appealed to him. On the day of the wedding he appeared at the breakfast table wearing a black tailcoat that he had liberated from his father's valet and proceeded to wait on the gentlemen—the ladies were busy fussing over the bride—without putting a step wrong. Only the spark of mischief in his eye kept him from being the perfect servant.

Harry might have been impressed if he had been able to pay attention. Unfortunately, he could think only of the things that could go wrong. He checked to make sure the bags were all gathered together. He checked to make sure the travel documents were all in order. He checked to make sure the travel documents were still where he had left them. He checked to make sure Pip had the ring. Finally Pip led him off to dress.

Pietro came along, delighted to show his skill in his new role. He deplored the gray waistcoat Harry proposed to wear until Pip pointed out acerbically that although this was a wedding, Doncaster was in mourning.

"Ah, how could I have forgotten!" Pietro struck his head. "A thousand pardons, a million pardons, my lord. I had forgotten the shadow cast upon this happy occasion. This waistcoat is most proper under the circumstances. You have exercised the nicest of judgments in choosing the richness of fabric to suit the joyousness of the wedding combined with the somber color."

Harry looked at Pip. "Crispin picked it out," he muttered.

The marquess's valet observed Pietro's antics with a jaundiced look and removed the waistcoat from his hands. "If you will allow me, sir." He then proceeded to shave Harry and snipped his hair lightly to subdue an errant lock. Under his skilled supervision, the bridegroom was dressed in sparkling white and freshly pressed linen, narrow trousers of dark gray, the offending silk waistcoat and a perfectly fitting morning coat. Pietro was allowed to tie the bow of Harry's tie, and Crispin acknowledged that it was well done.

Pip found himself enjoying Harry's discomfiture until his friend glared and reminded him that in a few months it would be his turn. "And don't think I won't enjoy seeing you sweat," said Harry.

❧

The small room off the consul's office had been transformed, with chairs set out for the family and guests and all other pieces of furniture reduced to stands for the masses of flowers lining the walls. The heavy velvet draperies at the windows had been replaced with thin silk in a pale yellow that made the room seem filled with sunlight.

In a vague sort of way, Harry did notice that the room seemed bright as he walked down the aisle created by the chairs. "The ring!" He halted halfway to the front of the room and patted frantically at his pockets. "I don't have the ring!"

"That's because you aren't supposed to have the ring." Pip grasped his arm and spoke in the tone adults use to calm a fractious child. "I have the ring. I will hand it to you when the time comes."

Harry allowed Pip to lead him to his place. Freeborn was standing there, his benign smile in place, holding a small book open. Harry barely noticed him but turned to watch the door. A young man, a friend of the Freeborns, began playing a melody, more dance than march, on the flute, and then Norrie appeared.

She was holding her father's arm, but her eyes fastened immediately on Harry's, and a smile tilted the corners of her mouth. She looked—beautiful was far too weak a word. There were no words to describe someone who was all his hopes and dreams, everything he had ever wanted and thought hopelessly beyond his reach. She was Norrie.

She came toward him, and her father took her hand from his arm and placed it in Harry's hand. He seemed to be smiling—Harry wasn't entirely certain. He was looking only at Norrie.

The ceremony proceeded, following closely the traditional words. "I, Harcourt Collingswood de

Vaux, take thee, Elinor Augusta Tremaine, to be my lawful wedded wife…" He spoke the words clearly, with no tremble in his voice.

She spoke clearly as well, and he listened to the words "…so long as we both may live."

And then Mr. Freeborn pronounced them man and wife.

Harry held her hands, rubbing his finger along the ring he had placed there, and felt such unspeakable happiness.

Freeborn cleared his throat and repeated, "You may kiss the bride."

It was no polite brushing of the lips then. Harry crushed her in his arms while she had her arms about his neck and clung fiercely. When they finally broke apart, laughing joyously, Freeborn was clearing his throat again. "A few formalities, my lord, my lady. Some papers to sign."

Harry went back to kissing her as soon as the formalities were over and the carriage door closed on them for the ride back to the palazzo. The too-short ride. But even Harry acknowledged that ceremony was necessary to mark the occasion. At least there was nothing now to take his bride from his side.

❧

The grand dining room at the palazzo was also bedecked with flowers. Since it had been decided that the Crescenzi daughter would be married in London, the marchese had insisted that the Crescenzi family would, if not provide, at least participate in the wedding breakfast for the Penworth daughter.

Deprived of the opportunity to supervise the celebrations for her own daughter's wedding, the marchesa had thrown herself into the preparations for Lady Elinor's wedding. The Crescenzi gilt and silver dishes had been polished to a mirror finish, the banquet cloth to cover a table that could seat sixty was blindingly white and showed not a wrinkle, and the plates edged with gold and painted with the Crescenzi crest set the table.

The Crescenzi staff of cooks and assistants had been quite as determined to show the English visitors what a wedding feast should be. There were dishes of risotto and of macaroni, there were croquettes and vol-au-vents, there were roasted capons and roasted lamb. Pastries abounded in curious shapes with fillings both savory and sweet. Bowls of strawberries and cherries glistened with drops of water. The wine was of the finest vintages from the Crescenzi vineyards.

Then there was the cake. Eduardo and Amelia had insisted on being allowed to prepare this as their wedding gift to the couple who were rescuing Pietro. Heavy with fruit, the cake was covered in a thick white icing that, in turn, was almost completely covered with swags and flowers and even butterflies made of sugar, a triumph of the pastry chef's art.

Still, what made it such a triumphantly joyous occasion was the almost palpable happiness of the newly married pair. She held his arm, he kept a hand clasped over hers, and they kept turning to smile into each other's eyes. They accepted good wishes and greeted all the guests, who were more numerous than one would have thought. The marchese, holding himself erect in his throne-like chair, smiled benignly at the couple for close to an hour before he withdrew, dignity intact.

Then there were dozens of Crescenzi relatives, eager to meet the English family to which they would be allied by Lissandra's coming marriage, scholars who had met Lord Penworth in the course of his studies and explorations and wished to honor such a learned and insightful English lord, and, of course, Prince Savelli. The contessa, in mourning for the loss of her jewels, did not attend. Elinor and Harry did not notice.

At one point, barely noticed by the others, Savelli was called from the room to receive a message. When he returned, frowning, he drew Lord Penworth aside for a brief word. The marquess frowned in turn and hesitated briefly as he looked at the bride and groom but then returned to his seat and to his meal without saying anything.

That did not suit Lady Penworth. "What was that about?"

"Nothing, I hope and trust. I'll tell you all about it later." When she looked dubious, he gave her a reassuring smile. "Truly, it can wait. We don't want to disturb the festivities."

Those were not words that reassured Lady Penworth. However, she was soon caught up in the flurry necessary to support the departure of the bride and groom. Elinor had, of course, to be removed from her wedding finery and inserted into a traveling ensemble suitable for the short carriage ride to the Hotel Europa in the Piazza di Spagna.

Harry bore the separation with ill-concealed

impatience. He was, it must be acknowledged, exceedingly impatient to arrive at the privacy of the hotel room. And on this occasion at least, Elinor had no inclination to linger over her toilette, though there were more tears shed as her mother helped her adjust her bonnet, a broad-brimmed leghorn trimmed with blue and green ribbons to match the plaid of her shot silk dress.

Lady Penworth stepped back to smile as she blinked back tears. "You look so very lovely, my darling daughter, so very lovely. You will have to go into black tomorrow for Harry's father, but at least today, today you are a bride, as radiant as a summer day."

Elinor was smiling through tears herself. "I am so happy. I didn't know it was possible to be so happy."

Then there were more tears, more farewells, more laughter, and Elinor was settling herself in the carriage. Something, someone caught Harry's eye, and he snapped his head around, but there was no one there.

"What is it?" she asked.

He shook his head, frowning. "Nothing. I thought for a moment I saw someone. But it's impossible." He stepped into the carriage, settled himself beside Elinor, took her hand, and the frown vanished.

⤝✦⤞

As the carriage rolled down the Corso and the well-wishers waved farewell, Lady Penworth turned to her husband. "Now will you tell me what the prince had to say that disturbed you?"

He smiled ruefully. "I thought you might forget."

She gave him a disbelieving look.

"Well, no, I didn't really think so, but I did hope." His smile faded to a look of concern. "Savelli had Landi imprisoned at one of his more isolated estates, but a message came saying that he has escaped."

Her eyes flew open, and she spun around to look down the street where the carriage had disappeared. "Do you think…? Shouldn't we warn them?"

"No," he said. "They will be leaving tomorrow, and Landi will be busy keeping himself hidden from Savelli's men. I don't see any need to distress them. They will have enough to cope with when they reach England without worrying about one Italian thief."

⁕

Lieutenant Girard fingered his moustache, torn between distaste for the man before him and hope that he might at last have the instrument that would bring Lissandra Crescenzi to him, that would make it impossible for her to refuse him. And destroy that pompous Englishman she pretended to prefer. "You are certain of this? The English are hiding him?"

"Why would I lie?" Landi lifted his hands in a careless gesture, but Girard could see the sheen of sweat on his upper lip. Few visitors were comfortable here in the Castel Sant'Angelo, especially those who were not certain they would be able to leave. The ancient building, first intended as the mausoleum of the Emperor Hadrian, had long served as both fortress and prison and was now the headquarters of the French Army in Rome.

Girard laughed shortly. "You would lie because you are a thieving dog who betrays his friends, his comrades, even his own family. You would lie about anything if you thought it would benefit you."

Landi flushed and straightened up, doing his best to project outrage despite his filthy appearance. "You dare call me a liar? Me, Cavaliere Landi? You know nothing of me."

A snort of contempt greeted that idiotic remark. "Everyone in Rome knows everything of you. You think people would hesitate to speak ill of you? You think servants and shopkeepers do not gossip? You have been stealing from your cousin, the Prince Savelli, and you are not even clever about it. You threaten his honored guests. The only reason you are not imprisoned here is that His Holiness chose to let your cousin deal with you to spare him the humiliation of having a member of his family brought to trial. Should I admire you for having escaped?"

"Should I spend my life bowing and scraping to a foolish old man in exchange for scraps? I saw a chance and I took it. That smug Englishman who has had everything in life handed to him, must I bow to him as well?"

"So you have a grudge against an Englishman as well as against Pietro Crescenzi. This should convince me that you are not lying to me? That you are not trying to use me?"

Landi lifted a shoulder in an effort to seem nonchalant and leaned back as best he could in the straight chair provided for visitors. "If you are afraid of the English…"

"Fear has nothing to do with it. I am a soldier. I have duties," Girard snapped. "England is not the enemy of France, no, nor of the Papal States. And these Englishmen are of the English nobility. It is no little thing to offend them, to charge them with a crime."

"I offered to tell you where Pietro Crescenzi is in exchange for my freedom. You accepted the bargain. If you are afraid to do anything about it, that is not my problem."

Girard paced back and forth across his small office. "There is no question of fear. There is, however, a considerable question of trust." He stopped and stared at Landi. "I would have to be a fool to simply accept your word for it that Pietro Crescenzi is in his family's palazzo being hidden by the English visitors."

"You will break your word?"

"Faugh! You stink." Girard wrinkled his nose and called for his sergeant. "Take this one down to the cells and lock him up." As Landi jumped to his feet in outrage, Girard held up a hand. "If you have been telling me the truth, you will be on your way soon enough. If not, our cells are no worse than you deserve."

He closed the door on the sounds of protest, and a slow smile spread over his face. Lissandra Crescenzi, the lovely girl he had first seen seven years ago, had grown into an even lovelier woman. A true beauty, but also a woman of courage and spirit. A woman who, he had seen, was willing to risk her life to help her brother. She had been impervious to his threats in the past because she was not a fool. They had both known that his threats were empty.

This time, if Landi had spoken the truth and Pietro was indeed being sheltered by the English milords, his threats would not be empty. What would she do to protect her brother? His smile grew broader. There was nothing she would not do.

Twenty-four

CONTESSA, THE MAN CALLED HER. ELINOR WASN'T QUITE
sure who he was, the gentleman who welcomed them to
the Hotel Europa. The owner? The manager? Certainly
nothing so minor as a clerk, not with that impressive bear-
ing, that exquisite tailoring, that enormous gardenia in his
lapel. But she hadn't caught most of what he said in his
greeting. The "contessa" had confused her, and her first
reaction had been to look around for Armando's mother.

Then she remembered that she was now Elinor
de Vaux, Countess of Doncaster. In England, people
would now call her Lady Doncaster, just as Harry
would be called Doncaster. And here in Rome, she
was *contessa*.

She let that unnerving thought float around in
her head as she walked along on Harry's arm. The
manager led them across the marble floor of the lobby
of the hotel, up the marble stairs, and into their suite,
which also had marble floors, though these were softened by thick carpets.

She stood in the middle of the sitting room of their
suite, opulently decorated in dark green plush and gilt.

The look on the manager's face, half obsequious and half proud, told her this must be the best suite in the hotel. Through the doors, a pair of French doors with gilded boiseries, she could see into the bedroom. To be more precise, she could see the bed, a huge bed covered with a gold satin coverlet and piled high with pillows. On the wall above the head of the bed, what looked like a large gilded crown gathered to itself the sheer silken draperies that drifted down over the sides of the bed. Her baggage had already been unpacked, because lying on the bed was her nightgown.

She stood there, staring at the bed and the nightgown. Just staring.

What was wrong with her? Why was she standing here dithering in her head? She was being ridiculous. There was no reason for her to be feeling shy and uncertain. She was Lady Elinor Tremaine, and she was *never* shy and uncertain.

Except that she wasn't Lady Elinor Tremaine anymore. She was now Lady Doncaster, wife of the Earl of Doncaster. Harry's wife.

Even so, that should hardly make her shy at the sight of a bed. Especially since she and Harry had already done *that*, and it had been lovely. The strange feeling of heat deep inside her grew just at the memory. She turned her head so that she could see Harry, who had finally managed to close the door on the manager's flatteries and assurances.

Was it her imagination or did Harry look uncertain too? He was standing halfway across the room, much farther away from her than he usually stood.

He looked around the room nervously and gestured

at the table by the window. "Would you like something to eat? We could send for some tea. Or wine, a bottle of wine."

Just like that her nervousness vanished and a smile tugged at the corners of her mouth. "Harry, we just left a room full of food and I couldn't eat any of it. Could you?"

"Is it too stuffy? It seems warm in here. I could open the window." He stepped over to do so, and the clatter of a passing carriage came in. "No, I probably shouldn't," he said, closing the window and letting quiet return to the room.

Her smile broadened. "Harry, maybe it seems warm because we are wearing too much clothing." She untied the ribbons of her bonnet, a frivolous confection of pale straw tied up in blue and green ribbons, and laid it on a cabinet. Next she slowly stripped off her kid gloves, finger by finger. The left glove was particularly snug, and she had to nip the tips of the fingers between her teeth to loosen them.

That halted him in his tracks. Finally he looked at her, and a slow smile spread across his face. "That is quite possible. If you like, I might be able to relieve you of some of the excess garments."

"That would be very kind of you. Perhaps I could even return the favor?"

He must have moved, or she did, or perhaps both of them moved, because suddenly there was no space between them at all. His arms were around her, crushing her against him so that even through all the corsets and skirts and petticoats she could feel him, the strength of him, the hard, powerful maleness of him.

"Norrie, Norrie…" Her name was coming out as a growl or a groan between the kisses that covered her face and neck.

She backed up, drawing him with her, as she moved toward the bed, tumbling onto it and bouncing on the silken coverlet. Bouncing together, and then sliding together on the slippery silk until they landed on the floor in a tangled heap of coverlet and laughter. He managed to twist them so that he was the one who landed on the bottom, but it had not been a dignified descent. His neck cloth was twisted and his waistcoat had come undone. Of course, that might have happened before their tumble since her hands were under his shirt.

"You are most chivalrous, my lord, to cushion the fall for your wife with your own body." The laughter was fading, and her voice was husky.

"Always, my lady." His smile was fading too, and his eyes darkened as he reached up to pull a pin from her hair, and then another and another until the plaits were loosened and her hair fell in a dark curtain on either side of their faces. She lowered her mouth to his in a secret, hidden kiss.

He stood up, lifting her in his arms as he did so, and she thrilled at the strength of him, that he should be able to lift her so easily. This time he laid her gently so that she sank without bouncing into the soft feather-bed. His hand trailed gently down her face before he began to unhook her bodice, slowly, as if unwrapping an unimaginable treasure.

When she reached to help him, he stopped her hand. "No. This time we will go slowly. Very slowly."

It was slow indeed, so slow that she thought she would go mad, for the unwrapping had been mixed with kisses and caresses, before they were finally together in the bed, skin to skin. His fingers were moving in that secret place between her thighs, making her twist and groan with longing. She reached down and wrapped her hand around him, caressing the silky strength of him.

"No," he gasped. "I won't be able to wait."

"Now," she said. "I want you now."

At last he was inside her, filling her, completing her. *Yes, yes, yes.*

❧

Lady Doncaster, who would have considerable difficulty thinking of herself by that name for some months, lay in the huge bed of the Hotel Europa's finest suite and smiled at the narrow strip of sunlight sneaking in where the curtains had been pulled not quite shut. She quite liked being awakened by sunlight and had always refused to close her curtains completely. She hoped that the Earl of Doncaster—Harry—felt the same way. It was one of the things to be discovered.

At the moment, she was discovering that when she lay with her cheek on Harry's chest, she could feel him breathe. She spread out her hand and brushed it back and forth over the hair on his chest, the soft, springy brown curls. She wriggled her body in a catlike movement and felt his naked body all along her naked body. She grinned. All these lovely sensations to discover.

"What are you doing?" She could hear the amusement in his sleepy voice.

"I'm exploring. Making discoveries. Did you know I can feel you breathe?"

He chuckled, and the sound rumbled deep in his chest.

"I can feel that too. Not just hear it, but feel it." She lifted her head to look at him in delight.

"You like to feel me?"

He pulled her a bit more on top of him and her hip brushed against quite another part of him. She sucked in a gasp and then noticed his small, smug smile. A slight wriggle made that smile disappear while the look in his eyes grew heated. She wriggled some more and his breathing changed. That was all it took? A little wriggle? The realization made her feel enormously powerful and she smiled down at him.

"You know what you are doing, don't you?" His voice was now hoarse. "You are a witch, a wicked, wonderful witch."

She laughed and he rolled her over, nibbling, kissing, caressing until the laughter dissolved in a maelstrom of sensations; indescribable, glorious sensations.

Sometime later—it had not seemed all that long but perhaps it was—Lord Doncaster finished tying his cravat while watching his wife get dressed. He was amazed at the pleasure this gave him—both the fact that Norrie was his wife, and the fact that he was sitting here watching her. First a black silk stocking slid up her calf, over the knee, where it was held up with a pink-ribboned garter. Then the other one. God, her leg was so beautiful. If he were a poet, he would write an ode to her ankle, another to her calf, her knee, and her thigh—an epic would be too short to do justice to her thigh.

She pulled on her drawers and tied them at the waist. Drawers trimmed with a wide band of lace—lace that no other man would ever see. Who would have realized the erotic power of a band of lace? It was just as well when she dropped the chemise over her head to cover her like a tent. He was getting uncomfortably aroused, and they did have to collect Pietro and Martha before they left on the steamer.

"You will have to do this." She stood before him, eyes dancing, and held out her corset.

He looked at it blankly. Did she want him to wear it?

"It laces in the back. I can't do it myself," she explained patiently. Then she put it on over her chemise, hooking it in front, and turned her back to him. He looked at the strings dangling there. "Just pull the laces nice and snug and tie them off."

He gave an experimental tug.

"No," she said. "You have to start at the waist."

He tried again, and after a few more false starts finally had the corset tightened to her satisfaction. "Women do this every time they get dressed?"

"Of course," she laughed.

"You are all quite mad." He shook his head in amusement as she donned her camisole, then her hoops, then a petticoat.

"And you show an admirable lack of familiarity with ladies' underclothing."

He smirked at that. "And you assume that women in all parts of the world dress like Englishwomen."

She turned a mock scowl on him.

Then it was his turn to scowl as she tied on a black silk skirt and buttoned up the black silk bodice.

"Black is not necessary." He bit off the words. "There is no need for you to be in mourning."

"There most certainly is." She looked in the glass and adjusted the ruffle at the neck of her blouse.

"No. You barely knew my…the earl."

"That has nothing to do with it. He was your father and I am your wife. It would be considered an enormous insult were I to wear colors, and you know it. Everyone who heard about it—and everyone would hear about it—would be horrified." She suddenly grinned. "I'm sure that we will find plenty of ways to horrify people. There's no point in doing so unnecessarily."

He was still scowling, so she stepped over to give him a quick peck on the cheek before she went back to the glass to tie on a bonnet. "Besides, it's not as if I am wearing bombazine. I think I look rather nice in black silk." She gave him a flirtatious glance over her shoulder.

He burst out laughing. "You're managing me. Not married a day, and you are already managing me." He pulled her up against him and nibbled on her ear. "The first chance I get, I am going to buy you a scarlet corset and a scarlet petticoat. Then the world can see you wearing black, but I will know that underneath all that prim and proper clothing you are a scarlet woman. My scarlet woman."

❧

In preparation for the departure of Doncaster and his bride, the Crescenzi palazzo seemed crowded to overflowing. Crates and trunks with the accumulated treasures of their travels, wedding gifts—including an Etruscan bronze statue of Hercules from Prince Savelli—and assorted items that would not be needed on the trip home were piled in one corner of the courtyard, awaiting shipment back to England.

The much smaller pile of trunks and portmanteaus that would be needed on the journey was in another corner, in the process of being loaded into the baggage carriage that would transport them to Civita Vecchia, where they would in turn be loaded onto the steamer for Marseilles. This endeavor was being supervised by Martha, who had learned enough Italian in the past months to enable her to conduct a very enjoyable shouting match with the driver of the carriage.

Upstairs was only slightly less chaotic. Lady Penworth had suddenly realized there were dozens—hundreds—of things she wanted to tell a daughter who was setting out on married life, especially married life with a mother-in-law who was likely to prove somewhat difficult. Lord Penworth was preparing for Doncaster a list of names—attorneys, accountants, stewards, bankers—who could assist him should his family's affairs be in confusion, as Penworth feared might well be the case.

Lissandra was on the fringes of the chaos, thinking that she should have asked Elinor more questions when she had the chance. She wanted to know so much about London—what life would be like there, what the people would be like, what she could expect and what would be expected of her. And she wanted to find out these things from someone her own age, someone like Elinor. Lady Penworth would probably tell her the sort of things her own mother would tell her, and that wasn't at all the sort of things she needed—wanted—to know.

She decided she should probably get out of the way now and trust that Elinor would be available in London, but just then one of the servants brought her a note. She frowned at it, unable to think of anyone who should be sending her notes. She frowned even more when she opened it and read:

Signorina Crescenzi—

I am waiting in the hall. If you are wise, you will come and speak with me.

Louis Girard

Her eyes blazed with fury. Not now! How dare he intrude on them now! She crushed the note and flung it aside before she rushed out into the hall.

He was leaning against one of the pillars, arms folded, his red trousers and blue jacket vivid against the pale marble. One ankle was posed casually across the other, his plumed shako sitting on the floor beside him. She halted abruptly when she saw him. He exuded an air of confidence and he was smiling. She did not like that smile. The kitchen cat looked like that when she had a mouse trapped.

She marched forward, head high, and halted a few feet from him. "What are you doing here?" she demanded, speaking in Italian. He did not speak her language well, but would doubtless know from her tone that she was speaking as if to a servant.

He did not seem in the least to be cowed by her.

Instead, the smile turned into something uncomfortably like a sneer as he answered her in French. "Ah, *chérie*, you must learn to speak to me more kindly." He unwound himself from the pillars and advanced on her like a predator.

She fell back a step but then determined to hold her ground. What could he do to her here, in her family's own palazzo? "I can think of no reason why I should ever look on you with kindness. How dare you intrude yourself on my family!"

"But it is about your family that I have come." His voice was all sweet reason. "I come to offer you a way to protect your brother. Even to save his life."

It was a bizarre conversation, as he spoke in French and she in Italian, but she had no difficulty in understanding him. She narrowed her eyes at him. "You are talking nonsense. My brother is off with Garibaldi. Everyone knows that."

"Do they? I have been speaking with an old acquaintance of his, one Armando Landi." She could not hide a start at that, and he smiled. "I see you know the name. I now know that your brother is here, in this building, and he is being protected by the Englishman, the one who looks like a brawler. Does your lover also hide him? Do the others all know about this? Does your father?"

She could feel the panic rising. It seemed to be coming up from her stomach. She swallowed to force it back down. "You would take the word of a dog like Landi? He would say anything to save his own skin."

Girard's grin broadened. "I see you know Signore Landi."

Stupid, stupid! If she lost her temper or, worse yet, panicked, everything could be lost. It would mean disaster not just for her brother but for Pip and for his family. She got control of herself and stiffened her spine. "What is it that you want?"

"But, *chérie*, you know what I want." He lifted his hands in a thoroughly Gallic gesture. "I want you." He seemed pleased to see her recoil.

"You are mad."

"Perhaps." He looked at her meditatively. "I think perhaps you have driven me a bit mad. I can think of no other explanation for this. So I think that you must be the one to cure my madness."

She shook her head, less in denial than in an effort to clear it, to make some sense of this.

"You have two choices," he continued. "Either you come with me, or I descend on this building with my troops and we search every inch of it until we find your brother and carry him off to the hangman."

"You cannot do that. You would not dare offend the English visitors. Your superiors would never allow it." She tried to sound certain, but feared she did not.

He smiled. "When I bring your brother before my superiors, they will pin medals on me. And the English will say nothing."

She chewed her lip. Why did he have to appear now? In another hour or so, Pietro would be safely away. "Time," she said. "You must give me some time to think. Come back in the morning…"

"You take me for a fool," he snapped, "one of your tame lapdogs like that oh-so-proper Englishman who dangles after you." He grabbed her arm to pull her to him. "Decide now, this minute. Either you come with me or I will have this place torn apart, and I do not guarantee the safety of anyone in it."

That was too much. When he touched her, her temper snapped. "*Vai al diavolo*," she shrieked. "Go to the devil." She clawed at his face with her free hand and kicked him, less effectively.

"Bitch!" He yanked her off balance and landed a backhand swing on her, knocking her to her knees. "I will teach you!"

❧

Downstairs, Rycote was having an ambiguous conversation with the marchese. It was clear that the marchese knew his son had been recuperating upstairs. Indeed, he obviously had known all along that his son was in Rome and had known precisely what had happened. On the other hand, he equally obviously did not wish to admit to having known any of these things. Now he wished to thank Rycote's family, his parents, his sister, and her new husband for smuggling Pietro out of Italy. However, he wished to express his thanks without ever saying precisely what he was thanking them for.

At least, this was what Rycote thought Marchese Crescenzi was saying. Rycote's Italian was really not very good, and the marchese spoke no other language. Not that Rycote's French was much better than his Italian, so another language would not have helped. He mumbled *per niente* and *prego* a few times. He thought that was something like saying that it was nothing. At any rate, the marchese seemed pleased with him and patted him on the shoulder as he departed. He would have to talk to Lissandra to find out what this had been all about.

He came up the stairs just in time to see Girard knock Lissandra to her knees.

With a roar of rage he charged at the Frenchman. Girard heard him just in time to shove Lissandra aside and turn to meet the assault.

They were both too blinded by fury to engage in anything resembling a scientific boxing match. It was nothing but a brawl as each one tried to hurt the other as much as possible, and no rules applied. In the end, the French soldier trained by the military was not a match for the English gentleman who had learned to fight from the stableboys on his father's estate and honed his skills in schoolboy battles at Rugby. Unfortunately for Girard, the uppercut that knocked him out came when he stood at the top of the stairs, and he landed motionless at the bottom.

The noise had drawn the attention of the entire household, who arrived in the hall to see Rycote, disheveled and breathing hard, looking down the staircase. Lissandra was wiping the blood from the corner of his mouth with a lacy handkerchief and murmuring endearments.

"What the devil is going on?" demanded Lord Penworth.

Rycote wrapped an arm around Lissandra and pulled her close. "Are you all right?"

"Yes, of course." She smiled up at him with adoration. "You were magnificent."

He turned to his father. "Girard was assaulting

Lissandra." He looked down to where Girard lay motionless, a garish doll on the pale stone floor. A circle of servants, carefully keeping their distance, were watching curiously. "Is he dead?"

Doncaster, who had arrived just in time to see Girard fall, ran to kneel by the body. He checked for a pulse and found it steady enough. After a quick examination he called up cheerfully, "He's alive, all right, but not undamaged. His arm is at a rather odd angle. I think it's probably broken."

Lord Penworth did not share the good cheer. He looked grim and spoke curtly to the servants. "Carry him upstairs. You'd better put him on a door or something, in case more than his arm is broken. And you, Rycote, will join me in the library."

❧

Lissandra insisted on being present in the library as well, since she, after all, was the one who knew what had happened. Rycote looked at his father and shrugged. Doncaster also came along, with his wife at his side and Pietro following behind. Bringing up the rear was Lady Penworth, who smiled at her husband and closed the door on the curious servants.

Lord Penworth heaved a resigned sigh, sat down behind the desk, and frowned at his son. "Well, Rycote, would you care to explain what the devil is going on here?"

He flushed. It was not often his father called him Rycote in that tone, and it meant his father was displeased. Very displeased. However, he was not about to apologize for his actions. "He assaulted Lissandra.

He struck her." There was an eruption of Italian from Lissandra's brother, but Rycote ignored it and looked full at his father. "I do not see that I could have acted in any other way."

Penworth's frown deepened. He looked at Lissandra.

"That is true, my lord," she said. "That pig of a Frenchman said that he knows Pietro is being hidden here. He says that if I do not go with him, he will call in his soldiers to search everywhere. They will find Pietro and hang him and make trouble for all of you."

Pietro's previous eruption had been mild in comparison to the one he produced now. It required the combined efforts of Doncaster and Rycote to keep him from charging out to slit Girard's throat, or dismember him, or simply geld him. A wide variety of possible punishments was mentioned.

Lissandra shook her head at her brother before turning back to Lord Penworth. "I tell that pig to go to the devil and then he hits me." She tilted her head and considered. "Well, I hit him first, but then he knocks me down, and Lord Rycote comes to my rescue." She turned a smile of blinding brightness on her betrothed.

"This is the devil of a mess," said Penworth under his breath. He picked up a pen and tapped it on the desk while he stared at the blotter. The others stared at him and waited. And waited.

"Very well," he said at last, lifting his head. "This is what we shall do. Harry—Doncaster—you and Elinor will set off for the steamer immediately. Crescenzi will travel in that hollowed-out seat Freeborn is so proud of. He will stay in there until you are safely out of the city. You have the passports Freeborn provided?"

"Yes, sir. For Elinor and myself and for the servants. That includes Crescenzi."

Penworth nodded. "Good." Then he turned to the young Italian. "And Crescenzi, you will obey Doncaster at all times. You will be silent, as a good servant should be. There will be no histrionics. No theatrics. None at all. Do you understand?"

Crescenzi started to speak, then swallowed and looked subdued. "Yes, my lord. I understand. You have all been put in danger because you have helped me. I will do nothing that might endanger you further."

Penworth nodded again and rubbed the bridge of his nose. "Now, we will have to deal with Girard." He thought some more, and the others waited. "The steamer leaves tonight at ten, is that correct?"

"That's right," Doncaster said.

"And it takes a horseman a good six hours to get to Civita Vecchia. It's longer by carriage, I know, but it is a fast horseman we must consider." He glanced at the tall clock standing between two bookcases. "It is almost eleven now. I will send a message to Girard's commanding officer, but I don't want him to receive it until four at the earliest. Let us hope that the streamer departs on schedule. Then it will not matter if he finds Girard's account of events more convincing than mine." Penworth allowed himself a slight smile. "But I doubt that he will."

There was a moment of silence. Lady Penworth spoke first. "Very good. And if Lieutenant Girard shows any signs of growing restive, a good dose of laudanum should render him tractable. Now come along, children. Elinor, Harry, Pietro, you need to be on your way. And I think you should explain to Martha what is going on. She is quite level-headed and unlikely to throw a fit. Pip…" She looked at her son consideringly. "I was going to say that perhaps you should remain disheveled, but I think not. We will have to do something about the lieutenant's arm, and no one could expect you to refrain from washing on his account.

"Lissandra, if you have no objection, it would be best for you to wear a bodice with short sleeves and a shawl when we receive the French commander. Then at an opportune moment you can let the shawl slip, exposing the marks where Girard grabbed you. That, plus that most impressive bruise on your cheek, should leave no doubt of his villainy."

The severity in Penworth's face eased a trifle, and a smile twitched at the corners of his mouth. "My dear, I have often thought that you would have made a marvelous director of theatrical pieces."

She turned to him and smiled. "I think so too. That is why I give such excellent parties." She continued out the door. "Now, about that arm, I do believe Crispin used to be quite adept at setting broken bones. He did it for a number of the children. Perhaps he has not lost the skill."

Twenty-five

PIETRO MANAGED TO SEEM TO BE NO MORE THAN ONE of the numerous servants carrying trunks and valises to the carriage, and no one peering into the courtyard would be likely to notice that one of the servants never returned to the palazzo.

Doncaster tenderly handed his bride, swathed in black, into the carriage and had barely seated himself beside her when the seat opposite popped up and a grinning face appeared. "You see, my lord, all is…"

The words were cut off and the seat crushed down as Martha settled herself firmly in the middle of it. "Silly jackanapes," she muttered. "Doesn't have the sense he was born with or he'd know to keep still."

"Quite right," said Doncaster. He stretched out his legs to give the side of the seat a kick and raised his voice. "I do hope we'll have a quiet trip. I wouldn't want my wife to be disturbed by unnecessary noises."

The rumblings ceased except for an occasional grunt when the carriage encountered a particularly uncomfortable bump, and not even half an hour had passed before they reached the city gate. A few soldiers leaned against the wall where an abutment offered a bit of shade. Doncaster and his lady descended and stepped into the tiny office where passports were presented for examination and stamping.

This was one of the danger points. They had to assume that the guards had been told to watch out for Pietro Crescenzi and might recognize him if they saw him. He was safe enough, hidden in the hollow seat. However, they needed a stamp on his passport, and a guard did not have to be a genius to realize that three travelers did not usually require four passports.

Elinor had insisted that she could provide the necessary distraction.

They entered with her leaning weakly on Harry's arm. The young guard half stood from behind his desk in a semblance of courtesy and put out his hand for the passports. He sat down again, gave the top one a cursory glance, and stamped it.

Elinor gave a sigh loud enough to attract his attention. She threw back the black veil that had hidden her face and his eyes widened. Gazing about her with a tragic air, she spoke in low, mournful tones. "Alas, that we must leave Rome for such a sorrowful reason." She bestowed a pained smile on the guard. "But the passing of a loved one is a grief we must all suffer, is it not?" She stepped slowly to the side, a hand pressed to her breast.

The guard, who could not have been more than eighteen, turned his head to keep her in view as he stamped the passports. "Ah, my lady, all sadness should be kept from an angel like you."

Doncaster slipped Pietro's passport under the stamp. The stamp came down.

Pietro's passport disappeared into Doncaster's pocket.

Elinor turned the full force of her smile on the guard and held out her hand to him. "It is the kindness and gallantry of gentlemen like you that will make Rome live forever in my heart." The young man turned a fiery red and bowed dramatically over her hand before he ushered them from the room.

Back in the carriage, the seat began to lift as they drove off, but Doncaster administered another kick. "Really, Norrie," he said.

"Do you think I overdid it? He didn't pay any attention to the number of passports."

"No, but you did such a good job that the entranced puppy is now staring after the carriage and we'll have to be a mile down the road before we can risk letting Pietro out."

❧

"Do you think I should give the lieutenant another dose of laudanum? He is beginning to wake up." Lady Penworth came into the library, where her husband had withdrawn into the simpler world of the Etruscans and was studying Dennis's chapter on Norchia. "I don't want him to be completely unconscious when his commanding officer arrives, but I don't want him quite coherent, either."

Penworth looked at the clock. "I should leave him be, I think. We don't want it to appear that we are keeping him drugged, merely that we are relieving his pain. Colonel Labouche should have received my note by now, and I made it sound urgent enough for him to come quickly." He looked up at her and smiled. "You have changed your dress. You look quite fetching in all that lace."

"Well, I thought I would aim for the frivolous and helpless look." She patted her lace cap and frowned a bit as she looked down at the six tiers of her skirt, all trimmed with lace. "Military men seem to like it. I told Lissandra to wear something pale so she would look helpless and virginal. And I thought we should each clutch a handkerchief. Do you think that would be overdoing it?"

Just then Rycote came in, Lissandra on his arm. She did indeed look fragile and helpless, making the bruise on her face all the more shocking.

Lady Penworth smiled at her approvingly. "I think you should sit over here on the right. That way the bruise on your face will not be immediately visible. It will be more effective if Colonel Whatever doesn't see it until you turn to speak with him."

"Really, Mother, I don't see any need for theatrics. I'll simply tell the fellow what happened and that will be that," said Rycote stiffly.

His mother and Lissandra looked at him pityingly.

"And I think he's coming now. I heard a bit of commotion downstairs when we were in the hall."

Just then the door was opened and the majordomo, in his most formal livery, announced, "Colonel Labouche of the French Army has come to call upon you, Excellency."

"Show him in, please." The marquess stood to greet his visitor.

In marched the colonel, his posture surely an inspiration to young subalterns. With his gray hair and lined face, he must have been well into his sixties, but his fierce moustache and eyebrows declared that no sign of weakness was allowed. He swept a quick glance over the others, but Penworth doubted that any detail had escaped him.

"Colonel Labouche, it is good of you to come so promptly." Penworth held out a hand.

After a moment's hesitation, the colonel took it with a firm clasp. "Your message implied that the problem is serious."

"Yes. Allow me to introduce my wife, Lady Penworth, my son, Lord Rycote, and his fiancée, Signorina Crescenzi."

Labouche nodded to them abruptly but looked at Penworth in inquiry.

"They are all concerned in this," he explained, a touch of apology in his tone. "You see, one of your officers, Lieutenant Girard, has been pursuing Signorina Crescenzi to an extent that has caused her considerable distress. Then today he came into this palazzo and assaulted her."

They all looked at her, and she turned her face so that Labouche saw for the first time the bruise darkening her cheek and eye. He drew a sharp breath and turned back to Penworth.

The marquess continued, "Rycote came to her rescue, of course, but Girard was—I don't quite know how to describe his behavior. He was acting like a madman. My son was forced to knock him down, and in falling, Girard broke his arm."

Maintaining impassivity, Labouche asked where Girard was at present.

Lady Penworth fluttered a bit, waving a lavender-scented handkerchief, as she explained that she had felt they couldn't, of course, leave the young man in such pain, so she had had his arm set and dosed him with laudanum. "He is just waking up now, if you would care to see him."

Lady Penworth took the colonel's arm to lead him into the small sitting room where Lieutenant Girard lay on a velvet settee, his bandaged arm and sling looking very white against the scarlet velvet. He raised his head groggily and fixed his eyes on Lissandra. He burst out in fury, "You! Your brother is a dead man! I will be avenged!"

"Such a foolish young man." Lady Penworth shook her head pityingly.

"Ah, Colonel, you see? Always he threatens to harm my brother." Lissandra raised her hands in a gesture of hopelessness. "My poor brother who had to flee from Rome six long years ago." She turned away to lean on Rycote's arm.

Girard managed to focus his eyes enough to see that his commanding officer was present. He struggled to sit up. "Sir, Pietro Crescenzi is one of Garibaldi's aides. He has been in Rome these past two months, and now these English are hiding him."

"Months? You have known that there is a Garibaldi spy in Rome for months? How is it that I have heard nothing of this?" demanded Labouche coldly.

Still half drugged, Girard failed to notice the icy note in his commander's voice and persisted. "He is here. The English are hiding him in their apartments. I know it."

Lady Penworth shook her head sadly. "He must be a madman. He has this bee in his bonnet about Miss Crescenzi's brother."

"I assure you, Colonel Labouche, that so far as I know, Pietro Crescenzi is not even in Rome. Neither he nor any other revolutionary is hiding in our apartments." Lord Penworth gave a small smile. "If it will make your mind easier, you have my leave to look anywhere you choose."

The colonel, who was scowling at his young officer, shook his head. "That would be absurd. I am hardly going to question the word of a man who dines with my emperor." He turned to give Penworth a wry smile. "We are notified when important visitors come to Rome, you see."

Penworth touched him lightly on the sleeve. "Then, if I might have a word?" The two men drew apart, and Penworth spoke softly. "My son was very angry at the insult to Miss Crescenzi, and I fear he wishes to challenge the lieutenant. I may not be able to dissuade him, and I know that a French officer would never refuse a challenge. Quite apart from the potential for tragedy, such a duel could be extremely embarrassing for me, for my country, and for yours as well when the incident that brought it on became known. And it would become known, as such things do."

Labouche looked at him consideringly. "Do you have a suggestion?"

"Obviously, no challenge can be offered while Lieutenant Girard is suffering from a broken arm. Is there any possibility that he might be sent elsewhere to recover?"

"Oh yes." The colonel's smile was grim. "He will indeed be sent elsewhere to recover. Algeria, most likely. I do not think you need worry yourself about him any longer. I will have him removed from here immediately."

The concord was sealed with handshakes, bows, and curtsies. The colonel departed and a guard of four men led Lieutenant Girard away in his wake. Rycote and Lissandra withdrew to converse, or perhaps to communicate in some other way, leaving Lord and Lady Penworth alone. She took his arm and said happily, "And I don't think we even had to tell any lies."

❧

It had grown dark by the time the borrowed carriage arrived at the customs house in Civita Vecchia, but the steamer could be seen pulling up at the dock. The coachman had taken to heart the order to travel with speed, and the passengers had been flung about mercilessly as the coach bounced about on the rutted roads.

"Tomorrow there will be bruises covering every inch of me," said Elinor, shifting uncomfortably. "I feared on occasion that we would be sending Mr. Freeborn's carriage back to him as a pile of splinters."

"I will treat you to a massage as soon as we reach our cabin," her husband promised with a grin. He lifted her onto the ground, holding her just a little longer than necessary.

She grinned back and then dropped the black veil Lissandra insisted she wear. Elinor had protested that only widows wore such veils, but Lissandra said that in Italy people would be most solicitous of a woman wearing one even for a father-in-law. Harry scowled at it, but did not protest.

Entering into the customs house, Doncaster looked about him scornfully and spoke in his best aristocratic drawl. "Good heavens, my dear, what a madhouse. Is there no order anywhere in this country?" He waved a hand at Pietro. "Go find out who is in charge here, if anyone is. We will wait outside where the air is at least fresher."

Pietro, throwing himself into his part, even gave his forelock a tug. Crouched over, he scurried off saying, "*Subito, subito*, immediately."

Elinor kept her hand on her husband's arm as he led her back outside, still peering down his nose at their surroundings. "You look supremely arrogant," she whispered. "How do you manage to keep a straight face?"

"Practice, my dear, practice. This is the way the rest of the world expects English gentlemen to act. Thoroughly pompous, self-important, and a bit stupid." He let his eyes roam over the crowd, apparently casual, but missing nothing, and moved his wife out of the path of the urchin who might be simply an urchin but was more likely a pickpocket. "Hush now. I think an officer is coming this way with Pietro."

She turned and saw a nervous-looking young customs agent accompanying an equally perturbed Pietro.

"My lord, I have explained to these officious fools that you are an English nobleman of the highest rank, returning home under circumstances of the most tragic, but they seem unable to comprehend." Pietro could not entirely subdue his usual dramatic flair, but his upper lip displayed a slight hint of moisture.

Doncaster looked at the officer wearily and spoke in fluent but atrociously pronounced Italian. "What is it now? Another series of stamps required?"

The agent, who could not be more than eighteen years old, whipped off his cap and jerked a bow. "Excellency, a thousand apologies, but my commander has received warning that a dangerous revolutionary may be in Rome. We must be on guard lest he try to escape this way."

"What has that to do with us?" Doncaster looked at the young man in amazement. "Do I look like a revolutionary? Does my wife?"

"Forgive me, Excellency, but..." He licked his lips and tried again. "My commander, he insists that he must interview you. Only, you understand, so that he can assure himself no one has imposed on you by inserting himself into your party."

Doncaster turned to his wife with an exaggerated sigh and spoke loudly in English. "So tiresome, these foreigners, my dear. But if this is what we must do in order to get home, this is what we must do." He put his hand over hers and gave it a warning squeeze.

The warning had not really been needed. Elinor had been startled by his play-acting at first, but was now ready to throw herself into the role of brainless ninny. She clutched a black-bordered handkerchief in her hand and pressed it to her breast with a sob. "This is really too much. But whatever you say, Doncaster. I am sure you know best."

She hung weakly on his arm as he ushered her through the crowd of people to the office at the rear of the building. Pietro and Martha followed behind, along with the young agent. Pietro attempted to look servile, but Martha marched forward militantly.

The commander of the post proved to be a weary fellow, perhaps fifty years old. His moustache drooped, his shoulders drooped, and his unbuttoned tunic revealed that his stomach drooped as well. Lifting his eyes from the paper he had been studying, he regarded them mournfully and then heaved himself to his feet. "Milord." He dipped his head in greeting.

"Ah, yes, Commander, is it?"

That produced a weary nod. "Commander will do," he said in heavily accented but perfectly clear English.

"Excellent." Doncaster beamed approval at him. "You speak English. Then we can get this nonsense over with quickly."

Elinor lifted her handkerchief to her mouth and made a sound that might have been a stifled sob. Or giggle. Doncaster patted her hand.

"Yes, of course. Quickly." The commander looked down at the paper before him. "You must understand my problem. I have been warned that a dangerous revolutionary, one of Garibaldi's trusted lieutenants, has been in Rome and is trying to escape."

Doncaster laughed lightly. "I assure you that I am not a dangerous revolutionary, nor do I associate with such creatures."

"Yes, of course, but I have this problem. Your manservant appears to fit the description I have been given. A young man, of average height, slim, with dark hair and eyes." The commander shrugged his shoulders.

Doncaster looked at Pietro. "Yes, he does fit that description, doesn't he?" He turned and looked at the young customs agent. "But so does your assistant here and, I dare say, half the young men in Rome."

The commander nodded acknowledgment of the point. "However, my assistant has been my assistant for over a year now, and what is more, his parents have been known to me for many, many years. May I assume you have known your manservant for no more than a few months?"

Doncaster tilted his head in apparent thought. "Yes, yes, a few months more or less."

"Then, you see, he could be my revolutionary, having wormed his way into your service as a way of escaping from Rome."

By way of reply, Doncaster burst out laughing. "Leporello?" He laughed some more. "Leporello a revolutionary? Oh my dear commander, the fellow is afraid of *spiders*!"

Pietro turned beet red as everyone turned to look at him.

The commander said, "Yes, but…"

"This is too, too dreadful," declaimed Elinor. "I cannot bear it, my love. In our time of sorrow, when we have so recently received word of your father's death, along comes this dreadful man"—she waved her handkerchief at the commander, who stepped back as if struck—"and his idiotic suggestion that Leporello—Leporello, of all people—is a revolutionary. When we must hurry to return to England…these dreadful delays… Oh…" With her hand to her forehead, she collapsed gracefully into Doncaster's arms.

"Now see what you've done," Martha scolded the commander. "You've gone and upset my lady when it took me half the trip here to get her calmed down." She fished around in her handbag. "I'll need her smelling salts. Leporello, you go and make sure the baggage is all in my lady's cabin, and my lord and I will get her on board so she can lie down."

Pietro hunched his shoulders as if expecting a blow. "Right away, miss, right away." He scurried off.

"And you!" Martha turned back to the commander. "You should be ashamed of yourself. Upsetting my poor lady with your nonsense. As if we'd have anything to do with any of your nasty revolutionaries."

"I think that is quite enough, Commander. I trust you have no objection to my taking my wife on board now?" Turning his back to the flustered officer, Harry put an arm around Elinor's shoulders as she revived enough to stand. "Come, my dear, I will help you to our cabin and then you can lie down. There will be no more interference from these gentlemen." He glared at them and they nodded quickly.

Elinor sobbed noisily into her handkerchief as he led her out of the office. She continued to sob, more quietly, as he led her up the gangplank and onto the steamer. By the time they had reached their cabin, the sobs had degenerated into giggles.

There Pietro awaited them. "Spiders?" he said in outrage. "I am afraid of *spiders*?"

As he stormed out of the cabin, they collapsed on the bed in laughter.

❧

A few days later, in the cells of the Castel Sant'Angelo, a guard was coming off duty. "Know anything about that Italian fellow who keeps complaining?" he asked his relief.

The newcomer shook his head. "All I know is, Lieutenant Girard said to keep him here until he said to let him go."

"Girard? Didn't he just get sent to Algeria?"

That produced a laugh. "Then I guess that complaining Italian will be here for a while."

Twenty-six

THEY LAUGHED IN MARSEILLES WHEN THEY READ Pietro's note saying that he had gone to Nice to join Garibaldi.

They laughed in Lyon when they went to visit the little priest who showed visitors the clock. He remembered them and laughed with them.

They laughed in Paris when Mr. Worth tried to maintain a solemn mien while Elinor ordered a dozen stylish gowns in mourning colors. They laughed even more at the look on Mr. Worth's face when Doncaster ordered a scarlet corset. And a scarlet petticoat. And scarlet garters.

The journey took much longer than might be expected. They stopped at each town on their route early in the afternoon and departed late the next day, looking blissfully contented. It was, after all, their wedding trip.

Their laughter slowed as they neared London. Messages had gone back and forth across the Channel, so that when they landed in Dover, the Doncaster carriage was there to meet them. Harry conferred with the coachman while Norrie settled herself into the well-padded plush interior and admired the little cut-glass vases by the windows, each one holding a small posy of rosebuds. It was the sort of detail her mother would have considered ostentatious, but she found it rather charming. But foolish. It was to be hoped that the carriage was well sprung. Too severe a bump would spill the water from the vase onto her dress. It might not harm the black poplin, but it would spot the velvet trim.

She took a deep breath. Harry was taking a long time with the coachman, and she was running out of trivialities to keep the worry at bay. Would they have to confront his mother today? Even in Paris they had heard whispers about her. It was not that Elinor doubted her ability to handle her new mother-in-law. She had seen Lady Penworth manage—or rout—everyone from the queen down to a recalcitrant servant, and what her mother did, she could do. It was tempting to get the confrontation over and done with, but it would be best to have a bit more information first. Her biggest worry was that Lady Doncaster, the *Dowager* Lady Doncaster, would make life difficult for Harry.

She was not going to allow that. His parents had done enough—too much—to torment Harry. His father was gone, so he could do no more harm. If his mother tried to do anything that would make Harry unhappy, she would discover that she now had Elinor to contend with. And no one was going to make Harry unhappy if Elinor had anything to say about it. No one.

The door opened, he climbed in, and the carriage slid smoothly into motion. Harry did not look too upset. At least there was no increase in the tension that had been growing in him since they left Paris. She took his hand, and he smiled and squeezed it back.

"We can safely go to Belgrave Square," he said. "My mother is at the Abbey. So I will be able to deal with the lawyers and all that sort of thing before I have to face her."

That was a relief, since it was obviously a relief to Harry. She did not doubt his ability to quickly grasp the essentials about the management of the estate, and that would ease his mind. There remained one question. "Are your sisters with her?" she asked.

"No, they are with Aunt Georgina in Richmond." He shook his head in disbelief.

Norrie frowned. "Is she unkind?"

He gave a short laugh. "She isn't even present. She is one of the family's ancient relics. The last time I saw her, she was waiting impatiently for this nonsense in France to be over so she could once more visit her friend Marie Antoinette. She thought I was some chevalier or other. Lord knows who she thinks the girls are."

"In that case, it sounds as if there will be no difficulty when we go to fetch your sisters tomorrow."

≪≫

There were difficulties, of course. The first occurred at Doncaster House. Harry knew where it was, but he couldn't remember if he had ever actually been inside it before. He certainly didn't know any of the servants.

He didn't even know where the bedrooms were. He covered his uncertainty by maintaining a frosty visage.

Elinor had no difficulty in matching his expression. She did not care for the fawning look of the butler and housekeeper, and she certainly did not care for the decoration of the house. She sincerely hoped that the estate was in healthy enough condition to bear the cost of new furnishings.

Advance warning of their arrival ensured that the rooms of the earl and countess were prepared, but nothing had been done about rooms for Harry's sisters. "Rooms for the young ladies?" a startled housekeeper said. "They've never been here these ten years or more, and then they were in the nursery. Always in the country they were."

Elinor ordered the two best guest rooms prepared for them. They were not rooms she particularly admired, but the girls might enjoy having a hand in the decoration. A smaller room would do for the governess, whoever she might be. And if she turned out to be a timid mouse or a gloomy drudge, she could be replaced.

The next difficulty came when Harry and Elinor arrived at Aunt Georgina's house, a Georgian villa in which nothing had been changed in more than fifty years. That was interesting, but it was not the problem. Or rather the problems.

Harry's sisters seemed reasonably pleased to see him. Or more than reasonably. Olivia had flown at him like a cannonball when she saw him. Julia was reasonably pleased to be told they were removing to London.

However, they did not seem pleased to discover

that Harry had a wife. When she was presented to them, they stood there in dresses of dusty black—obviously dyed by someone who had done a poor job of it—and stared at her with flat, unfriendly eyes.

"You never told us you were married," Julia said. The words were for Harry, but the glare was all for Elinor.

"Well, I haven't been married very long," Harry said, trying to sound reasonable. Elinor could have told him that reason wasn't going to work.

"Still, you could have written." The younger girl, Olivia, stuck out her lower lip. "I suppose this means we will have to live with Mother."

"It means nothing of the sort," said Elinor briskly. "Your brother would not hear of such a thing, and neither would I. You will be living with us." She was not accustomed to being disliked, certainly not at a first meeting, and was not sure how to proceed. However, acting confident was probably a good idea.

"Off in the nursery wing, I suppose, so you can ignore us while still doing your duty," Julia said bitterly.

"We thought you would come back and this time you would make things better." Olivia looked at Harry reproachfully.

Julia sniffed. "We should have known better. Nothing will change."

"Stop this nonsense." Harry seemed to grow taller as she looked at him, and his sisters seemed shocked into silence. "Of course things will change. Didn't I promise that when I came back I would take care of you?" His voice softened. "Well, I have come back, and now I can take care of you. I am the earl now, remember?"

His sisters looked at him uncertainly. "What does that mean?" asked Olivia.

"It means," said Elinor, smiling proudly, "that your brother is the one who decides things like where you will live and what you may do."

"Not our mother?" Julia looked doubtful.

"Definitely not our mother," Harry said firmly. "Now, do you have a governess with you? Any maids of your own?" They shook their heads. Their governess had been dismissed when she protested that old gowns dyed black made inadequate mourning attire for an earl's daughters.

Not even a governess. Elinor shook her head. Olivia was only twelve. What had her mother been thinking? Stupid question. Had she ever heard anything of Harry's parents that would lead her to think they were capable of rational thought? That would lead her to think they gave their children any thought at all?

Harry turned to his wife. "It was sensible of you to bring Martha. She can supervise the girls' packing."

She didn't remind him that he had been annoyed to find the maid in the carriage on the journey down. She simply nodded and said to the girls, "Bring only the things you want to keep. We will do some shopping in London. You obviously need new clothes."

They looked at their brother, who nodded in turn. As they left the room, Elinor could have sworn she heard a small giggle. The thought of new clothes, even mourning clothes, can do that.

❧

The new Lady Doncaster decided to place household concerns far down on her list of priorities. She contented herself with a quick tour of Doncaster House with the housekeeper. This was followed by a short—one might say terse—chat, during which she pointed out that she had no intention of retaining servants who were not up to the job. She expected a far higher standard of cleanliness and service than she had seen so far and gave a brief rehearsal of what she expected to see. An appointment was made for two weeks hence, at which time the situation would be evaluated. A shaken housekeeper tottered off to the kitchen to confer with her colleagues.

Then Elinor turned her attention to important matters—family matters.

Julia and Olivia were at the top of her list. Well, second on it. Harry led everything else, but at the moment he did not seem to require a great deal of her attention except, of course, at night. Just thinking about what happened at night made her stop whatever she was doing and sigh blissfully. Being married was so delicious that she could not imagine why anyone remained single. Other people weren't married to Harry, so that probably made a difference.

During the day, she began making rapid progress with the girls after she went through their wardrobes and threw out practically all their garments.

"Mother said that since we are in mourning and no one will see us, it would be more sensible to simply dye our old dresses black," Julia said.

"What utter nonsense. We don't dress to impress other people." Elinor paused to consider. "Well, sometimes we do. But for the most part the way we dress reflects the way we think of ourselves. A woman who goes around in worthless rags will begin to think she is worthless even if she didn't think that way in the first place. And you, my pets, are not worthless."

As she noted the girls' surprised confusion, her mouth tightened. Their mother had apparently considered her daughters worthless and had not even tried to hide her opinion from them. Elinor picked up a chemise with at least a dozen patches, made a sound of disgust, and ripped it across.

The new Earl of Doncaster was spending his days in conference with lawyers and men of business. To his enormous relief, the estate was actually in healthy condition. The late earl had preferred brandy to business, but was not entirely a fool. He had left his affairs in the hands of a highly capable man of business. Nor had the earl's wife been able to run up disastrous bills. She received her allowance promptly each quarter, and jewelers, milliners, and all others had soon discovered that neither the earl nor his man of business could be induced to pay a penny more to cover her bills.

No one was inclined to mention the rumors about how those bills were paid.

There was more relief when he learned that the Dowager Lady Doncaster was entitled to a perfectly respectable widow's portion, including either a country house in Wiltshire or a house in London, as she chose. It was all settled, and he did not have to make any decisions about it.

In the will, Harry was named guardian of his sisters, with no role for their mother, and quite respectable dowries had been set aside for them. That rather bothered him, he told Norrie in the early hours of the morning when confidences are exchanged. "I suppose he didn't know me well enough to realize that I would take care of them."

"Nonsense," Norrie said. "It was only sensible to make provision for them in his will. You might have died on your travels, and they would have been left to the tender mercies of whoever inherited the title. Who is next in line, by the way?"

He frowned. "I don't know. There must be a cousin or two someplace."

"You see? They would have been left to the care of a total stranger who might have felt no obligation to them at all. That provision is an indication of your father's good heart, not his distrust."

A resigned smile slowly spread across his face. "You'll make a saint of my father yet."

Eventually Harry had dealt with all the problems that could be dealt with in London. It was time to travel to Bradenham Abbey and deal with his mother.

"I think I should go down to the Abbey by myself first," he said, standing in front of the mirror trying to tie a neat bow in his cravat. He still had not hired a valet. Norrie seemed to enjoy helping him out of his clothes.

She did not, however, seem to enjoy his remark.

"You think you should do *what*?"

"Go down first by myself. You know, make sure everything is put to rights before you see it for the first time. After all, it's going to be our home. I don't want you to have a poor first impression of the place." He was still facing the mirror, but she was perfectly visible in it, and she was not looking happy. Angry was more like it. Furious might be an even better description.

"What absolute twaddle. As if you would have the least notion of how to put a house to rights. What is this all about?"

He gave up his struggle with the cravat and turned to face her. "My mother is there."

"We knew that, didn't we?"

"I don't want her anywhere near you."

"Oh, Harry, I know that's what you want, but it's not going to be completely possible. Sooner or later we will have to deal with her, and it might as well be sooner."

"It's not that." He stood there frowning. "We don't have to deal with her. I have to deal with her."

"Well, I'm not going to let you face her by yourself, and that is final."

The frown eased, and he shook his head at her in fond despair. "It's just that…I can't think of any good way to say this. She isn't alone."

"Surely she isn't hosting a party?"

"Only a party of one. A gentleman at my club wanted to be sure I knew, since I had been out of the country so long. She is accompanied, as I am told she often is of late, by Lord Percival Winters."

Norrie stared at him for a moment, and then sat down abruptly. "I am not certain I understand what you are saying."

He raised his brows but said nothing.

"All right, I am not certain I *want* to understand what you are saying." She shook her head as if to clear it. "It is barely two months since her husband died, and she is—at least ostensibly—in deepest mourning, accompanied by her lover? Is that what you are telling me?" He nodded. "Thank heaven your sisters were deposited with Aunt Georgina, at least." He shrugged, and she relapsed into silence.

She was shocked. Wonderful. He—and his family— had managed to shock her. Never before had he seen her shocked. Angry, yes, and even frightened. She had been angry with Landi, with Girard, even angry at the way his sisters had been treated, but never shocked. This was what he had succeeded in doing for her. Instead of protecting her, he had exposed for her the vileness that was his mother.

He cleared his throat. "So you see, there is no need for you to come with me. I can see to it that she never crosses your path."

She looked up, startled. "No need? Of course there is a need for me to come with you. To be honest, I am looking forward to seeing you throw Lord Winters out of your house. I know his wife, you see. After that, I am sure I can help you convince your mother that she will be happier if she departs immediately for whatever residence she chooses."

It was Harry's turn to sit down abruptly. "You're serious." Her shock had apparently been replaced by anger.

"Of course. We are married, aren't we? That means that we face things together. If you confront her alone, you may be held back by some nonsensical notions of the duty owed to a mother. I will have no such qualms." She began to pace back and forth, tapping a finger on her cheek. "The only question is whether your sisters should come with us."

"My sisters!" Now she had shocked him. "They're children."

"Yes, they really shouldn't witness this, though they would probably enjoy seeing you toss Lord Winters out on his ear. However, there could be an ugly scene, and we do not want them to witness that." She frowned. "The problem is that they really shouldn't be left alone."

"They'll be safe enough here, surely, with a house full of servants."

"It's not their safety that worries me. They still half expect us to go off and leave them."

"They can't seriously think…" He heaved a sigh. "Of course they can. A week isn't enough to overturn a lifetime of experience. You'd best stay here with them. I can come and get you all when it's safe."

She shook her head dismissively. "Absolutely not. I know you want to protect them, but they also need to know that we are all part of a family, that they belong with us. No, I think what we will do is go down in two carriages. You and I can set out early in the morning and be there shortly after noon. The girls can set out later with Martha so that they arrive in the early evening. That should give you enough time to send Lord Winters on his way, and any eruptions from your mother should have subsided by then." She looked up at him with a smile. "It was clever of you to have your estate so close to London. It makes it so much easier to get away for a while whenever we choose."

Suddenly Harry was feeling cheerful again. "We have some other places farther afield," he said. "Even one in Wales if we ever want to get away from everything."

⁓

Despite the gloom of the day, chilly and damp even for England in June, Harry had been looking at the countryside with considerable interest earlier in the trip. The world looked rather different when one owned a large chunk of it and was responsible for those who lived on it. Buckinghamshire was pleasant to look at, with gently rolling hills covered with what appeared to be fertile fields. Norrie shared his interest, and they wondered whether those fields were really sufficient to support the prosperous towns they passed through.

As they neared Bradenham Abbey, the landscape continued to be attractive, but Harry's spirits fell. "We must be getting close. I recognize the names of some of the places we've passed. But I don't recognize the places themselves." He shook his head. "All my life, this has been my home, at least nominally, and so little of it is familiar."

Norrie, who had been holding his hand, gave it a sharp shake. "Well, it soon will be familiar, so stop feeling sorry for yourself. Just think of all the fun we will have exploring and discovering."

He grinned. She never let him feel sorry for himself. Or rather, she always showed him that there was no reason to feel sorry for himself. "What, no words of sympathy, no pity for my benighted childhood?"

"Nary a one. Look! Is that it?"

They had just crested a hill and could see in the distance an enormous rambling building of gray stone. Actually, it looked more like a series of connected buildings, none of them very high, wandering across a valley.

"Yes, my dear. That is your new home. Bradenham Abbey."

She seemed to be looking at it with delighted surprise. "It really is an abbey? I mean, most of the time when things get called an abbey, it only means that there once was an abbey, and they used the stones to build a new house."

Harry smiled and realized that he was looking at it with a certain fondness. "It really is an abbey. After the monks were kicked out, the new owner was a frugal sort who just knocked down the church and adapted the rest. It's been adapted a bit more since then, and it's really quite comfortable inside as I recall."

"Oh, Harry, I can't wait to see it." She was practically jumping up and down on the seat.

"Just remember what—or who—is waiting for us there."

She lifted her chin. "Nothing and no one we can't handle."

❧

The coach pulled up at the entrance to the Abbey, where a roofed staircase was guarded by Gothic arches. There was a pause before the door opened and a footman hurried down to help them. A second and a third followed to carry their luggage, and by the time Harry and Elinor had reached the door, an august personage was standing there to greet them.

"My lord, I must apologize for the inadequacy of your welcome. We had not expected you."

"It was a sudden decision." Harry, with Elinor on his arm, walked into the entrance hall, a rather gloomy, square room with doors leading in all directions. "My dear, may I present Bidewell, our butler." While Elinor smiled a greeting, Harry continued, "Have my wife's things and mine taken up to our rooms. I trust they are ready for us."

"The earl's room has been kept in readiness for you, of course, but…" Bidewell did not seem to know how to continue.

"But you did not know I had married." Harry smiled. "Never mind. Just put Lady Doncaster's things in there with mine. And my sisters will be arriving later today. Have their rooms ready too."

Bidewell blinked.

Harry sighed. "My sisters do have rooms, do they not?"

"The nursery has always provided them with a certain degree of privacy, my lord." The butler seemed to be choosing his words with care.

"Privacy. Good God." Harry closed his eyes. "Prepare two of the guest rooms for them. We won't be having any guests for a while, and they can choose different ones tomorrow if they like."

By this time Elinor had passed her bonnet, gloves, and mantelet to a waiting footman, and Harry had also been divested of hat and gloves. "Is my mother about?" he asked casually.

"I believe she is in the blue drawing room." Bidewell hesitated, as if about to say more, but closed his mouth and stepped back.

"We will join her," Harry said. "Have some tea brought to us there."

❧

A footman flung the door open and they entered the blue drawing room together. Elinor had her hand on his arm and his hand was protectively over hers. The couple on the settee sat up abruptly, the woman turning angrily to face the intruders. The man beside her jumped to his feet. Elinor felt a momentary confusion. She had expected to be encountering Harry's mother, but this woman, although of a suitable age, was dressed in a gown of orange and red plaid.

"Hello, Mother," said Harry.

Oh goodness, thought Elinor. This is his mother. She felt glad that she was wearing one of Mr. Worth's creations, a fine black wool trimmed with black velvet at the bodice and on the bell sleeves. She had chosen it because it would not get too wrinkled on the journey, and it gave her spirits a boost to know that she was now the one dressed properly.

"Harry. What are you doing here?"

As a welcome to a son not seen for years, it sounded inadequate to Elinor. She tightened her hand on Harry's arm.

"This is my house, if you recall," he said.

She made a dismissive noise and looked at Elinor. "And this is…?"

"Allow me to present my wife." Harry's smile barely touched his mouth and reached no higher.

"Your wife? Since when have you been married?"

Elinor was rather pleased to see that Lady Doncaster

looked annoyed. She bowed her head slightly to her mother-in-law to acknowledge the introduction, and said, "Please allow me to offer my condolences on the death of your husband. I understand it was quite sudden and unexpected." Her eyes swept down over Lady Doncaster's dress and back to her face. The annoyance changed to a flush of anger.

"We were married in Rome," said Harry calmly. "I regret we were unable to inform you, but when the news of my father's death reached us, we decided to simply hurry home."

That did not appear to placate his mother, who turned on him with an angry frown. "I had plans…"

A loud harrumph from her companion interrupted her. He looked uncomfortable, and that discomfort increased when Harry turned to him.

"Ah, yes." Harry smiled coldly. "My dear, may I present Lord Percival Winters?"

"Oh, I know Lord Winters," Elinor said with a polite social smile. "We have met at my parents' home."

"Indeed, indeed, I have known Lady Elinor since she was a little girl. How are you, my dear?"

"Actually, it's Lady Doncaster now," Elinor said.

"Of course, of course." He made a choking noise before he turned to Lady Doncaster with a warning look. "Penworth's daughter, you know."

Elinor could almost see the wheels turning in Lady Doncaster's head as she assimilated this information and tried to decide how to use it. Just then Bidewell appeared with the tea tray. He stood there uncertainly until Elinor waved him to the tea table and seated herself behind it. "How do you take your tea, Lady Doncaster?"

Such an ordinary question with which to announce who was now the lady of the house. Such a bloodless coup d'état.

The older Lady Doncaster recognized precisely what had happened and looked for a moment like a fox at bay. She managed to recover enough to say, "Just a drop of milk, if you please."

Harry stood beside Elinor, leaning with studied casualness on the mantelpiece. "What brings you here today, Winters?"

Winters darted an uncomfortable glance at Lady Doncaster, who said smoothly, "Winters is an old friend of the family. He came to commiserate with me on the loss of my husband."

"Dear me," said Elinor. "There seem to be no more cups. Does Lady Winters not take tea?"

There was an uncomfortable silence. Lord Winters finally harrumphed and said, "My wife was unable to accompany me."

"You must miss her dreadfully," Harry said. "Do not let us impose on you any longer. Feel free to leave at once. We will have your things sent on after you."

Lord Winters put down his teacup and got to his feet with a quick, nervous smile. "Excellent idea."

"Don't be absurd, Winters," said Lady Doncaster, reaching out to grab his sleeve.

Winters shook his head and pulled away. "Much the best thing, don't you know. After all, you have your family with you now." He hurried from the room.

Lady Doncaster turned on her son. "How dare you march into my house and interfere in my life this way?"

"Actually, it is *my* house," he said mildly.

"And you haven't set foot in it in years. I will not allow you to meddle in my affairs. If you propose to stay here, I will go to London."

He shrugged. "Do not let me hinder you. But don't plan on going to Doncaster House. That also is now mine."

She stared at him openmouthed. "Do I understand you correctly? You are throwing me out of my own home?"

"As I said before, it is now my house, not yours. Did Dalrymple not explain the situation to you? He assured me that he had. You have your income, a quite generous one, and either a house in London or an estate in Wiltshire. Have you decided which you will choose?"

"Although there is more entertainment to be found in London, there is, perhaps, more privacy in the country," Elinor put in. "Fewer people to be shocked if you choose to put off your blacks."

Lady Doncaster gave the younger woman a look of loathing. "Do not be an insipid fool."

Harry choked down a laugh.

She turned to her son. "And your father would never have expected me to pretend grief at his death, any more than he would have mourned me. Don't try to claim that you ever thought us a loving couple."

Elinor looked to see if there was enough tea in the pot for another cup. Regrettably, she decided, there was not. "It is not the dead who care whether we wear mourning or not. It is the people who make up society. And they seem to care a great deal."

"Will you be quiet!" Lady Doncaster glared at Elinor before returning to her son. "You know I could never live permanently in the country, and you cannot expect me to live in that pokey little London house. It's practically in Pimlico."

Harry said nothing.

"Think of your sisters. In a few years they will be grown. You can't expect an earl's daughters to be brought out from a house in Pimlico."

"That is not a problem," said Elinor. "Harry's sisters now live with us, and I am sure I can manage to bring them out. If I have any difficulties, I can always call on my mother." She smiled serenely.

Lady Doncaster looked at her son, suddenly uncertain.

He smiled. "You don't really think I would allow my sisters to remain with a woman who thinks nothing of entertaining her lover in what should be a house of mourning?"

She stared at her son with narrowed eyes. "He told you, didn't he? The old fool."

"Told me?" Harry was trying to appear imperturbable.

"Told you what I said to him when you were born—that you probably weren't his. God, he was so stupid. Such a stupid, boring prig."

"A prig? The earl? That is hardly the way I would describe him."

Harry was still leaning casually against the mantel. Elinor wondered if his mother could see how tense Harry really was, how coiled, ready to spring. Probably not. She did not seem to be a perceptive woman.

The countess laughed shortly. "You should have seen him back then. Chortling with delight over a puny, mewling infant. And I was feeling sick as a dog. I couldn't stand it. I had to do something to prick that inflated bag of smugness."

"Do you mean to tell me that you lied to him?" Harry's hand was clenched so tightly the knuckles were bloodless. Elinor didn't think the countess could see it from where she stood, but she reached up to put her hand on his anyway. If he struck his mother, he would regret it later. His hand was icy, and she wrapped her fingers around it to try to restore some warmth. Slowly it relaxed and wrapped around hers in turn.

Lady Doncaster looked at her son, an unpleasant smile twisting her lips. "You'd like to know, wouldn't you? You would like to be certain that you are Doncaster's son. You might be. You're smug and self-righteous enough. But that means the uncertainty will be good for you." She stood and strolled to the door. "Very well, I will leave, and I think it unlikely that we shall meet again. I will let Dalrymple know when I decide which house I want." She turned to look back. "It will take me a few days to pack, but this house is big enough for us to avoid unpleasant encounters."

"Wait." Elinor stood up.

The countess raised her brows, but paused.

"Excuse us, Harry. I need to speak to your mother." He scowled and began to protest, but Elinor shook her head decisively and pushed him toward the door. "We need to come to an understanding. You can go give orders about having Lord Winters' things sent after him."

Once the door was closed firmly behind him, she turned to face the older woman. They were of a height. The equal footing made it easier to speak without any pretense of subtlety. "You will not cause Harry or his sisters any further distress."

"I? How could I possibly distress them?" Lady Doncaster looked amused. "I see them so rarely I hardly recognize them."

Elinor was not amused. "You will create no more scandals. You will behave with at least outward propriety. And you will continue to keep away from your children."

That ended Lady Doncaster's amusement as well. "Why, you sanctimonious little brat. How dare you presume to order my behavior? I will live as I please, just as I always have."

"No. You have shamed Harry and his sisters enough. There will be no more of that."

Lady Doncaster's smile was more like a sneer. "And just why do you think I should pay any attention to a child like you? Do you think I am powerless? I have friends who could make your life miserable if I choose."

"Do you? I think not. You forget that I have a family and friends myself, and I do not think your friends would care to make enemies of mine. You saw how quickly Lord Winters took his departure. He knows how much difficulty my parents could make for him, were he to offend me."

Elinor saw doubt begin to creep into Lady Doncaster's expression and smiled implacably. "You see, the queen, who rather admires my mother, wrote to Harry and me, wishing us well in our marriage. Her

Majesty also expressed the hope that this meant an end to scandals in the de Vaux family."

"As if it matters what they say of me in that pompous, prudish court."

"You will find that it matters to many people, even to those you call your friends. I doubt you have any who care for you enough to risk their own positions in society. If you do not wish to change your habits, I suggest you take up residence abroad. It's a pity you can't enter a convent, but you might like Vienna, or perhaps St. Petersburg."

"I don't believe it. You can't be serious."

Elinor shrugged.

"Harry would not let you…"

"Do you seriously think that Harry would come to your defense? You have brought him and his sisters nothing but shame and scandal all their lives. Be grateful it has not occurred to him that he could have you clapped into an asylum as a depraved lunatic."

Elinor almost laughed at the expression of horror on the woman's face. She truly did not know her son at all. Harry would die before he did such a thing to anyone. Fortunately, he had a wife who would make any threats necessary to protect him, and his sisters as well. "Your departure from England would be the least painful solution for all of us," she said.

A snarl escaped from the countess before she caught herself up and looked coldly at Elinor. "I will consider what you have said."

"One more thing. Harry's sisters will be arriving later today. You will not distress them with your complaints."

She shrugged. "Why would I even see them? There is privacy enough for all of us. We need not meet again."

Then she was gone, leaving Elinor half triumphant, half aghast. She collapsed into a chair to collect herself, hardly believing her own success. Without the tension that had held her upright, her legs would not hold her up. When she was able, she hurried off to find Harry.

He was in the library, staring at the portrait of the late earl. She wrapped her arms tightly around him, wanting to wrap him in her love, and could feel the trembling begin. It grew stronger until he wrapped his arms around her, holding her tight until it subsided. He was still pale, but he seemed to have regained control of himself.

"She may have lied just to make him miserable. She destroyed him in a fit of pique. What kind of woman would do that? Is that my heritage?"

"You inherit nothing from her. She gave birth to you. That is the only connection between you."

He shook his head. "Now you know why I wanted to keep you far away from her."

"She is nothing to me, so she cannot hurt me. But she had the power to hurt you. I didn't want you to have to face her alone."

"He may well have been my father. I should have…"

She put a hand to his lips to stop him. "There is nothing you should have done, nothing you could have done. When did he ever take on a father's role? He was no more your father than she was your mother. He made his choices just as she did, and you are not responsible for them."

He cupped her face in his hands and moved his thumbs across her cheeks in a gentle caress. "I do love you. You are a very fierce champion, wife."

"That I am." She smiled and tugged at him. "Now come along. We have to locate the housekeeper and find out where your sisters should be put. Then we have to make this a home for them."

"And then we will build our own life with our own family. Not like mine."

"And not like mine, either. But our own. After all, we make a good team, do we not?"

"We do. Oh, indeed we do."

Epilogue

"MAMA, MAMA, THIS WAY. COME SEE." HIS LITTLE legs churning, young Viscount Tunbury raced at surprising speed down the neglected portrait gallery of the Abbey. It had become a favorite rainy-day play-room ever since he and Nurse discovered it. Its length offered space for running with a minimum of things to crash into. He stopped before a large family group near the end of the gallery. "Here."

His mother, laughing gently at his excitement, fol-lowed at a somewhat more subdued pace. "What have you found, Will? Another knight in armor?"

"Me," he said proudly. "My picture."

"Oh, I don't think so." Then she stopped in front of the portrait. Most of the paintings in this gallery were mediocre portraits of unimportant and long-forgotten members of the family, and this was one she had never noticed before. She glanced at it, and then she stopped and stared. It was a family portrait, the father in a dark coat with one of those elaborate neck cloths wrapped around his throat, the mother in a simple white dress that looked almost like a nightgown, and a child, a little boy, wearing a red velvet jacket.

Will pointed at the little boy in the painting, a little boy with the same brown curls as his, the same brown eyes, even the same way of standing with his head tilted to the side. "It's me."

The silence stretched out as she stared at the painting. "No, my sweet," she said at last, "not quite you. That's a portrait of your grandfather, Papa's father, when he was a child."

He frowned. "It looks like me."

"Yes it does, indeed it does."

"I like it."

"I like it too."

"Will Papa like it?"

She bent over to hug her son. "I think that when Papa sees it, he will like it too. Very much indeed."

Constantinople, March 1861

THE BRITISH EMBASSY IN CONSTANTINOPLE WAS A major disappointment. With its neoclassical facade and geometrical flower beds, it would have looked right at home had it been set down around the corner from Penworth House in London. Inside it was furnished in the latest English style, with Scottish landscapes hanging on the walls and Wilton carpets on the floor.

Emily heaved a sigh. Constantinople had looked so promising when they arrived this morning, with the city rising up out of the morning mists, white and shining with turrets and domes and balconies everywhere. The long, narrow boats in the harbor all sported bright sails. It had been so new and strange and exotic. Now here she was, walking with Julia behind her parents on Wilton carpets. Wilton carpets imported from Salisbury! When even she knew that this part of the world was famous for its carpets.

The doors at the end of the hall were flung open and a butler, dressed precisely as he would have been in London, announced, "The Most Honorable the

Marquess of Penworth. The Most Honorable the Marchioness of Penworth. The Lady Emily Tremaine. The Lady Julia de Vaux."

They might just as well never have left home.

Emily smiled the insipid smile she reserved for her parents' political friends—the smile intended to assure everyone that she was sweet and docile—and prepared to be bored. She was very good at pretending to be whatever she was expected to be. Next to her, she could feel Julia straighten her already perfect posture. She reached over to squeeze her friend's hand.

"Lord Penworth, Lady Penworth, allow me to welcome you to Constantinople." A ruddy-faced gentleman with thinning gray hair on his head and a thinning gray beard on his chin, inclined his head. "And this must be your daughter, Lady Emily?" He looked somewhere between the two young women, as if uncertain which one to address.

Emily took pity on him and curtsied politely.

He looked relieved, and turned to Julia. "And Lady Julia?"

She performed a similar curtsy.

"My husband and I are delighted to welcome such distinguished visitors to Constantinople," said the small, gray woman who was standing stiffly beside the ambassador, ignoring the fact that he had been ignoring her.

Emily blinked. She knew marital disharmony when she heard it. She also knew how unpleasant it could make an evening.

"We are delighted to be here, Lady Bulwer," said Lord Penworth courteously. "This part of the world is new to us, and we have all been looking forward to our visit." He turned to the ambassador. "I understand that you, Sir Henry, are quite familiar with it."

"Tolerably well, tolerably well. I'm told you're here to study the possibility of a railroad along the Tigris River valley. Can't quite see it myself." Before the ambassador realized it, Lord Penworth had cut him out of the herd of women and was shepherding him off to the side.

In the sudden quiet, Lady Penworth smiled at her hostess and gestured at the room about them. "I am most impressed by the way you have managed to turn this embassy into a bit of England," she said. "If I did not know, I would think myself still in London."

Lady Bulwer looked both pleased and smug. She obviously failed to note any hint of irony in Lady Penworth's words. Emily recognized the signs. Her parents would out-diplomat the diplomats, smoothing over any bumps of disharmony in the Bulwer household, and conversation would flow placidly through conventional channels. Boring, but unexceptionable. And only too familiar.

Then Julia touched her arm.

Still looking straight ahead, and still with a faint, polite smile on her face, Julia indicated that Emily should look at the left-hand corner of the room. Emily had never understood how it was that Julia could send these messages without making a sound or even moving her head, but send them she did.

In this case, it was a message Emily received with interest. Off in the corner were two young men pretending to examine a huge globe while they took sideways glances at the newcomers. This was much more promising than the possibility of trouble between the ambassador and his wife. Refusing to pretend a lack of curiosity—she was growing tired, very tired, of pretending—she looked straight at them.

One was an extraordinarily handsome man, clean-shaven to display a beautifully sculpted mouth and a square jaw. His perfectly tailored black tailcoat outlined a tall, broad-shouldered physique. The blinding whiteness of his shirt and bow tie contrasted with the slight olive cast of his skin. His hair was almost black, and his dark eyes betrayed no awareness of her scrutiny. He stood with all the bored elegance of the quintessential English gentleman. Bored and probably boring.

The other man looked far more interesting. He was not so tall—slim and wiry, rather than powerful looking—and not nearly so handsome. His nose was quite long—assertive might be a polite way to describe it—and his tanned face was long and narrow. Like his companion, he was clean-shaven, though his hair, a dark brown, was in need of cutting. While his evening clothes were perfectly proper, they were worn carelessly, and he waved his hands about as he spoke in a way that seemed definitely un-English. He noticed immediately when she turned her gaze on him and turned to return her scrutiny. She refused to look away, even when he unashamedly examined her from head to toe. His eyes glinted with amusement, and he gave her an appreciative grin and salute.

The cheek of him! She laughed out loud, making Julia hiss and drawing the attention of her mother and

Lady Bulwer. Sir Henry must have noticed something as well, for he waved the young men over to be introduced to Papa.

They both stopped a proper distance away, and the handsome one waited with an almost military stiffness. Sir Henry introduced him first. "This is David Oliphant, Lord Penworth. He's with the Foreign Office and will be your aide and guide on the journey. He knows the territory and can speak the lingo. All the lingos, in fact—Turkish, Kurdish, Arabic, whatever you run into along the way."

Oliphant bowed. "Honored, my lord."

Lord Penworth smiled. "My pleasure."

"And this young man is Lucien Chambertin. He's on his way back to Mosul where he's been working with Carnac, digging up stone beasts or some such."

"The remains of Nineveh, Sir Henry." Chambertin then turned to Lord Penworth with a brief, graceful bow and a smile. "I am most pleased to make your acquaintance, my lord, for I am hoping you will allow me to impose on you and join your caravan for the journey to Mosul."

He spoke excellent English, with just a hint of a French accent. Just the perfect hint, Emily decided. Sir Henry was not including the ladies in his introductions, to her annoyance, so she had been obliged to position herself close enough to hear what they were saying. This was one of the rare occasions when she was grateful for her crinolines. They made it impossible for the ladies to stand too close to one another, so she placed herself to the rear of her mother. From that position, she could listen to the gentlemen's conversation while appearing to attend to the ladies'. What's more, from her angle she could watch them from the corner of her eye without being obvious.

"I cannot imagine why you should not join us," Lord Penworth told the Frenchman. "I understand that in Mesopotamia it is always best to travel in a large group. You are one of these new archaeologists, are you?"

Chambertin gave one of those Gallic shrugs. "Ah no, nothing so grand. I am just a passing traveler, but I cannot resist the opportunity to see the ruins of Nineveh when the opportunity offers itself. And then when Monsieur Carnac says he has need of assistance, I agree to stay for a while."

"Well, my wife will certainly find the ruins interesting. She has developed quite a fascination with the ancient world."

Oliphant looked startled. "Your wife? But surely Lady Penworth does not intend to accompany us."

"Of course." Lord Penworth in turn looked startled at the question. "I could hardly deny her the opportunity to see the ancient cradle of civilization. Not when I am looking forward to it myself."

"I'm sorry. I was told you were traveling to view the possible site of a railway."

"I am." Penworth smiled. "That is my excuse for this trip. General Chesney has been urging our government to build a railway from Basra to Constantinople. His argument is that it would provide much quicker and safer communication with India. Palmerston wanted me to take a look and see if there would be any other use for it."

The ambassador snorted. "Not much. There's nothing of any use or interest in this part of the world except for those huge carvings that fellows like Carnac haul out of the ground."

The handsome Mr. Oliphant looked worried. Before he could say anything, dinner was announced, the remaining introductions were finally made, and Emily found herself walking in to dinner on the arm of M. Chambertin. He had behaved quite correctly when they were introduced and held out his arm in perfectly proper fashion. He said nothing that would have been out of place in the most rigidly proper setting imaginable. Nonetheless, she suspected that he had been well aware of her eavesdropping. There was a decidedly improper light dancing in his eyes.

She liked it.

About dinner she was less certain. The oxtail soup had been followed by lobster rissoles, and now a footman placed a slice from the roast sirloin of beef on her plate, where it joined the spoonful of mashed turnips and the boiled onion. The onion had been quite thoroughly boiled. It was finding it difficult to hold its shape and had begun to tilt dispiritedly to one side.

"This is really quite a remarkable meal," Lady Penworth said to their hostess. "Do you find it difficult to obtain English food here?"

"You've no idea." Lady Bulwer sighed sadly. "It has taken me ages to convince the cook that plain boiled vegetables are what we want. You can't imagine the outlandish spices he wants to use. And the olive oil! It's a constant struggle."

"And in that battle, the food lost," muttered Emily, poking the onion into total collapse.

A snort from M. Chambertin at her side indicated that her words had not gone unheard. After using his napkin, he turned to her. "You do not care for *rosbif*?" he asked with a grin. "I thought all the English eat nothing else."

"We are in *Constantinople*, thousands of miles from home, and we might as well be in Tunbridge Wells."

He made a sympathetic grimace. "Perhaps while your *papa* goes to look at the railway route, Sir Henry can find you a guide who will show you and your friend a bit of Constantinople. You should really see the Topkapi—the old palace—and the bazaar."

"Oh, but we aren't going to be staying here. Julia and I are going with my parents."

Mr. Oliphant, who had been speaking quietly with Julia, heard that and looked around in shock. "Lady Emily, you and Lady Julia and Lady Penworth are *all* planning to go to Mosul? Surely not. I cannot believe your father will allow this."

Emily sighed. She was accustomed to such reactions. *Lady Emily, you cannot possibly mean… Lady Emily, surely you do not intend…* All too often, she had restrained herself and done what was expected. She intended this trip to be different. Still, she was curious as well as annoyed. Was Mr. Oliphant about to urge propriety, or was there some other reason for his distress? "Why should we not?" she asked.

Mr. Oliphant took a sip of wine, as if to calm himself. Or fortify himself. It was impossible to be certain. He cleared his throat. "I fear Lord Penworth may not be fully aware of the difficulties—dangers, even—of travel in this part of the world. The caravan route through Aleppo and Damascus and then across the desert is hazardous under the best of circumstances, and these days…" He shook his head.

"My friend does not exaggerate," put in M. Chambertin, looking serious. "Although the recent massacres in the Lebanon seem to be at an end, brigands have become more bold, and even the largest caravans—they are not safe."

"But we are not planning to take that route." Emily looked at Julia for confirmation and received it. "We are to sail to Samsun on the Black Sea, travel by caravan over the mountains to Diyarbakir, and then down the river to Mosul. And eventually on to Baghdad and Basra. Papa discussed it all with people back in London when he and Lord Palmerston were planning the route. So you need not worry." She smiled to reassure the gentlemen.

M. Chambertin and Mr. Oliphant exchanged glances, trying to decide which should speak. It fell to Mr. Oliphant. "I do not question your father's plan, Lady Emily. These days that is by far the safer route, though no place is entirely safe from attacks by brigands. However, he may have underestimated the physical difficulties of the trip. The mountains—these are not gentle little hills like the ones you find in England. They are barren and rocky, and we will cross them on roads that are little more than footpaths. It is impossible to take a carriage. If they do not go on foot, travelers must go on horseback or on mules. And this early in the year, it will still be bitterly cold, especially at night."

"You needn't worry," Emily assured him. "We are all excellent riders, and I am told that the cold is preferable to the heat of the summer."

M. Chambertin smiled at her and shook his head. "I do not doubt that you are a horsewoman *par excellence*, and your mother and Lady Julia as well. However, the journey over the mountains will take weeks. We will encounter few villages, and those are of the most poor. There will be times when we must sleep in tents or take shelter in stables. Nowhere will there be comfortable inns where ladies can refresh themselves."

Emily and Julia looked at each other, sharing their irritation. Male condescension was obviously to be found everywhere.

"I believe you misunderstand the situation, gentlemen." Julia spoke in her iciest, most superior tones. "We are not fragile pieces of porcelain. We are grown women, and English women at that. I do not think you will find us swooning at the sight of a spider. Or, for that matter, at the sight of a lion. Since Lord Penworth has determined that we are capable of undertaking the journey, I see no need for you to question his judgment."

Author's Note

The book to which Lord and Lady Penworth frequently refer is *The Cities and Cemeteries of Etruria* by George Dennis, a two-volume work of more than a thousand pages, first published in 1848. It is still regarded as an important reference on Etruria. Unfortunately for Mr. Dennis, he never received the honors he deserved during his lifetime because of his lack of academic credentials. His book was, of course, appreciated by perceptive readers like Lord and Lady Penworth.

Around the time of our story, Prince Torlonia retained the Florentine archaeologist Alessandro Francois to conduct explorations of the Etruscan necropolis of Vulci on his estate. In 1857, the archaeologist discovered what is now known as the Francois Tomb, with its magnificent frescoes. I transported it to Prince Savelli's estate so that my characters would not have quite so far to travel from Rome and pushed its discovery up by a year. Carlo Ruspi was an artist noted for his drawings of works discovered by archaeologists, and he did indeed do the drawings of the Francois